MW00710535

Poolside Sting

A Fargo Blue Mystery Series

Poolside Sting

Don McKenzie and Ron McKenzie

Poolside Sting Copyright © 2006 by Donald E. McKenzie and Ronald A. McKenzie

All rights reserved. No part of this book shall be reproduced or transmitted in any form or by any means, electronic, mechanical, magnetic, photographic including photocopying, recording or by any information storage and retrieval system, without prior written permission of the publisher. No patent liability is assumed with respect to the use of the information contained herein. Although every precaution has been taken in the preparation of this book, the publisher and author assume no responsibility for errors or omissions. Neither is any liability assumed for damages resulting from the use of the information contained herein.

This is a work of fiction. Names, characters, places, and incidents either are the product of the author's imagination or are used fictitiously. Any resemblance to actual events or locales or persons, living or dead, is entirely coincidental.

ISBN 0-7414-3186-6

This novel was previously published as *Las Vegas Comp: Murder at Emerald Towers*.

Published by:

INFINITY
PUBLISHING.COM
1094 New DeHaven Street, Suite 100
West Conshohocken, PA 19428-2713
Info@buybooksontheweb.com
www.buybooksontheweb.com
Toll-free (877) BUY BOOK
Local Phone (610) 941-9999
Fax (610) 941-9959

Printed in the United States of America

Printed on Recycled Paper

Published May 2006

Dedication

To our Dad, Alonzo Max McKenzie (1919 - 1961), a proud member of the U.S. Coast Guard during World War II, who loved a good detective story. We wrote it for him, and for our Mom, Janis Grace McKenzie (1928-2003) who bought us all the comic books we ever wanted. Ever since then we have been filled with stories we had to write.

Acknowledgments

The authors developed the Fargo Blue character in a television pilot named *Courier*, at their writing weekends on the campus of UCLA in the early eighties. They then developed the Fargo Blue character into a mystery series in 1995 sitting at the off track betting lounge at the Excalibur Hotel in Las Vegas, Nevada.

*   *   *

We both thank our wives, Sandi McKenzie (Don) and Pamela McKenzie (Ron) who always give us the time to write. Also a special thank you to My Advertising Partner© who designed the cover for Poolside Sting.

We would also like to thank Chris Roerden of Edit It who guided the manuscript with suggestions and critiques, and made our efforts worthwhile. However, the authors accept all responsibility for any errors or mistakes.

Don McKenzie
Ron McKenzie

Introduction

From the Las Vegas Times

Blue Not Blue About Final Wrap

(Las Vegas, Nevada)   Fargo Blue, known as Fargo, long-time homicide inspector for Las Vegas Metro Police ends a distinguished career after solving the latest in a series of puzzling homicides.

"I feel good about moving to the private sector," says Fargo, as he checked in for his last day on the job with the Las Vegas Metro Police.

Fargo's career started over ten years ago when he made Homicide Inspector at the ripe old age of twenty-five. "First day out I found myself at the Sands Hotel where I was put in charge of a double murder. I was scared to death," says Fargo.

One would never know it. Fargo, who believes in a basic "follow the clue" crime-solving approach, was able to trace the killings to a robbery gone badly on Fremont Street. The search ended with the arrest of one man who eventually confessed to the murders and is now serving life at the Nevada State Prison.

The Las Vegas hotels have been Fargo's best friends over the years. He developed a reputation within the department that when a casino had a problem, they requested Fargo Blue by name. Now that Fargo is in the private sector, he will be working for many of those same hotels as a private investigator on a case-by-case basis.

"I've busted down a few doors in my time," says Fargo. "Even went through a couple of locks, but I did what I had to do, to give the bad guys a new address behind bars."

Fargo Blue was all smiles on his last day. He says, "The fun has just begun.

Poolside Sting

A Fargo Blue Mystery Series

One

I introduced myself over the phone as Fargo Blue, but she didn't seem impressed. Said she already had that piece of information. She was different. She called herself Pleasure and said she knew Uncle Leo. Intriguing. I was to visit her poolside at the MGM Grand, which is always a good way to start Monday morning. But I had a bad feeling, like the dice rolled a seven on your last ten spot. It just doesn't feel good.

I had met Uncle Leo when I was working homicide in south Vegas. Every time I made a good collar, they called their Uncle. He was the public defender learning his trade and fast becoming one of the most popular guys in Vegas. Now he is retired with more connections than he knows what to do with. And it was the connection to Uncle Leo that bothered me.

I'm a full-time P.I. and part time treasure hunter. It's a passion where I can use my detective skills to track down the loot of the world. I wear a gold Hong Kong Jockey Club ring on my right index finger. I travel to Hong Kong every year to visit my sister, and on one trip helped a friend of hers. The ring was a gift, which I will always remember.

At six foot two, with thick almond brown hair, and somewhat on the lean side, I always look good in what I wear. Most of the time it was the same - a five-hundred-

dollar sport jacket over a hundred-dollar shirt. But no ties
- that is my concession to Las Vegas heat. The jacket hid
my 9-mm Glock I always carry. Black, so it won't reflect
light. Today it was under my arm, tomorrow on my leg or
on my belt in back. Keep them guessing is all a part of
the game. When things get tough I also carry a SIG .40
S&W, and a snub nose .38 in an ankle holster for extra
protection.

I backed out of my garage in Summerlin, went
through the security entrance and headed south toward
Sahara on Rampart Boulevard. After several blocks, I
turned east onto Sahara headed toward the Strip where I
turned right. I passed the Wynn Las Vegas casino and the
Fashion Show Mall. The Strip continued to be the best
real estate investment there was as evidenced by Trump's
new condominium tower. Eventually I could see the New
York, New York Hotel that dominates the famous four-
corner intersection on the south end of the Strip. Though
I had an old Cad Seville I used for stakeouts, the car I
loved was the 635 SCI BMW I was driving. Solid black
with smoked windows; it had a black interior, and at
three years old, the engine purred. That's where all the
money went in this car. You have to have religion when
you want to leave some place fast, and I bought my
religion under the hood. It could catch the last rays of a
dying sunset.

Las Vegas doesn't change much if you live here. It
changes only if you visit. The buildings get taller, and
more of them appear, each a little different. Only in
Vegas can you have a New York skyline on one corner, a
castle on the next, with Egypt just down the road. But
one thing never changes; the cash drawers are just as
deep. You can still lose money in the desert, and millions
come back every year to make another deposit.

Then there are the bad guys who want to play
with guns. Where there's money, there's trouble.
Someone either wants more or wants someone else to

have less. Sort of like treasure hunting. Same thing any way you cut it. When it gets serious it leads to murder. That's where I come in, but I come in through the back door. Murder is not something the Strip hotels advertise. When hotel security wants to level the playing field, they call Fargo Blue. I pulled into the MGM Grand's back lot and found a space. I backed in, which is just a habit. It's easier to leave.

I entered the MGM Grand from the basement garage like everyone else. Two things happen when I walk into a casino. I feel the chilled blast of the air-conditioned air, thanks to that big dam up the road a bit, and I have an overwhelming desire to check my loose change. A normal Las Vegas habit, but I beat it. Well, sort of. I put only three dollars in a slot at the first casino I walk into every day. It drives the tourists crazy when I hit one. On this day I selected a slot with a sense of history. I cranked the handle and watched it spin. Red, white, and blue sevens lined up will pay ten thousand for a three-buck investment. This one didn't, which continued to prove I wasn't good at history, either.

I crossed the marbled lobby floor and took a hard right. After a short walk I approached the Sport's Bar and off-track betting area. This was right next to the poker area and I could see several games of Hold'Em poker being played. I stopped long enough to look at the morning line in the Daily Racing Form. I glanced at the pages and settled on a horse running in the fourth at Bay Meadows. A three-year-old filly coming down in class with a good win record but placed out of the money last three times at the gate. Odds were just under twenty-to-one, but I knew the horse would be trying just as hard as the favorite. I put ten down on the nose and headed for the pool.

I left the track betting area and walked straight toward the mall at the rear of the casino. I passed Wolfgang Puck's where I had enjoyed many fine meals there. I walked past the fine shops and restaurants and headed toward the pool and spa located at the end of the mall. I took the escalator down. To the right was the entrance to the convention center and meeting rooms. I slowed a bit as a beautiful number came out of the spa on the left. Nice town to work in, I thought to myself. Coming out into the bright sunlight I found myself in one of the most attractive poolside settings that Las Vegas had to offer.

Sometimes casino security gives you a problem if you can't show them your hotel key, but I have one of the most extensive collections around. Even though I had a key in my pocket, I didn't need one today. At the MGM Grand you can sometimes crash the pool. Other hotels require a room number or a key card, but not the MGM Grand. Not many people know this. The trick is looking like you belong. You can also get out the back way by the tennis courts if you have to. A potential security problem waiting to happen. My job is to notice these things.

I glanced around the pool, which was surrounded by the emerald green towers of the hotel. It was about eleven o'clock, and beginning to get busy. The air was filled with the sounds and smells of a Vegas pool. Happy kids played with endless energy on the man-made sandy beach at the pool's edge, while parents nursed headaches of one kind or another from the night before.

Everybody comes to Vegas thinking they can get the perfect tan in three days. Not true. It takes a real effort over a period of weeks. If you're not careful, the only thing you'll end up with is the perfect burn, the Las Vegas red badge of courage. Something to take home and show off at the office.

I spotted Pleasure right away. She commanded the center of attention on the far side of the pool that was surrounded by palm trees. She was stretched out enjoying the sun. It's funny how some people have an aura about them. She had it. A pool attendant was delivering a second set of towels, probably just to get a closer look. A few hotel guests had arranged their chairs to get a better view. Male and female, I might add. I walked carefully around the pool and I approached her with caution. Sort of like handing bloody meat to a hungry lion.

"Mr. Blue, I believe," Pleasure said as I approached. She extended her hand. We shook. Her hand was warm and comfortable. She held on longer than necessary.

"Have we been introduced?"

"You're Fargo Blue, the detective."

"Fargo Blue Investigations at your service." She was around thirty-three and a delight to look at. It was all I could do to keep my eyes locked on her eyes hiding behind those dark glasses. A once-over would be too obvious. Her attitude told me to go ahead anyway. But I didn't. I was a tough guy. It was killing me, and she knew it.

"Could you hand me that towel?" She indicated the one by her feet. She was making it easy for me to check her out. I liked politeness. There's not enough of it anymore in the world. I wasn't disappointed. She was tan and voluptuous, with hair the color of coal. She was built and she knew it. She wore a white two-piece with enough cleavage for everybody. A bead of sweat rolled down her breast and disappeared into her top. A guy in my line of business has to pay attention to the details. I'm a real pro when I have to be.

"Yes, I'm Fargo Blue, and you're Pleasure...?"

"Pleasure ought to be enough for now."

I tried to keep a straight face, even though I suspected you could never get enough pleasure. "How can I help you?"

She slid her Ralph Lauren wrap-around sunglasses down her nose to get a better look at me. A chair appeared out of thin air and I was delighted to sit down. I was the doctor and she was my patient. "I have a friend who needs help," she said.

"What's the name?"

"Jody."

"Jody who?"

"Judith S. Barrett. Jody for short."

"Why don't you have Jody call me?"

"That's the problem. I can't find her. She arrived yesterday on the noon flight from New York. She picked up a room key, left her baggage in her suite, and vanished. It's not like her."

"Call the police and ask for missing persons. They can help."

"I can't."

"Why?"

"She was carrying a great deal of money!"

"Whose money?"

"My money!"

"Are you interested in finding the money or her?"

"Do you want the truth?" she answered coyly.

"Lie to me."

"My friend and the money."

"Tell me about your friend."

"She's even more beautiful than I am. But I'm not the envious type."

"I'll file that away."

"Might come in handy. You never know." She leaned over to reach for something under her lounge chair. My pool mates were getting jealous. She pulled out a small black gym bag. On the side was written MGM Grand in gold letters.

"I didn't bring you anything."

She slipped her Ralph Lauren sunglasses down over her nose again, looked at me over the top of the rims, and ignored my comment. She didn't appreciate good humor.

"Will you take my case, Mr. Fargo? I need private help, and I hear you're good."

"How do you know Uncle Leo?"

"A long, long time ago I helped him out of a jam. So I called him and he recommended you. How about it?"

"Maybe, maybe not."

A small smile appeared at the corners of her lips. "Why not? I pay dividends when I have to." She stretched her arms over her head and closed her eyes. She was playing with me.

"I need more information. Like, who are you? Where did you come from? Where did the money come from and where do you think it went? This is a big town, Ms. Pleasure, and people play for keeps."

"I need your help," she said talking to the sky. "I'll make you a deal." Her eyes were on me again. "I'll hire you and if you find something you don't like, you can drop the case. How much to start?"

"A thousand a day plus expenses. Two-day minimum."

"That sounds fair to me." Pleasure reached into the bag and pulled out a hotel key card and tossed it to me.

"Combination for the room safe is in the upper left-hand side of the bureau. Looks like a phone number. Just drop the first digit and reverse the numbers. It's the standard right/left/right combo. Give it a spin, and pull out four days' pay and a thousand for expenses."

"What about your card key?"

"Keep it. I have another one."

"Sounds great," I said, always happy about being paid up front.

"You sure you don't mind me opening your safe?"

"You work for me now. I trust you."

"Why?"

"I think you'll stick around for awhile." Pleasure adjusted the top of her suit.

Can't say I have any complaints about the scenery.

"How long are you going to be here?"

"Long enough. Part vacation. Part work. Having fun. The usual."

"Doing what?"

"You're the detective. Go detect. And one more thing," she added. "In the bag there's a gun. Could you put it back in the safe for me?"

"What are you doing poolside with a gun? This is the MGM Grand. Most people would consider this a safe area."

"This is the wild, wild west," she said without smiling. "One has to be prepared for greatness."

I had to agree with her. She needed the bag so I stuck the gun in my belt hidden by my jacket. A nice 9-mm Beretta with good balance. I admired her choice. Pleasure rolled over onto her stomach and tossed her hair up and held it with one hand.

"Since you work for me, I don't suppose you'd have a problem putting some suntan lotion on my back, would you? Your hands will get all greased up."

"A P.I.s work is never done."

She undid the bikini top and arched her back. It dropped a little bit farther down than she probably wanted, or maybe not, but I didn't complain. Neither did she. I applied the lotion with interest and conviction, the secret to my success. There was a little hope and exploring at the same time. I was going to have to thank Uncle Leo when I saw him this afternoon.

"Emmmmm, that feels good."

"My pleasure," I said as straight as I could. "Anything to please my boss." That's the kind of guy I am. Always ready to pitch in and help. Las Vegas, I love this town.

Two

I was ready with Pleasure's room key to get me past elevator security. Didn't need it, which surprised me. I made a mental note as I approached her room. The habit of a detective. When I have a case I always work backwards and then forward. I go as far back as I can, and then work through all the events leading up to the incident. I check out the who, what, where, when and how of all the people I meet on a case. Then I follow the clues. Most people look for the obvious. I look for the clues. The ones you can't see. The ones begging to be found. Room 2438. The key card worked fine. I snapped on the light as I pushed the door shut. I stood silently and listened. I smelled the air. Nothing.

The suite was spotless. Maid service had come and gone. The dark emerald green carpets flowed from one room to another, and the decor reflected wealth. Clever of those hotel moguls. Make the guests feel as they have a lot of money, and they will tend to gamble more. This was more than a hotel room. It was a small suite for special people. It made me wonder about my client. I passed a built-in bar and entertainment center and moved into the bedroom. The bed was huge. So was the mirror on the opposite wall. The bed was on a raised platform that overlooked the Jacuzzi, which was next to floor to ceiling windows that overlooked the pool area.

Something always overlooked something in Vegas. The bathroom was spacious and well appointed. Just as my client was. Fitting.

I entered the second bedroom and spotted luggage in the center. Evidently it was Jody's luggage she had left. I reentered the master bedroom and located the bureau. The upper left-hand drawer was, what can I say...filled with silk undergarments. Pleasure was a crafty little thing. I got the combo and headed toward the safe. Three spins and a crank and the door swung open with a typical creaking sound. Right out of a movie. Why all safes do that I'll never know. Peeking in I found large stacks of hundred-dollar bills. I removed a stack and counted out five thousand dollars. Four days' pay plus a thousand for expenses. Pleasure was becoming one of my best clients. I could get used to this.

I replaced the rest of the money and estimated she had about twenty-five grand in the safe. Was she a high roller, or into something else? I'd have to check. If she had this much here, how much was Jody bringing in? Curious, I pulled out several envelopes, all addressed to a Ms. Kimberly P. Weber of Pacific Palisades, California. I wondered if that was Pleasure's name. They were empty. I made a note of the name and return address to check out later. I pulled Pleasure's Beretta from my belt and placed it in the safe. As I did so, I noticed the sulfuric smell of a fired gun. I probably hadn't caught the odor before with all that chlorine and distractions by the pool. This made me uncomfortable. I checked the clip, and it was full. Safety on. No round chambered. Pleasure had some explaining to do. I placed the weapon in the safe and swung its door shut, puzzled.

I gave the combination a spin as I stood up. Just then the hotel door opened and two figures entered. Both had weapons, and they were leveled at me in the standard two-handed arm-extended police stance. I felt like I was on the wrong end of a police training film.

"Hold it right there!" yelled the first figure as he came through the door.

My hands went over my head as a natural reaction whenever a gun is aimed at me. Sorry to say, but I've had a lot of experience at this. Damn. Something's wrong with this picture. Then I saw who it was. An old friend, Detective Jack Johnston. "Hello Johnston. Nice to see you again. Johnston was a taller then I was, but was just as quick.

"Fargo! What the hell are you doing here?" He pulled his gun up and off me, and motioned that it was okay to the man behind him. Evidently it wasn't okay with the second guy because he kept his firearm pointed directly at me. Then I saw who it was. I didn't care for him. Not in the slightest.

"As usual, I'm one step ahead of hotel security," I commented trying to keep the sarcasm out of my voice. I failed miserably.

"Not in my hotel," said Vince Olsen as he waved his gun at me. Olsen was chief of security at the MGM Grand Hotel. We didn't get along. The guy's a jerk. Used to be a good cop but he went bad, got kicked out, and landed a hotel security gig.

"Couldn't you knock?"

"There's been a murder by the pool," Johnston said. "Lower your gun, Olsen." Johnston put his hand on Olsen's arm and forced him to lower it. Olsen was muscular and stubborn, which is why he was hired by the MGM Grand. He was also pudgy.

"A murder in broad daylight!" I exclaimed. "Good job, Olsen."

"Screw you, Fargo."

Johnston indicated the window. "Take a look and see for yourself." I walked around the Jacuzzi and peered through the floor-to-ceiling window. The far side of the pool area had been closed and Las Vegas Metro Police were stringing yellow crime tape around the palm trees.

It looked familiar. I had just been there.

"What happened?" I asked, knowing the answer wasn't going to be good.

"Somebody took out one of the guests just as she was reaching for a Bloody Mary," Olsen said. "What do you know about her?"

"Who?"

"The victim."

"Did I know her?"

"You're in her suite."

"You're kidding."

"Wouldn't joke about a thing like that."

"You know her long?" asked Johnston.

"Whose her?"

"You tell me," Olsen said.

"Don't know who you're talking about."

"Try guessing," said Olsen. "Try real hard."

"I'm in my client's room. What about you?"

"Your client?"

"Yep."

"Maybe your client is dead," said Johnston.

"And maybe you did it," finished Olsen.

Johnston turned to the head of security. "Cut the comments, Olsen. Fargo was putting bad guys away while you were trying to break out of a crib."

"Yeah, right. That's not what I heard," commented Olsen.

Johnston turned and gave another hard look at Olsen, who turned away. I directed my conversation toward Johnston. "What name do you have?"

"She went by the name of Pleasure."

I had that sinking feeling when you know things were going to turn out bad and there was nothing you could do about it. "I haven't known her that long. Not long enough, that's for sure," I said. I wondered if Pleasure's death was connected to Jody. "What do you know about her?" I asked.

"Not much," said Olsen. "We're pulling her hotel records now. You working for her?"

"Yeah. I had some business to take care of for her. Nothing important."

"Care to tell us about it?" asked Olsen.

"Not right now. It was personal. You can understand that."

"Sure, I can understand that. Humor me. Tell me about it anyway."

"It's on a need-to-know basis. You don't need to know yet...privileged information."

"This is my hotel," Olsen yelled. His face flushed with anger.

"Great, hire me. We can work together."

Olsen shook his head in disgust. "Are you protecting her?"

"No. Nothing like that."

"We'll leave it at that right now, but we'll need to talk more later."

I turned my back on Olsen. "You need me anymore, Johnston?" I asked as I walked through Pleasure's bedroom and took one last look around.

"We'll need a statement."

"I'll take care of that right away. I'll prepare one from my notes and get it to the station. If there's any questions, you can give me a call."

"Fine."

"Yeah, and remember, you're a suspect," Olsen said in his most pleasant manner.

"Find anything of interest?" I asked as I stalled to collect my thoughts. Two problems. One, if I'm a suspect, I'm not giving them a statement. Definitely Uncle Leo time on this one. Second was the question of the gun in the safe. I would have loved five more minutes before the crime lab arrived. Johnston was also going through the room carefully before he brought in the lab. Even though the murder was committed by the pool, they would probably declare Pleasure's hotel room part of the crime scene so they could do a detailed forensics' inspection.

"Nothing," said Johnston. "This room is about as clean as they come. The desk called up. She checked in yesterday. Paid cash. Room reserved for a week. No record of any airlines she flew in on, or how she was going to depart. There are some clothes in the closet and in the drawers, and a set of luggage in the corner. No room service. Just the maid this morning cleaning her room. She ordered lunch at the pool."

Olsen had pulled out his cell phone and asked for an update on what was happening down by the pool. He was observing the scene from the window. Dead bodies created special kinds of problems that were handled with a great deal of concern toward the bottom line. Publicity. They just don't want the public to know about any kind of death in the hotels. Especially murders. If a customer dies in his sleep, that's okay, but they'll still try and move the body out in the middle of the night just so the other guests won't see a gurney roll by with a black bag on it. For a nighttime party town, this was easier said than done.

"Come on, Fargo, I want some answers." Olsen put away his cell phone.

"Hey, Vince, you know me. I'm a detective. I'm here to help you guys out. I expect you're going to want to hire me."

"What for?" Olsen said.

"To find the killer. I know you guys are sharp. But the police, no offense, Jack, will drop this one when somebody doesn't confess in the next twenty-four hours. The hotel will want to find the killer. I'm already working for the victim, so you get a lot of information for gratis."

"We'll see about that," Olsen said. "For starters, who's Pleasure anyway?"

"Haven't the foggiest idea. I got here just before you did."

"Why are you here?"

"We've been over that. One thing leads to another," I said, meaning it. A little interview down by poolside, a visit to the hotel room, and then Pleasure's dead. Boy, I wish that hadn't have happened. Really wrecks the day. "How did somebody get into the pool area with a gun?" I asked.

"How do you know she was shot?" asked Olsen.

"I don't. Just digging for information." I watched Olsen get steamed. "Just a guess. I wanted to see your reaction. After all, it's the Las Vegas way of doing things." I couldn't imagine somebody smothering a hotel guest by poolside, or even a knife attack. I was shuddering from the bad publicity this was going to give the hotel.

"Not a chance," said Johnston. "We think she was hit with a poison dart."

"A poison dart!" I blurted.

"Yeah," said Olsen."

"Maybe on Safari, but not by the pool."

"Right out of a Hollywood movie," said Johnston joining our conversation.

"Just like a bad guy would do right up there on the silver screen," added Olsen.

I shook my head. "Boy, that does take the cake," I said. In all the years I've been a homicide detective, I've never investigated a murder by poison dart. That was a new one on me. "Listen, guys. I've got to get going. I've just got one question for you."

"Yeah?" said Olsen.

"How come you knew it was a guy who murdered my client?" I turned and stared at Olsen.

"I never said it was a guy..."

"You said, 'Just like a bad guy would do right up there on the silver screen.' "

"It was just a figure of speech."

"You know something about this you're not telling me, Olsen?"

15

"Hey, listen. I ask the questions here," he said sharply.

"What about witnesses? There had to be somebody who saw what happened," I commented. I figured I better start gathering some facts because I knew I was going to be drawn into this one.

Olsen leaned against the dresser. "You know what happens in a crowd scene. We'll be lucky to get two stories the same. We've got other crews checking the rooms all along this wing of the hotel. We might find a witness. It was just a few minutes ago that we found out this was her room." Olsen changed again to his violent personality. "Let me ask you again. What the hell are you doing in a dead woman's room?"

"It's personal," I answered.

"How did you get into her room?"

I held up a room key. "She gave me her key."

Olsen grabbed at it. "I'll take that evidence!"

I pulled back and Olsen grabbed at thin air, almost losing his balance. "No you won't." I tossed the key to Johnston. "If it's evidence, let's give it to the responsible person in charge."

Olsen ignored my insult. I thought it was pretty good.

"How did she find you?" asked Johnston.

"Just lucky, I guess. Call on the answering service early this morning. Said she knew Uncle Leo. Wanted my service for a few days."

"And now she's dead," said Olsen.

"That's what you're telling me. When I left her, she was alive. You know, if your security was a little bit better, maybe she would still be a guest of the hotel."

Olsen made a move toward me, but I was ready to take him to the carpet.

Johnston intervened. "Now let's not get personal."

"Well, somebody should," I said. "I'm just doing my job. I'd like to see Olsen do his."

"I'll do mine, Fargo. You just stay off this case. You're a suspect. You hear me?"

"Yeah, I hear you. Don't screw this up. You're dealing with my client. And I take everything you do personally. You have to answer to me now. And I don't like slackers."

"All right you guys," said Johnston. "Cut the crap. Take your personal differences someplace else."

"Yeah. I'm outta here," I said. "You need me, you know where to get hold of me."

Vince Olsen turned his back on me. "Yeah, under a rock."

"Beats slumming on Fremont," I said as I slammed the hotel room door. Fremont Street was a darker part of Olsen's past before he got busted. I figured it would piss him off. I could hear Olsen shouting through the closed door.

"Cram it, Fargo! You're prime number one as far as I'm concerned. It's going down in the report that way."

He was furious, which is what I wanted. He'll try harder. Not that Vince Olsen didn't need some pissing off, but I had to get the hell out of there so they could leave. I needed time to think. I had this sick feeling in my gut of what would happen if they found a recently fired 9-mm in the safe with my prints all over it. I wondered what other prints were on the gun. It was a crime scene now, and I wanted the gun. But I had a secret weapon; I still had the room key. I had switched it for the phony one I'd brought from the office. A neat little Las Vegas trick -- like switching dice.

Three

I saw the hotel guard walking out of the elevator on the twenty-fourth floor, and I knew he was going to be posted outside Pleasure's door. Tough break. I had intended to get back inside just as soon as I could. I headed straight for the elevator. It was not going to be easy to get the gun back. I was also concerned about an obstruction of justice charge. There was a lot of money in the safe, and although I had not been hired to represent her financial interests, I felt obliged to help. After all, I had been hired to find Jody and the money she was holding for Pleasure. Who it rightfully belonged to was another story. Follow the money, somebody once said. It has solved more crimes than Batman. And in Vegas, loose money has a habit of disappearing.

I worked my way back to the pool area, as I wanted to observe the crime scene. I spotted Peter Daily, a cop I had once worked with. Peter had just made detective. Good guy with a big family and a large mortgage. A harder worker there never was. His personnel file had "motivated" written all over it.

Yellow ribbon wrapped the area completely. The body had already been removed. Being at Poolside the crime scene had been cleared quickly after forensics had investigated. I can imagine the problem of this crime scene with so many people around her a the time of death. Daily was making sure the area wouldn't be contaminated as crime scenes always attracted a lot of people. We both knew that forensics would be back for further investigation.

The public's fascination with crime is unbelievable. If a person had a choice of watching a film about a dog and cat, or a romance movie, or the typical action adventure everyone-has-an-Uzi movie -- the action adventure would take a glittering first. No way around it, crime pays at the box office.

"Pete, what's the scoop?"

Peter smiled when he saw me, and we shook hands. "I've never had one like this. Looks like a pro. They probably looked like a tourist and walked in just like all the hotel guests. One bumblebee dart in the butt, and then they exited the area. Probably several ways out of here. That's my take on what happened. No emotion, no fear. Brutal."

"Bumblebee dart! Never heard of such a thing."

"Yeah. A dart with a stinger. Take a look at this." Pete walked over to the yellow tape outlining the crime scene and lifted a plastic lid that was used to cover evidence. He leaned over and pointed at a small black and yellow furry looking dart lying on the ground. "This is what killed her. She was spotted by a lifeguard when she rolled off her chaise lounge. He ran over and pulled the dart out of her butt and threw it on the ground. Most of the employees around here think she died of a bee sting."

I bent down and looked at the dart. Looked like a bee to me. I wasn't exactly an expert, this being the first one I had examined. "Never seen this used before. Anything about the victim?"

"Just a guest. Her name was Pleasure. At least that's what we have right now from the Stage Deli records. She ordered pastrami on rye with a Bloody Mary, and signed for it about an hour ago. Are you working this case? You're on the scene fast."

"Well, to be honest, she's my client," I said as I stood and examined the area around me. Typical hotel pool area. Nothing out of the ordinary.

"Pleasure was your client!" Daily said rather surprised.

"Ahaaa, I guess I should say she was my client. I just met her. Any other witnesses?"

"The usual. Nothing that will help. Your client, huh. Was she in trouble?"

"No. Just someone who needed some help. What did the witnesses say?"

"No one saw a thing. You know...vacation. No one wants to get involved."

"Well, with a figure like hers, I know someone was watching."

"Yeah, you're probably right about that. I've got a complete list of everyone here at the time of the hit. But they'll be scattered to the four winds. I don't think I'll be able to track all of them. Not that it matters any. I heard you bumped into Olsen?" Daily indicated his walkie-talkie.

"Yep. Happy-go-lucky guy."

"Sounds like Olsen didn't buy your story about her being your client?"

"Not a chance. He said I'm the number one suspect."

"Olsen's full of crap. He couldn't find sand in a desert. He's always been ticked off at you since you caught him planting evidence on Joey Santino. You sent Santino up the river later anyway. Olsen should have been with him. He'd frame his mother if he thought it would get him a promotion and a feature story in the paper."

We talked shop a bit and I left. Had some things to do. First, I had to worry a lot about the Beretta. The worrying part would be easy. I also needed to talk to Uncle Leo about my client, and I had to contact MGM Grand's management and see if I could get hired. Then there was the dart. I was going to have to learn a bit more about the capabilities of a flying bumblebee. Another piece of information to check on was the luggage in Pleasure's room. Some of it should be Jodys'. The police didn't know that yet. Might give me an advantage. I wanted to work this case from the inside. Being an intruder always worked the best. Boy, old Vince is going to have a cow when I show up working for the MGM Grand.

It was time I got hold of Abby. I had not seen her in a couple of days and usually stopped by when I could and when I knew there would be a break. I headed straight for the Tropicana, which is right across the street. Abby appeared as a line dancer in the Folies Bergere show. When looking for Abby, I always entered through the stage door. The one reserved for the showgirls. It suits me. There were mandatory rehearsals required of the entire dance line, so I expected Abby would be here. On top of that, if the showgirls were just a little off on their performance the night before, they had to put in extra hours under the work lights.

The stage was naked minus any of the glamour props. The dancers were just going through a dance routine for the benefit of two new girls who were breaking into the line over a period of several weeks. You think the gambling business is rough? It gets pretty hot in the changing rooms between numbers when they have forty-five seconds for a costume change. Grab the wrong costume and you'd hear about it.

Abby saw me leaning against some flats. She is dressed in black dance leotards, bright red warm-up leggings, and a cut-off sweatshirt to keep the chill off. Her blonde hair is pulled up in back to keep it out of the way. It always impresses me how good dancers look in leotards, and how bad everybody else looks at the gym.

Abby is like all the dancers who'd made it this far. Lean. Good figure. Her muscles are taut, showing the exertion of the workout. A glow radiated from her even more than usual. This is her life, her passion, and her dream. She is going to dance until they carry her off the stage. This is why I love her.

"Hi there. How's my favorite dancer?"

"About exhausted," said Abby, dropping to the wooden stage floor for some touch-the-toe stretching exercises. "I can't believe I have two shows tonight."

"You always have two shows. That's what you do. Myself, I'm thinking about going home and taking a nap."

"Typical."

"See, I'm the stable working guy who wants to take care of the dancer."

"I'm not the mortgage kind of girl. We've been over that. Someday. Sometime."

"I love you anyway. It's just a matter of time."

"You're as free as a hawk of prey," Abby said.

"I was hoping you were a wounded dove."

Abby just stared at me. She hated crummy lines.

"Time for a quick lunch?"

"Nah. I have another short rehearsal this afternoon. Working in some new moves. Maybe my feathers won't piss off Rhonda who is behind me."

"Bummer."

"What about you? What are you up to?"

"Got a new client this morning."

"Terrific. What kind of help does your new client need?"

"My client's already dead."

Abby stopped her stretching exercise and looked up at me. "You've got to be kidding."

"I'm talking dead. Nothing to laugh at."

"A hit?"

"Poisoned dart got her."

"Poison dart?"

"Yeah. A dart disguised as a bumblebee."

Abby gave me a quick look of surprise. She had the same reaction as I did. "The old bumble trick, huh," as she continued her stretching exercises.

"Dart right in the butt. It'll do it every time."

"In the butt?" I knew Abby hated doctors, and the mention of the weapon made her cringe at the thought of getting another needle jammed in her own backside, like when she was a kid.

"Yep."

"That's got to hurt."

"Only till you're dead. Then the pain goes away."

"Thank goodness for little favors," Abby said, crinkling up her nose in a way I love. "So, what's your involvement now?" asked Abby as she leaned forward and held her shoes with both hands without bending her legs. I winced at the possible pain.

"Don't really know. I've been hired for several days, so she'll get my full attention. I think I have an obligation to my client to make sure the villain in this case gets the one-way ticket on the bad guy express."

"The hero syndrome is once again upon us."

"She's dead. There will be no rewards."

"I take it she was good looking."

"Very. But dead is dead."

"In this town, anything is possible. Help me up."

She raised her arms and I pulled her to me. We were alone on the stage. I started to dance. Timing is everything.

"You're so romantic," she said.

"Thanks. I needed that." We continued to dance. We made a striking couple. Her blonde locks contrasted with my thick brown hair. And we're both tall and athletic. We glided around the stage, which was lit only with the work lights. There was just enough light to see what we were doing. I pulled her closer to me and then spun her around.

"This is a new side of you I haven't seen before." Her green eyes sparkled.

"I'm a great dancer."

"I don't hear the music."

"That's the romantic part. Maybe someday you can tell our kids how we danced on the most famous stage in Vegas."

"They'll think it's dumb."

On that comment I swung her around and then confidently lowered her to the floor. She moved with style. It was then I accidentally dropped her. She landed on her butt with a thud.

"Ouch. Damn it, Fargo."

"Sorry about that. Something to tell our kids about. The mysteries of the stage. Working the boards. Slipping and falling." I was in trouble.

"I'm going to be black and blue tomorrow."

"I think maybe by tonight." I picked her up. She wasn't happy about it. "We'll have to work on the spin part of the routine."

"Yeah. We'll work on it all right. We're going to drop it from the act."

"Pick you up tonight."

"I've got my own car. Thanks."

"Special meal. I'll pick up the tab."

"I don't think so. Not after the stunt you just pulled."

"I'll pick you up at eleven-thirty right after the last show." I started to walk away.

She stuck out her foot and tripped me. I fell flat on my face. Wasn't expecting it. I thought she would never stop laughing. Applause greeted me from the wings. I looked up to see the gang entering the stage for more rehearsal. They arrived to see me go splat. Great. Perfect timing. I imagine I will be reminded of this moment just a couple of times in the future.

Four

I left the Tropicana and headed back toward the MGM Grand using the overhead bridge connecting the two casinos. Traffic swept under me in a river of metal and plastic that flowed day and night. Places to go, money to lose. The New York, New York Hotel made an impressive skyline on the opposite corner. Some say better than actually being in New York. Where else can you take a roller coaster ride, check out the tug boats, walk over the Brooklyn Bridge, and take a close-up look at the Statue of Liberty? Then you can check into the Trump Tower and have dinner at Gallagher's Steakhouse, followed by a drink at Coyote Ugly, a southern style saloon featuring hot female bartenders who have elevated pouring drinks to an art form. All of this wrapped up in the same hotel, and if that's not enough, you can always place any number of different bets on the casino's elaborate gambling floor. Every tourist has cash to gamble, and the lure of the tables is too much for many who are just walking through the casino. No matter what you do, the edge is always with the casino.

I called Uncle Leo on my cellular. It turns out that Uncle Leo had headed for the off-track betting lounge at the MGM Grand when he'd heard that I had an appointment with Pleasure this morning. We always met someplace on Monday, and the MGM Grand was one of the best. The advantage of being self-employed. Not to mention one of the nicer betting boards in Vegas. I wanted to start hanging out at the MGM Grand to get a feel for the place. Pleasure's killer was probably not in residence, but I needed to get as close to the action as I could.

I took the escalator down from the Tropicana overpass to the street level, walked a short distance and then took the escalator back up the next overpass, which put me at the entrance to the MGM Grand. I walked in and stopped at the railing above the Race and Sportsbook and Poker Room.

I spotted Uncle Leo right away in the Sport's Bar. You could always find the horse junkies. They had the day's racing form spread out in front of them. Sometimes they carried small computers for handicapping, but more often than not, they relied upon their own systems. Uncle Leo always placed bets based upon the morning line and then handicapped each race throughout the day, looking for a good overlay. He always watched the races on a small monitor that was suspended overhead. The final clue to his whereabouts was the cigar smoke that swirled around his table. Lots of smoke indicated a loser.

I stopped at the Stage Deli and picked up a pastrami on rye and moved up a couple of steps into the lounge betting area. I waved down the hostess and signaled for two more draft beers to be delivered to Uncle Leo's table. He was into the Daily Racing Form. We're both suckers for the ponies, but I couldn't match him for track knowledge and betting experience. I was in training. Uncle Leo was always looking for the big ticket trifecta. He'd hit it once on a triple long shot and has been coming back ever since. Of course, everyone in the casino had hit something at some time. It's why they keep coming back, to pay for the last time they hit it big. You always end up putting it back into the casino.

I sat down next to Leo and unwrapped my pastrami sandwich. "Hear about my new client?"

"You mean Pleasure?"

"She's dead."

Uncle Leo lowered his racing form. "I heard about the murder by poolside, I didn't know it was Pleasure." Uncle Leo stared into space for a few seconds to gather his thoughts. I let him. "I'm sorry." He glanced at me, then his eyes flitted back to the monitor, but I saw his brow knit in puzzlement. He squinted at the monitor, creating more lines in his already wrinkled and tanned face. He had seen a lot in his time.

"Yeah...not so good," I said, with the full weight of it hitting me.

"You could have done better. When they die right away, it makes me look bad. You don't make so much money. End of the billing period. Time for a new client."

Uncle Leo's flippant remarks were cleverly disguised to bring the seriousness of the problem into focus. I had a dead client. She deserved better. Everyone does.

"Where did you know her from?" I asked. I spread more mustard on my pastrami and took another big bite.

"She's from the very distant past. Family connection." Uncle Leo watched the tote board as the clock ticked off the minutes for the next race. Track money, or stable money, came in last, and the experienced watched for which way the inside money went. Last-minute money bet on the second or third favorites might indicate the insiders know of a problem with the favorite, or another horse is in prime shape and ready to run.

"Olsen made me the number one suspect," I added, watching the odds change from the morning line.

"Right away you know you're not having a good day. Did she hire you?"

"Yep."

"Did she pay you?"

"Yep."

"For what?"

"Wants me to find somebody named Jody who has a lot of her money."

"Sounds like Jody might be a good suspect."

"That's what I thought."

"Where there's money, there's trouble."

"I knew I heard that someplace."

"You heard it here first. Any other complications I should know about?"

"Well...my fingerprints are on Pleasure's 9-mm Beretta handgun in her hotel room's safe, and it was recently fired. Other than that, no problems."

"I have some advice for you," said Uncle Leo as he watched the ponies enter the gate for the fourth race at Belmont.

"I like Redwine to win," I said. "What's that?"

"Get yourself a good attorney, and learn something about choosing horses. Redwine hasn't got a chance."

"Sort of like me. Is that what you're saying?"

"You picked the horse, I didn't... and besides, you're going to need something like red wine or stronger before this is all over."

"What should I do, from a professional legal posture, of course?"

"Punt."

"Seriously."

"I wouldn't worry about it," said Uncle Leo. "I've got Make-a-Wish, Guild-7, and Wind Dancer on a trifecta. You know where the Beretta is. I would try and find out where the bullets are that were in the gun."

The noise of the track came up as the horses left the starting gate. "...and they're off. Race'n Run breaks from the pack and is leading by a head as they approach the first turn...Make-a-Wish and Wind Dancer bunch in the middle with Quake and Guild-7...Redwine brings up the rear along with A-Million, and Winner-Takes-All."

I lost my thoughts as the roar of the crowd coaxed the horses around the first corner. Good point. Uncle Leo was always one step ahead of me. I'm a detective, but I had to ask anyway.

"How do you find where the bullets are?" I asked as the horses reached the backstretch.

"Read the paper, check out the police. Detect. You only care if the bullets slowed someone down. Might even run it past your cute little nurse friend over at Midland emergency. You know the one."

"How can I forget? But a gun shot wound would be reported to the police," I said.

"Then the police would be one step ahead of you," said Uncle Leo.

I had to agree with his logic.

The horses were rounding the final turn and approaching the stretch. The race track regulars were on their feet to route home their bets. "...Guild-7 leads by a neck and is followed by Wind Dancer and Make-a-Wish...and here comes Redwine out of no where weaving her way through the pack." The crowd continued to call out their favorites as the pack began to fold. "...from behind and now breaking wide to the outside, Redwine is number four, now number three, no... number two and giving Guild-7 a run for the money. They are neck and neck and it's...it looks like Redwine by a nose."

I sat down with as much pride as if I personally owned, trained, and rode Redwine across the finish line. This was what Monday was all about. Beating Uncle Leo at his own game. "Sort of looks like Redwine broke up your trifecta plans. Your ponies finished two, three, and four, I see."

Uncle Leo stuffed his tickets back into the track book he always carried with him. Tax back-up. "Doesn't mean a thing. You can call him all day long, but if you can't put your money where your mouth is, it doesn't mean a damn thing to a pony jock like myself."

I pulled from my pocket the ticket I had bought earlier that morning and dangled it in the air. "A ten spot on a twenty-to-one shot ought to buy me dinner for a couple of nights."

Uncle Leo shook his head. He hated it when I won after he spent long hours studying the handicapping charts and the morning line.

"Let me buy you another beer. We can discuss this further."

"What's there to discuss? When they get the Beretta, they will have you for lunch."

"No, no," I said. "I was talking about how I picked Redwine."

Uncle Leo laughed and we settled in for the next race of the day.

I arrived back at my house a little after seven after spending the remainder of the day trying to develop leads in my office. Nothing turned up. Summerlin was quiet this time of the evening. I owned a large two-story stucco home with a pool and very private yard. The Spanish tiled roof helped to keep it cool. The pool was next to a covered patio area that was an extension of the family room. It had a large built-in barbeque and an outside fireplace for fall days. It was really too big for one person, but it was my reward for a hard days work. The house was in a gated Summerlin community in a cul-de-sac providing a little bit of security. I also had my own system installed that I could monitor from the office. True, I wasn't close to the Strip, but it gave me a rest from what Las Vegas is all about - action. I enjoyed the morning drive to my office located east of Decatur. I occasionally drove past my office to the Sahara Casino for breakfast, or just stopped at Starbucks at Decatur and Sahara for coffee and a bagel.

I had a couple of hours to get cleaned up before picking up Abby for a late night snack. I planned to visit the MGM Grand in the morning to see what I could develop, but first I settled in at my desk and wrote up the day's notes. A detective's job is not always on the street. Paperwork. Substitute for memory. Kept me out of court more than once. Fragments of information. Details. I went to work on my Pentium workhorse. After about thirty minutes I had a pretty detailed description of the day's events. I also added the following questions. What will happen with the gun in the safe? Who gets the money in the safe? Are there any relatives? Witnesses? I had a lot of questions to answer.

Five

MONTOYA MARTINEZ COLORADO stepped out of a black limousine that had pulled under the emerald green Portico entrance of the MGM Grand shortly after 9:33 P.M. The limo departed and Colorado, which she liked to be called, strolled into the MGM Grand. She is noticed. She always is. Tall, with a figure a Hollywood starlet would die for, she is dressed neatly and conservatively in a skirt, blouse and jacket. Her light makeup accented her desert tan, which contrasted with her red hair. She was rich, confident, and carried a metal attaché case. An accent scarf and an expensive leather handbag made up the rest of her accessories, except for the jewels.

Colorado wore a pear-cut diamond pendant offset by brilliant cut diamonds on each side. A diamond-studded tennis bracelet hung loosely from her left wrist adorned with a double row of brilliant cut stones. She had a single solitaire diamond ring on her right hand. All total, probably about eight carats' worth. Colorado strolled through the Portico entrance and into the casino, turning heads as she went. She kept to the right and ignored the temptation of the slots. She eventually was at the beginning of the Studio Walk where the shops and restaurants were located. Colorado entered the Desert Sage Jewelry Company without glancing back over her shoulder.

"It's wonderful to see you, Ms. Colorado," greeted Walter McCaddy. He quickly locked the front door and led her through the retail space. "Las Vegas has missed you."

"And I've missed Las Vegas," replied Colorado. McCaddy guided her to a small parlor in back reserved for diamond buyers. Tonight, McCaddy was the buyer. He was about six-foot tall and on the puffy side, with a reddish face and a small brown mole alongside his nose. His eyes, now glowing upon seeing Colorado, were blue.

The viewing room was designed for the rich, and reserved for high rollers whose credit line could buy most of the jewelry McCaddy's store displayed. It also impressed the short-term winners, who suddenly found themselves with a large bankroll, courtesy of a good run at the tables, and a hot number that needed impressing. The room was practical as well as comfortable. It contained a small table with a light box, which was color balanced for the viewing of precious stones.

Once they were seated, Colorado pulled out two small black bags from her metal case and placed them on the table. She carefully closed the case and placed it at her side.

"I'm so happy you have been able to return to my hideaway, if you might call it that," the jeweler said as he eyed the bags, and then Colorado. McCaddy, thinking of nothing else but of the intimate possibilities between them, had envisioned this woman in his arms, naked and trembling, wanting more. It was his dream.

"May I?" asked McCaddy, indicating the two black bags.

The tall beauty smiled. "Please, be my guest."

McCaddy opened the first small bag. Inside he found two parcels. He opened them carefully and examined one hundred carats of brilliant cut diamonds. Their sizes ranged from one-half to two carats. Against the black velour of the table, they glistened of untold stories from the past and the promise of future adventures.

"These are magnificent, Colorado. You have done marvelous per our little agreement."

"You can still handle two packets a month?"

"Of course. That should be without question. Money is not the problem. As you know, the owners of the Desert Sage have no ancestors in the business. Even though I've been in this business for nearly forty years, when I go to New York or Amsterdam, I'm treated like an outsider."

"That's the diamond business."

"Yes, you're right. Irish I am, but Jewish I'm not. You have solved a great problem for me."

"I'm glad to be of service," smiled Colorado. "And the other package..."

"Of course," said McCaddy. Gently, McCaddy opened the second bag and was pleased to see a startling display of designer jewelry by Carrera and Mavado.

"You are pleased?" questioned Colorado, who took no interest in this dazzling display of jewelry.

"Just like I ordered. And the grades look good."

"You'll still have to sort and grade the loose stones yourself, but I think you will find they're all E in color, or better. I believe you said you were putting together a custom necklace?"

"Yes. This will be just perfect," said McCaddy as he examined several of the stones with a loupe.

"I'm glad they have met with your approval."

"I'm delighted, my dear friend. And you're making a profit?"

"I'm very comfortable with our business relationship."

McCaddy looked up. His eyes sparkled as much as the diamonds did. McCaddy did love his diamonds. "Can I ask who you're getting the stones from?"

"You may, but I'm refusing to answer," smiled Colorado. "I work both Hill Street and the New York diamond market. I also travel overseas to Hong Kong on a regular basis, but I prefer to deal out of Amsterdam and India."

"Very wise, I might add, to deal directly overseas with the wholesalers. Why have I not heard of you before?"

"I'm new to the trade," Colorado said coyly. I spent my time in London training under a couple of East End diamond dealers. Long family history in the trade. I moved on to the United States and then the New York market."

"Do you have contacts on the floor of the New York Diamond Exchange?"

"Of course."

"I do have one question, if you don't mind."

"Anything I can do to help," said Colorado.

"We always like to have a reference on the dealers who we buy from, and it turns out, how can I say, since we began working with you, we haven't been able to obtain a reference on you."

"Is that all," laughed Colorado. "I have become a very private person. It's not wise for a young lady to travel with tens of thousands of dollars of jewelry, is it?"

"This is true, but..."

"I can provide you with background references, but not specific as to where I purchase the stones," said Colorado. "My goal is to deal with only reputable dealers in my field on both sides. I provide a special service of delivering high-end goods at a cost well below what the normal wholesaler can provide you with. I target stores like yours that are reputable, but don't have the inside connection to really make a good profit. I have a small company in Europe with ties to the largest diamond suppliers and cutters in the business. It has taken me years to put all the contacts together. You must understand that I cannot just give this information away. I have to protect my interest, my business. How do I know that you're not wanting to cut me out of the middle and make even more of a profit?"

"No, no. I have no such interest. But I do have to document where the stones come from. For the records."

"If you would like to continue to do business with my company, then we'll do business. As we get to know each other, then I will provide you with references in the future, providing, of course, orders are forthcoming."

"I can assure you, there will be no problem."

"Have you made arrangements to pay me in cash, like I requested?"

"Of course. Just like last time." McCaddy stood. "If you will excuse me, I will be back shortly."

"If you don't mind," said Colorado, "I would like a tour of your operation here. I'm very interested in the security problems a firm like yours has. I'm thinking of opening a small retail establishment in the east, and I'm unfamiliar with the security necessary for retail opera-tions."

"Why, that won't be a problem. I'd be delighted to help. Perhaps you would care to share in a glass of wine after the tour. A celebration of our successful business arrangement. I have a very nice North Coast Pinot Grigio that I've been saving for a special occasion."

"How thoughtful of you," said Colorado, shoulder-ing her handbag. "A delightful way to end the day." She picked up her metal attaché case.

"Please. It's not often that a young lady requests the services of an old-fashioned diamond dealer. Let me carry your attaché case for you." McCaddy offered his hand.

Colorado smiled. "Ahhhh...but you need to carry all your diamonds."

"You are correct," conceded McCaddy, with a slight bow. He made a striking pose in his gray pin striped suit, and enjoyed the advantage of being taller then Colorado as he guided her on a tour of his retail jewelry operation. When they returned to the back offices, McCaddy described the walk-in safe.

"It's one of the newest models. It works on a time lock system. Only two of us have keys. It takes only one key to open plus a combination code. If we open it at off hours, it takes two keys to gain entrance."

"But what about the casino? They're open all night, and if they get a big winner, won't they want to come in here to purchase something?"

"It's rare that actually happens, but we do have the merchandise out front for them. Even casino shops can't stay open all night. It's tough enough being open seven days a week, twelve hours a day."

"I'm very impressed with all of this. Your security here is top rate," said Colorado.

"Thank you. We have spent a great deal of time perfecting it." McCaddy placed the diamond packets on a small table just outside the walk-in safe.

"Not exactly foolproof though."

"Pardon...?" McCaddy turned around.

Colorado held a S&W 9-mm handgun leveled at McCaddy's chest. "You should have done a better job checking out my family!"

"This is a robbery," stuttered McCaddy.

"Why, of course. That's why I like having the jewelry store closed when I visit your fine establishment."

"But I thought...that...you...and me...."

Laughter filled McCaddy's ears. "Please, that was part of the plan. Women's charms can be very seductive, don't you think?

McCaddy's face turned red with anger. He was being made a fool of. He'd had all these plans. She was so sincere.

"Turn around, McCaddy," said Colorado. The Irishman turned around. "Put your hands behind you.

"Please...don't use the gun...I..."

Colorado pulled out a set of cuffs and snapped a loop around his wrist in one fluid motion. As she moved to place the other one, McCaddy shoved her backward knocking her to the floor. As her hand braced to soften the impact, the stainless steel automatic slid across the tiled floor. Colorado crawled after it. McCaddy also lunged for the gun, but Colorado was quick and gripped the gun around the handle. But she was fully stretched out and had no leverage.

McCaddy swung his body over hers just as she twisted around to face him. He collapsed on top of her, something he had only dreamed about. He struggled for the gun, and then surprised Colorado by making a move to shut the safe door. His elbow hit Colorado's arm.

"No, noooo..." yelled Colorado. A muffled pop, and McCaddy slumped on top of her, emitting one long groan of fright, terror, and agony. Then nothing.

"Ahh crap," said Colorado. She waited, but heard nothing. She rolled McCaddy off her. He had received a bullet directly in the heart, and had bled all over her and onto the floor. She grabbed McCaddy and pulled him aside. Pulling his jacket off him, she rubbed it against her clothing trying to get rid of the blood. Too late now, she thought. I was only going to tie McCaddy up for a while, and now he went and got himself killed. She tossed the jacket back on top of McCaddy.

Colorado did a sweep of the room and outer office area for surveillance cameras. Two cameras, she had been informed. She took a can of black spray paint from her bag and sprayed each one making them useless. She was already on tape, but she would worry about that later. Then she reached into her handbag and quickly put on a pair of rubber gloves. Colorado retrieved the two black bags of loose stones and finished pieces, and dropped them in a pouch on the inside of her metal attaché case. She glanced at the clock on the wall, then entered the safe.

Moving efficiently, she located a series of locked boxes. Colorado pulled small wads of plastic explosives from her case and stuck them to the locks on the boxes. The inside of her bag was extremely well organized, with Velcro holding everything she needed in perfect position for quick access. In a period of sixty seconds she prepared all ten locked boxes. Each wad of the explosive material had a thin wire attached to it, which ran to a small electronic black box she had retrieved from her attaché case. She connected the last wire, walked out of the safe, and closed it behind her leaving it slightly open. She then pulled a small stool into the middle of the room, and climbed up to disengage the smoke detector. She then kicked the stool out of the way, moved behind the work counter, and punched a button on a remote control unit. A muffled explosion occurred, followed by smoke streaming out the cracks of the safe's door. Colorado donned a small gas mask complete with a portable light on top, and reentered the safe. The floor of the safe was littered with both diamonds and shards of metal.

Colorado moved methodically from box to box, scooping up packets of precious stones and dropping them into a series of small bags she carried. She was out of the safe within ten minutes. Setting down her case, she picked up McCaddy's arms and pulled him into the safe. She dropped him with a thud. She did one last check for anything that could incriminate her, and exited the safe.

Colorado looked at her watch, closed the safe, and gave the combination a spin. She then pulled a small tube of super glue from her pocket and squeezed half the tube into the key openings of the safe. So much for that lock. She squeezed the remaining super glue around the large combination lock. The tube went into a plastic bag that went into her metal case.

She then went to a locked cabinet in the far right corner under one of the video cameras. She jimmied the door opened and removed three security video tapes. She tossed these into her bag. So much for store security.

She then stripped down and put on a knit dress that had been rolled into her attaché case. She pulled off her red wig, revealing thick lavish blonde hair, placed her clothing in the case, and took one look around for any forgotten items. She moved cautiously toward the front of the store wiping any fingerprints she might have left, even though she knew this was not necessary. She had touched nothing in the office.

When Colorado appeared outside the Desert Sage Jewelry Company, no one would have noticed her. Just another customer leaving a store. She locked the front door with the keys she had taken from McCaddy. She looked into the reflection in the store window to check for anything irregular. She had planned everything. Most people never do the fine tuning it takes to plan a crime to perfection. She had spent the necessary hours to work out all the details. Partners never did that. They were dumb and stupid and didn't pay attention to details. She was a planner, leaving nothing to chance. She negotiated deals, and demanded others to perform to her satisfaction. She reached the visitor parking lot at the rear of the casino, climbed into a nondescript rental car, and pulled into traffic. No decals indicated the car was a rental. Another precaution. All stickers had been peeled off earlier after she'd stolen the car. Rental cars were the best to steal because they contained lots of fingerprints.

Colorado was lost in traffic within a matter of minutes. As she drove, she had only one thought on her mind. Her unseen partner. He had given her good information, but she didn't like working with partners. This one knew too much and he would have to be made a silent partner. Something to think about as she drove through Vegas' dazzling Strip of flashing neon lights, which promised to entertain and delight while skillfully reaching into your pocket and stealing your dreams.

Six

I felt refreshed and ready to go. It was Tuesday morning.
I had spent the late evening and early morning hours
with Abby lingering over a long dinner at the Hard Rock
Café. Amateur gamblers arrived to give themselves
energy for the night's run at the tables. The pro gamblers
had their own special spots always located not far from
the action. For Abby and me, it was a safe retreat into the
anonymity of the Las Vegas scene. No one would
recognize her as a lead dancer at the Trop, and any local
crime buster wouldn't be seen in a place like this. We
ordered pasta. Mine was a broiled chicken over pasta
with a ton of garlic. She had a dish that looked more like
a pizza in a bowl. We shared a bottle of Cabernet
Sauvignon from Nelson Family Vineyards, a California
winery located near Hopland, California in Mendocino
County. Caramel crowned steam-baked apples made to
perfection ended our late-night snack.

   Abby was the woman I loved, but she was unwill-
ing to make the big commitment. For the moment, she
was living the life she wanted as a dancer. She enjoyed
the pain, the sweat, the glamour, and most of all the
applause. As a private detective I was living the life I
wanted. Every day different, new people, new problems,
and sometimes, new dangers. And when I didn't have a
case, I always had a treasure to find. Sometimes it was

gold in the desert. Sometimes pieces of eight in old wrecks at sea. Sunken Spanish Galleons have led to many adventures, and I'm sure will lead to more. I have even tracked down Civil War battles looking for coins that had been lost by soldiers, who were often paid just before going into battle so they would be motivated to fight to win.

My only problem was that I wanted Abby as part of my life. She insisted that we were both free as birds. Our different goals were the source of a long outstanding rift between us. This left my love life somewhat in limbo. But there were still times when we shared the day's events. Our happiness, and our sadness.

In the back of my mind I kept thinking of Pleasure and how this whole thing had started. I swung my car into the MGM Grand's covered parking area, walked into the casino, and headed for the main offices. I had a plan; a good one, I might add.

But first I stopped at a dollar slot machine and fed in three coins. I had a stash of dollar coins in my car. I hit two watermelons out of three and got back two dollars. As I left I was almost knocked over by three ladies who went for the machine like it was free food after a starvation diet. They fought amongst themselves for the machine's future.

"I saw it first," yelled an obese woman.

"I'm the one who taught you to never let a single play from a stranger go by without following with at least another nine dollars to clear the machine," her friend screamed at her.

Everybody had their own ideas of how to hit a winning slot. I made it a practice to never look back just in case they were right. I hated it when I heard bells go off with accompanying screams of joy. I passed the reception desk and moved over to the bank of elevators. I rode to the second floor and entered the Casino's general management lobby. The name on the desk said Susan H. Roberts.

"Good morning, Susan," I said.

A very attractive woman in her late twenties looked up. She had a soft sensuality about her. Not like the showgirls, who radiated a flash of beauty under the lights. Susan had the figure, and the looks. Her dark auburn hair cascaded down to meet her shoulders. Her suit was well tailored and she was well groomed. She appeared comfortable and secure.

"Hi. Call me Susie. Everyone else does around here. How can I help you?" Her voice carried a slightly southern accent.

"I would like to see Mr. Lanning."

"Do you have an appointment?" Her eyes never left mine. She paid full attention to my request, which I took as a compliment. Not like most receptionists who keep right on working and never give you the time of day. She was professional and protective at the same time. You sort of wanted to take Susie home with you and make sure nothing ever happened to her.

I unfolded my detective's I.D. "No I don't. I'm a P.I. and I have some information regarding the murder yesterday at the pool."

"A murder! We all heard she had an allergic reaction to a bee sting. Oh my."

Hotel spin doctoring at work. "Is Harry in?"

"You know Mr. Lanning?"

"We go back a long way."

"Well," she glanced at the badge again as I put it away. "Mr. Lanning is in the casino at the high stakes slot area welcoming a group of Japanese visitors to the hotel."

I headed for the door. "Thanks Susie...."

She cut me off. "He doesn't like surprises."

I gave her a wave as I left. "I'll catch him there."

I hurried down the set of stairs adjacent to the elevator and then checked to make sure Lanning was not headed up. The sounds of casino action met me. Even for early morning, the casino was a busy place. I moved toward the high stakes slot area, which had everything from twenty-five-dollar to five-hundred-dollar slots. Bigger money likes to feel important. Put a velvet rope in front of the gaming area and that made the players feel exclusive. The casino also threw in some one-hundred-dollar slots, which always sucked up the winnings from the twenty-five-dollar players. It's just a game, and all the casinos have a million tricks to separate you from your money.

I saw Harry moving toward me with the usual entourage. He was dictating a memo. He was famous for these. Harry "Legs" Lanning was the manager responsible for the entire casino and all of its complicated operations. Everybody knew him as "Legs" because he was six-foot-six inches tall. He was one-hundred percent Italian and looked the part: dressed immaculately in the finest Armani suits I have ever seen.

"Good morning, Harry. It's been a while." I stuck my hand out and he caught it. I turned and fell into his stride as he worked his way back to the management area. The others formed a group in back of us. Harry watched everything as he walked the casino. He waved at a pit boss as we went by the tables.

"How you doing, Fargo? I figured I'd see you sooner or later."

"Are you referring to that bee sting out back yesterday?"

Harry stopped short. "Well, you know how it is. I've got a casino to run, and I can't let the wrong story get around. Bad for business."

"That's what I want to talk to you about. You know she was my client?"

"No, no I didn't. Olsen never said anything in his report I read this morning. He did say you were the

44

number one suspect. Happiest I've seen him in a long time."

Harry pointed to a black chip lying on the carpet and waved one of his assistants over to it. Harry had the best eyes in the business. He could spot a chip a mile away. Makes the floor personnel feel like crap. The assistant picked it up and walked over to the pit boss working the dice tables. The pit boss would record it, and later they would play back videos to find out who was its owner. At the MGM Grand the chip would be credited to the rightful owner's account, if they could be identified. A message would follow explaining the credit. Makes them come back, and you want the hundred-dollar betters to come back.

But not everybody plays with hundred-dollar chips. Someone might be working the tables by skimming chips. These end up on the floor kicked aside for a later pickup. Usually it was a woman with a very low cut dress. This always distracted the players. The chips would be knocked off the table for later removal. Everyone likes a hot table with cleavage -- except management. Makes them nervous. They don't like skimmers. The customers love the ladies, and always bet more to impress them with their wealth. The casinos tolerate the female skimmers because it makes the customers happy. It was a love-hate relationship.

"I can help you with this case. You know Olsen hasn't the time to work this thing. And the cops will give up within a couple of days. Particularly when there isn't a lot of good, hard evidence at the crime scene. The case will always be open, never closed."

"What do you want?"

"The crime was committed here. There is reason to believe a missing person may be part of this crime, or have information about it. I don't have a client. I want you to hire me and comp me a room. I need to spend a lot of time here. If there is something going on, it would be in your best interest to find out right now."

"That's Olsen's job."

"Yeah, right. Olsen's job. My dead client in your hotel. Doesn't look too good."

"Olsen will be pissed."

"When was the last time Olsen wasn't pissed about something?"

"Well, you're right about that." Harry walked while thinking. The group followed in pursuit. "What's in it for me?"

"You get the best P.I. in Vegas. And you get the only person who had contact with the victim before she got stung."

"You mean I get the number one suspect."

"Yeah, right. Me, the best cop in this town. I turned P.I. because I want to enjoy life before it's over. I like what I do. Now Olsen, he's the one who got kicked off the force. He hasn't liked me since I got the goods on him on the Fremont job."

"Olsen gets the job done. He keeps this place in shape."

I stopped him. "Harry, you need me."

Harry stopped walking. "Look, let's get something straight. I don't need you. I don't care about you. I don't care what happens to you. You're a suspect. I've got a murder case on my hands, and I've got people breathing down my neck to take care of it. As far as I'm concerned, it's a P.R. problem. Nothing more."

"P.R. isn't going to help if there's another murder."

"No, but if they arrest you I can spin it so everyone here can sleep at night."

"Until the next killing. Look, let's get to the bottom of this and move on. I don't like my clients being murdered in your hotel any more than you do. I can't count on Olsen. I've got to do the job myself. I'm just asking so I can help you."

"And what are you going to do for me?"

"Another set of eyes."

"That's it?"

"I'm the only one in any kind of position to help you."

"The entire Strip is going to be laughing at me for hiring the suspect. They'll think I'm nuts."

"Or they'll think you're a genius."

Harry turned around and observed the action at the tables while he thought about what he should do. Suddenly he waved over another member of his entourage. She was tall, and her very dark red hair was so straight it looked ironed. She wore dark-rimmed glasses and carried a steno pad.

"Julie, this is Fargo Blue. Fargo, this is Julie Fuller. She's new here. I want you to set Fargo up in a mid-level suite overlooking the pool. It's to be comped by the casino with all expenses. The works. No questions. He gets VIP all the way." Julie wrote furiously. "He needs complete freedom to move throughout the casino. Take care of it at the front desk and put a memo out to those that need to know. For the record, Fargo is a high roller from Chicago."

Harry shook my hand and then walked away. He turned, and came back and put his hand on my shoulder. His cold steel gray eyes were six inches away. "I want a personal report for my eyes only every morning when you have something of significance to report. On my desk at seven A.M. Olsen will run his operation independently from you. If there's anything he finds out, I know he's not going to tell you. But I will. I'm your go-between. I want the killer more than you do. Like I said, it's bad for business. If you screw up in any way, I'll drive you to the station myself and turn you in. You got that?"

"Clearly."

He was gone. I walked with Julie toward registration. It was obvious she was comfortable with her position within the casino. Dealers and pit bosses acknowledged her as we walked through the blackjack line and swung around past one of the slot pits. Like Harry, Julie worked the casino as we walked. Nothing escaped her attention. We arrived at the front desk and after a short conversation with the head manager, she was handed a room key. She turned and handed me the key.

"You're all set. Top of the line three-room suite for two weeks. I've upgraded you. VIP treatment. The room will be ready in a half hour." She flashed a smile. "Just use the room key and it will get you everywhere. Any questions, here's my card. I'll take care of it."

I took the card. "Thank you, Julie. I appreciate your help."

"Anything to help a high roller from Chicago."

"One more thing. When you get a chance, could you ask Harry for any notes that Olsen put together? Whatever you can obtain, it will help."

She made a note. "Sure, no problem. Just check your hotel voice mail for messages. Whatever I get, I'll put in an envelope at the front desk, and leave you a message. Look for it in the morning."

"Thanks."

"Bye." She left giving me a big smile, turning heads as she went.

I made my way back to my BMW, where I picked up a bag with some overnight necessities and a change of clothes. I grabbed my portable phone, computer, and multi-channel police radio and headed back to the casino. I traveled light and compact. This time I took a right and headed toward the pool area. I flashed the real key card and walked over and sat down.

I wanted to study the scene of the crime, which was on the other side of the pool. People had begun to arrive to secure their pool positions for the day. Peter Daily had said the shooter most likely came in from the entrance on my immediate left, crossed behind the pool, made the hit, and then moved off to the right, probably leaving by way of the tennis courts. There was something wrong with this picture.

"Mr. Blue, sir?"

I looked up to see a pool attendant hovering above me. "Call me Fargo."

"Mr. Fargo."

I laughed.

"Mr. Fargo, can we get you anything? Compliments of the house. Perhaps a Bloody Mary, or a light snack this morning."

Word gets around fast. "That sounds fine. But make it a dill pickle instead of celery. And a bagel and cream cheese would be nice."

"Toasted?"

"Ahhhh, yes please."

"Right away, sir."

What the hell? This was what life was all about. At least part of it. I mean, think about it. Most people work their entire lives at a job they hate. Me, I love my work. Be happy in your work. That's my motto.

I focused my attention back to the crime scene. What was wrong? What didn't fit? Several young women, who were obviously traveling together, arrived on the scene and secured their lounge seats. They moved the chairs to get the best of the sun. A pool attendant helped them. They started to remove their clothes get down to their swim-suits. Strip was a better word for it. It's one of the mysteries of Vegas. They come from all over, and when they get here, they do things they would never do at home. They all wore the briefest of bikinis and tried to outdo each other. One of the great sporting events was watching these housewives, secretaries, and lawyers undress in public. Every once in awhile you were rewarded when one simply took off her top and slowly changed into a new bikini top. Of course everybody pretended not to watch, but everybody did. That was the game, not to get caught. I watched behind my dark sunglasses. Las Vegas. This was the life.

"Mr. Fargo, sir. I hope this meets with your satisfaction?" A platter was placed beside me with the bagels, lox, and cream cheese presented on a leafy background of spinach lettuce that would make Martha Stewart proud and envious. The Bloody Mary looked good, and large. The garlic dill pickle made it work. The biggest one I had ever seen. I signed the chit and noted that the tip was included.

"Sir, if there is anything else we can help you with, please just give us a wave. And, I will check back with you to make sure everything is in order."

"Everything looks great. What's your name?"

"Randell, sir."

"Thanks Randell. Oh, one thing. The door that is over there on the right. Where does it go?"

"It goes to the women's Spa, sir."

"And that connects around to the series of doors which are in back of me?"

"Yes, sir."

"I see. Thank you, Randell."

"Very good, sir." Randell gave a slight bow and started to depart.

"One more thing. Were you working here yesterday when the unfortunate bee sting incident happened?"

"No sir."

"Who was?"

"That would be Williams, sir. We alternate our shifts. He'll be here tomorrow."

"Thanks Randell, thanks a lot."

"Very good, sir."

Interesting, interesting indeed. If the killer went through that door, then the killer must have been a woman. The perfect place to commit murder. Everybody's lying on their backs looking at the sun. Nobody sees anything. But the real problem was, there was more than one way to get in and out of here. I had walked right in that morning with no room key. And you could easily get out by the tennis courts. Easy in, easy out. Even a killer could figure that out.

Seven

I fought off a bellhop and then caught the elevator to the 30th floor. Everyone is always so helpful at the MGM Grand. It's either that or they're after tips. Three corridors branched off from a common area, and Room 3032 was about midway down the central corridor. I used my hotel key card and entered a fabulous MGM Grand hotel suite. It started with a sunken living room/bar area off the entryway, which was accented by beautifully polished dark hardwood floor. A fruit basket with my name on it sat on the bar as well as a bottle of champagne and two glasses. A smaller bedroom was on the right, the master suite opposite it. I walked into the master suite and saw a sunken hot tub tiled in a dark green. This led into a spacious bathroom and steam bath. What a setup. I was home.

I unpacked my bag and computer and set up shop. Once the portable ink jet printer was in place, I accessed the free WI FI provided by the MGM Grand. I passed on setting up my police scanner because I didn't think I would have much opportunity to use it. I took a careful look around and marveled at the view of the pool area with the skyline of the New York, New York hotel in the background. The MGM Grand had all the conveniences of home for us high rollers from Chicago. The phone rang and broke my spell. I picked it up.

"Hello, Mr. Fargo. This is the MGM Grand Concierge speaking. I wanted to check with you to make sure everything is all right. Can we get you anything?"

Why can't they get my name right? "No, no, everything is fine here. And thanks for your consideration."

"Will you be dining with us today, sir? Can I arrange lunch for you? Perhaps in the MGM Grand Cafe, or would one of other establishments be more suitable? Perhaps something brought to your room?"

"No, I'm just fine. Haven't thought that far ahead."

"Very well, sir. Good day, sir."

"Thank you." When I hung up the phone I thought about how much attention I was getting. Was it because I was good looking? I doubted that. Was it because I was a reported big roller from Chicago? Was it because I was hot on the trail of a killer? Or was it because the hotel wanted to keep an eye on me? I didn't know, but I would find out. All a part of my investigation. There were traps to set. At that moment the red light on the phone started to blink. Already a message. I dialed three-two-two to pick up my message. A recording came on. The message was from Julie. She indicated that the hotel gossip was that Olsen is out to get me. He was telling everyone that I was the target, and that I would be going down for the count in a matter of hours. He said he didn't care about promotions. His job was to get killers off the street and out of his hotel.

I wondered if he knew I was here already. Just wait until they discover my prints on that gun. Then he'll really get excited.

The lox and cream cheese were working on me. I wasn't as hungry as I was thirsty. I left the room after setting everything right. I left my computer so you would have to move a sheet of printing paper to get to the keyboard. The computer was password protected, but the point was, I didn't know if any angel was looking over my shoulder. I always checked for bugs at night.

Video and audio. Briefcase was also set so I could tell if anyone tried to open it. A paper clip rested vertically on the backside. Anyone picking up the briefcase would never notice the clip, or notice it was placed exactly three inches in from the right side.

Once I got downstairs to the casino I headed over to the Turf Club. I ordered a cold draft beer, flashed my key card, and then moved to the Sports Bar, where the horse betters were just getting into the day's race action. I sat in the corner and watched. I didn't watch the races, I watched the people.

Sure enough, a thug dressed as a tourist came up to the snack bar with a two-way radio, running a continuous line of chatter. I unfolded the Daily Racing Form and punched a hole in the page. I could see everything that was going on. It was Olsen. He talked to the server behind the counter, who pointed in my general vicinity. Olsen moved in my direction, still not suspecting the man behind the newspaper. When he was right in front of me I lowered the paper, and we locked eyes. He knew I had him, and he had blown his cover. I beat him at his own game. He was embarrassed as he turned and moved away, talking into the security radio.

"Can I buy you a beer?" I shouted after him. "Or are you working," I yelled, adding insult to injury. It wasn't my imagination or a wild guess: I was being followed by the hotel, and that meant Olsen had been tipped off by Harry. I had to understand their viewpoint. I was, after all, the number one suspect. Made sense. I pondered the thought as I drank my beer. A cheer went up in the turf club and I looked up to see a sleek-looking filly named Follow-Me cross the finish line. Perfect, just perfect.

It was almost one o'clock by the time I reached the office I shared with Uncle Leo and Sheri. Located in a small commercial complex on Sahara just past the In & Out drive-in, we were isolated in five offices on the second floor. Several fountains in the courtyard below were visible and provided a welcomed relief on hot summer days. A small reception area was in front and the offices were along one side and in back. One office was mine, one Leo's, and the third was Sheri's. Computers were everywhere as we had invested in a network computer system that was online twenty-four hours a day. The fourth office served as a storage room and lock up area for our surveillance gear and firearms safe. We also kept overnight bags in there for when we had to make a mad dash to the airport. We tried to be prepared for every possible situation.

The Most important room was used by everybody. The law library and conference room provided us with research tools to solve important issues and a place to meet. It also acted as a command center when something was going down. The library was wall-to-wall books, which provided insulation from office and street noise. Shut the door, and it was quiet. An old lawyer trick.

We had just recently moved to this location on Sahara as we had outgrown our former office located off of Charleston near The Gambler's Book Shop. They sold gambling systems to tourists who came to Las Vegas in search of the perfect system. 'Dream sellers' are what we called them. But they did fulfill a service to those in search of instructional manuals that would train them in the art of blackjack dealing or being a stick man at a crap table. Uncle Leo spent a lot of time there.

Uncle Leo was not in. I greeted Sheri, a former U.S. Coast Guard officer turned P.I. No office is complete without a beautiful redhead who runs the entire show. Thirty-five years old and very accomplished. Besides having her own detective practice, we made her in charge of the office and computer systems. When she tried to explain our computers to us, we gave her a raise. Leo and I had formed a pact: if we lost her we agreed to quit the biz. We gave her a salary for taking care of the computer system, and also to administrate our books. It worked out fine and everyone was happy.

How a lady of the sea ends up working as a detective is another story. I, for one, believe that women are naturally good detectives. Must be all that shopping. Sheri had helped me out in a number of situations. In the detective world, women can solve problems a man can't even guess at. I classify it under the heading of woman's intuition. They can also get into places men can't, and that's always helpful.

"Hi, Fargo," said Sheri. "You're late."

"Been one of those days."

"Hey, when are we going to do a stakeout together? I'm free Saturday night."

"You don't make dates for stakeout," I said, smiling.

"I know. I just don't have anything to do Saturday night. Probably end up at the shooting range."

I laughed. "Probably the safest place to be anyway. In parts of Vegas they still shoot back at you."

"That's called a war zone. Been there, done that."

I had to laugh. "Any phone calls?"

"You've got two. Some woman named Pleasure called and said she'd catch up with you later. And...."

"Pleasure!" I said surprised. "When did that call come in?"

"Let's see...Well, let's see, it came in late this morning. Late."

"Are you sure it wasn't yesterday?"

"Positive. I log the voice mails and delete all entries at the end of the day."

I sat down heavily in a chair. "This morning you say...." I now started to think about what was going on. It raised a lot of questions I had to answer.

"Yeah. Is it important?"

"She was murdered yesterday."

"Impossible," said Sheri, now very interested.

"You can prove the time the call came in?"

"Sure. It's on voice mail. I missed the call and by the time I got to the phone she was gone."

"Play it back."

"Okay."

Pleasure's voice crackled through the answering system. "This is Pleasure calling for Fargo. Fargo...I will be tied up for a couple of days so I hope you can find Jody for me. Thanks for taking the case and coming by and seeing me yesterday. Hi to Uncle Leo. I'll be in touch. Thanks. Bye."

"And you went out to lunch around eleven-thirty A.M. and came back at noon?"

"That's right. I just picked something up and brought it back here. What happened?"

"I met with her around eleven yesterday morning. Then I went up to her room and almost immediately was told by hotel security that she had been murdered at poolside."

"You're kidding!"

"Nope. If the call really came in after eleven today, then she was alive after she was dead, if that makes any sense."

"Then who's the dead girl?"

"That's what makes a mystery," I said. "Write up a memo of everything you did this morning setting down a time frame of events. I'll catch up with you later. Do you know where Uncle Leo is?"

"He said something about Belinda. Who's Belinda?" Sheri asked.

"Sounds like a pony to me."

Eight

I got out of my office as fast as I could. Maybe Pleasure was still alive! The only place I would find an answer was the morgue. Was she still alive, or had I just listened to the last phone call my client ever made? There was some hope here. I don't like any of my clients getting taken out. If she was alive, then who was dead? What kind of game was Pleasure playing?

As I drove down the Strip, I wondered who had done the I.D. on the body. When I'd gotten to the crime scene the body had already been removed. As far as I knew, I was the only one who knew what she looked like. A lot of questions were starting to come into focus and I made mental notes to follow up on them. I pulled into a covered parking lot and hesitated before getting out. This was not my favorite place, and I always had to stop for a few seconds to get ready for what the morgue offered. Dead bodies.

It was even more depressing than I had remembered. The odor of sour-smelling bodies, overpowered by the sharp scent of chemicals known only to the medical examiner, assailed my senses. This strange world of death belonged to Las Vegas Medical Examiner Herman D. MacMillan. Herbie, as everyone called him, has seen more death in his thirty years than a hit man from New York. I filed my request in the reception area and found him reviewing his notes in his office.

"Fargo. I'm glad you dropped by."

"Not my first choice of places to be on a nice afternoon."

"At least you walked in."

"Yeah. There is that aspect of it. I feel better already."

Herbie wore a white lab coat and was about my height. Brown hair with a tint of gray. A receding hairline gave him a distinguished look, but the dark eyes revealed many hours of autopsy work. He unwrapped a huge sandwich and took a bite before looking up. "What brings you down here? This is not your normal neck of the woods, and you're not the social type."

"You had a body come in here yesterday afternoon. Pleasure was her first name. Don't know the last."

"Weber, Kimberly P.

"Weber. That's her last name?" I remembered the envelope in the safe.

"That's what I was told. She died at the MGM Grand yesterday morning. Haven't done the exam yet. Supposed to have died by a poison dart."

I ignored him. "Who did the report?"

Herbie picked up a clipboard and flipped through several pages, and then put it back down "It was signed off by Peter Daily."

"Good," I said. "He's good with details at crime scenes."

"One of the best."

"I'd like to take a look at the body."

"No problem." Herbie took another huge bite of his sandwich, got up from his desk, and put back on his reading glasses that he wore most of the time. A national symbol for hitting fifty. The eyes are second to go. At least that's what they used to say around the station. "Any particular reason?" he mumbled through salami and corn beef.

"She died between eleven and twelve yesterday. I got a phone message from her between eleven and noon this morning. The voice was the same. I've got to check out the body."

"Curiosity got the best of you, I take it?"

"Yep."

We turned left, going through the metal swinging doors, which lead to the cold storage department where the corpses are held before any autopsies are performed. Other lock ups held the bodies that had been released for pick up by the relatives.

As we entered another swinging door, Herbie picked off another clipboard as they walked into the Parts Room, as it's sometimes called. "Looks like twenty-seven-B is her unlucky number." Herbie placed the clipboard back in its spot, pulled out several plastic gloves from his pocket, and threw one pair to me. I pulled them on. He also threw a nose mask to me, and I snapped it into place.

We walked into a room of bodies. If I had not been here before, I would have found it an upsetting experience. The first time I witnessed an autopsy for the department I nearly lost it. I barely made it through that morning, and the images stayed with me for years. It was part of the routine I eventually got used to. You have to remind yourself that these are not living, breathing humans anymore.

Herbie stopped in front of a rolling table and checked the number. The table contained one body wrapped in a plastic sheet.

"How come you never checked the body at the MGM Grand?" he asked me.

"Her body had already been removed from the site. I had just been hired to perform some domestic chores for the deceased. It caught me off guard when she was reported dead about a half hour later."

"Well, here she is." Herbie pulled back the top plastic sheet to reveal a woman, late thirties. Naked. Dead. Defenseless. She had short chopped hair, fairly good figure, but no tan, as Pleasure had. I breathed a silent sigh of relief.

"That's not my client. That's not Pleasure," I said.

"Ever seen her before?"

"Nope. Can you show me where the dart hit her?"

Herbie rolled her over and showed me the red swollen spot on her left buttock. "I'll have the final autopsy done by tomorrow, and that will list the official cause of death. But she does show signs of an allergic reaction typical of a poison." Herbie rolled her back over.

"I take it you haven't finger printed her yet."

"Will get on it right away. I'll make a temporary name change." Herbie checked his clipboard. "Looks like it will be a Jane Doe number ZV2336. You want to be notified when I make it official that it's not Kimberly Weber and I.D. the Jane Doe?"

"As soon as you I.D. the victim, call Uncle Leo's office and leave a message who she is. I'm staying at the MGM Grand if you need to get hold of me. Just leave a message on my voice mail. No wait, just call my office. Don't call the MGM Grand."

"Will do. Glad it wasn't your client," said Herbie as he finished tucking the plastic sheet around Jane Doe. We pulled off the gloves and aimed for the waste can. Herbie's was a straight jumper, and I went for a hook. Both landed neatly in the basket. Nothing but plastic. Four points. No comment necessary, as we had played the game for years. The nose masks followed.

"Makes me feel a little better," I said. "I still don't know what I've got hold of. When do you notify homicide?"

"In my autopsy report, unless they come down here for a reason."

"Good."

"Why are you so concerned about Homicide? Weren't you on their side at one time?"

"I'm the number one suspect."

Herbie gave me a look of surprise. "May I ask who is leading the charge on that one?"

"Olsen, from the MGM Grand."

"Olsen's been dirty ever since he was kicked off the force."

"Listen, don't tell Olsen until he asks. This could turn out to be the real Pleasure, and I need some time to check things out."

"I just file reports," said Herbie. "Sometimes they take awhile."

I gave Herbie a wave of thanks as I headed out of the morgue. I figured he was going back to finish his sandwich.

Nine

I checked my suite and it was clean and undisturbed. The autopsy room had given me the feeling I had death all over me, so I took a shower, and changed clothes. It felt almost as it I was on vacation, which is why I like being comped. I checked out the view from my room. Las Vegas was turning from day into a magnificent night of dazzling neon lights.

I grabbed the first empty elevator and headed down to the 24th floor. I knew the hotel maids had left the floors early in the afternoon after taking care of the last rooms that needed to be readied for late check-ins. Even though housekeeping was on call, I didn't expect to find any maids on Pleasure's floor as I got off the elevator. I stalled as two Japanese tourists entered their room. They paid no attention to me as I wandered down the corridor pretending to look for a particular room number.

When they closed their door, I quickly moved to room 2438. There were no telltale signs of an investigation typically found at most crime scenes such as tape across the door, or black smudges where the forensic team had attempted to lift prints. I expected this, as it would have been bad advertising for the hotel to constantly remind the guests of a crime scene right next to where they were sleeping.

One thing I did not expect was an additional lock on the door. It took the form of a keyed padlock that had been attached with a clasp and two hinges that fit together, and had been bolted into the door. If you did not pay close attention, you would not have seen this additional lock. A "Do Not Disturb" sign partially obscured it.

I removed a lock picking-kit from my breast pocket, slipped the rake into the lock, and gave it a feel. Six pins, at least, which would take some time. I began the process, bringing in the pressure bar to turn the cylinder when I had everything in place. My father had been a locksmith, and it was from him that I learned the trade. It helped me out more than once - even when I had found a locked safe while on a treasure-hunting trip. It wasn't easy, but I opened it. The contents paid for the trip and a couple more on top of it. I had paid my dues in the back of my dad's Lock Shop, which contained hundreds of daily challenges. Most kids played football or baseball after school; I went on field trips to pick locks. There is nothing more challenging than a combination lock with an unknown number of spins. A kid can't have too much fun.

I focused on the end of the rake as it moved each of the pins into place. A time-consuming process. Within two minutes, I heard a slight click. The pressure bar turned and I was able to snap the lock open. I pocketed the lock, took out the hotel key card, and hoped they had not changed the code to the room. I was in luck. I turned the knob to the door and it opened, letting me slip into the room without being noticed.

I stopped for a few seconds, letting my eyes adjust to the darkness of the room. A bead of perspiration slid down the side of my face. Since I was officially on the case, from the hotel's perspective I really was not committing too great a crime. Fat chance they would buy that story, but I like to think positively. I could argue with the police that I had a right to be there because the hotel employed me. Anyway, they weren't going to like it, as I had not followed proper procedure. I hadn't gone through Olsen or Las Vegas Metro. Olsen would have said no, and that would have been the end of it. I would have to deal with him sooner or later. A detective's job is to solve the mystery. Nothings illegal till you get caught; then you'd better have a good story.

I debated about turning on the lights and decided against it. No use in attracting unnecessary attention. I went with my instinct of working in the dark. The chance of Olsen or the police making a surprise visit was slim. If Olsen came in I'd just shoot him anyway. I laughed. I wondered if Olsen would find it funny. Probably not.

As my eyes adjusted, I looked around. Pleasure's hotel suite was as empty as I had figured it would be. The police had taken everything and tagged it as evidence. I would have to make an official visit to view the evidence. I moved into the bathroom and noticed it had been stripped clean of all of Pleasure's personal items. The police had dusted everywhere, and the entire room was covered with smudges of black powder and signs of the removal of fingerprints with tape. I am sure the entire suite would have been photographed as it was originally found, and then detailed photographs of anything deemed interesting by the forensics' team.

One fact about hotel suites is that the cleaning staff pretty well keeps the rooms spotless and the surfaces wiped down. When a print is found, it is a good chance it belongs to the current occupant of the room, or possibly the previous guest. But if the murder occurred in a bar or restaurant, the police end up with hundreds of unknown prints. Always a huge mess to pick through and find the one print which was the killer's.

I clicked on my portable mini-flashlight and held it between my teeth as I checked the safe. It had one stripe of police tape across the combination lock, which probably meant the police had not opened it yet. Maybe Pleasure's stash of money and her handgun were still there. I gave it a spin, went through the right, left, right spinning of the combination from memory, and pulled down on the handle. Click, and I was in. I swung open the safe door and peeked in. I saw a soft and rather heavy gray bag with some sort of insignia on it. I unfolded it and discovered fifty or sixty diamonds flashing their brilliance back at me. I was stunned, to say the least. These hadn't been there before. What was going on?

Suddenly my eyes closed involuntarily by a flash of blinding light. Someone had turned the overhead lights on. I spun around, going for my 9mm Glock in one smooth motion. I was staring down the gun barrel of Peter Daily's Colt .45, my gun only half drawn.

"Freeze, Fargo."

I had no idea what was happening. I dropped the flashlight and kept the Glock pointed at the floor.

"What the hell are you doing here?" questioned Daily. He took his gun off me. Courtesy goes a long way.

"Just doing my job," I said.

"Slowly put your piece away, Fargo."

"No problem," I said, as I slid it back in my waist holster behind my back. "Where did you come from, Daily?"

"I'm on special stakeout. Ahhhhh...Keep those arms in the air. I got to call this in." He waved at me with his gun to raise my hands.

"I'm working for the hotel. Just checking things out."

"Yeah, that may be so, but right now I've got you opening a safe at a crime scene as well as breaking and entering. We've been waiting to see if anybody was going to visit the victim's hotel suite, and what they would do."

"Playing with the evidence, huh. That won't look so good in court," I said, thinking as fast as I could.

"What do you mean?"

"I assume you opened the safe and know exactly what's inside."

"Nope. We haven't been able to open the safe. A real screw up. Hotel is going to have their man up here bright and early tomorrow morning."

"Everything in this safe belongs to my client."

"Nobody knows that for sure...."

"Look, I swear to you that I'm on this case for the hotel."

"Maybe so. But I still got to call it in."

"You're going to call Olsen?"

"Olsen! Hell no, I'm calling Johnston. He's the one who set this up. I'm just trying to get in a little overtime."

"I know the feeling." I looked down at the safe and wondered what I should do next. "You go ahead and call it in. I want to look at the contents of the safe."

Daily radioed dispatch and started the process in motion that was going to cause me a lot of grief. I looked into the back of the safe and saw Pleasure's 9mm. I took a chance. I reached in and grabbed it.

"Look what we have here," I said, pulling out the weapon and making sure my fingerprints were all over it.

"Hey! Put that down," yelled Daily.

I looked up. "Oh...sure. No problem." I placed the gun down on the carpet next to all the small parcels of diamonds. Those really had me confused. Who the hell had been in this safe?

"Listen," said Daily, "...you just back right up and sit down on that couch. They're going to be here soon. And just to make it look good, put your hands in your pockets and sit down."

"I can do that," I said as I moved carefully back. I decided to play it like it was no big deal. After all, I had been hired by the hotel and was being comped. I just had to explain that Pleasure wanted me to take care of some personal property inside the safe.

"Let's make this look as official as possible," said Daily. "Why don't you hand over your piece? You know I hate doing this, Fargo."

"I know Daily, it's all part of the job. I'd do the same if I was in your position."

"Thanks." I removed my 9-mm and gave it to him butt first. I shoved my hands in my pockets and sat down on the couch. "How's the wife and kid?" I asked.

At that moment, Olsen burst in the room followed by Johnston and a couple of street cops. Olsen walked right over and gave me an upper cut, catching me in the jaw. "We got you now, you bastard," said Olsen, massaging his knuckles. "I'm glad to put some hurt on you." I rolled off the couch and onto the floor bleeding. With my hands in my pockets, I had been caught completely off guard.

Daily, Johnston, and the cops immediately jumped to my aid and pulled Olsen away from me. Daily and Johnston helped me up to a sitting position. At the moment, I wasn't so happy with Olsen. I fantasized I could feel my hand being crushed as I pushed Olsen's nose down his throat. A pain I was looking forward to. I gave Olsen a look to let him know he was in trouble, and then focused on the problems at hand, which were many.

Ten

It took an hour of fast talking, much to Olsen's protests, before I was allowed to leave Pleasure's hotel room. I proceeded to have a couple of draft beers thinking things over in the Sports Bar. After working out a few details, and getting over being slugged by Olsen, I left and was I standing in the Porte Cochere outside the MGM Grand's registration waiting for my car to arrive when four police officers approached me on what I knew was going to be official business. The squad of men was lead by Olsen, who actually pointed his finger at me, and told the police officers, "to watch him carefully." Johnston was also there, but acted very uncomfortable.

"What's this about?" I asked.

"You're under arrest," Olsen said.

"You can't arrest me. You're just a hotel cop."

"That's why I brought your buddies along."

"Under arrest for what?"

"Breaking and entering a crime scene at the MGM Grand, plus the robbery of the Desert Sage Jewelry Company, and suspicion of murder."

"Why didn't you arrest me in the hotel room?"

"Breaking and entering is the minor charge," smiled Olsen. "Besides, I wanted to have time to bring in the press." I glanced at my friend Johnston.

Johnston stepped in front of Olsen. "We just got a follow-up call about the robbery at the Desert Sage. It doesn't look good. There might be a chance that the diamonds found in Pleasure's safe might have originated from the Desert Sage."

I turned around to see several vans pull up with camera crews unloading and shouldering video cameras. "Nice move. I'm sure management is going to love it."

"We always get our man."

"The idea is to get the right man," I said as two officers grabbed my arms. The camera crews moved in. A reporter was setting up for a live feed.

"Handcuff him, boys. He's a slippery one," said Olsen, enjoying his newfound fame.

"I don't think handcuffing me will accomplish anything."

"Gives me a lot of satisfaction," smirked Olsen.

"Hands behind the back," said a young patrolman. It went downhill from there. I was handcuffed in front of a gathering crowd of press. I was then frisked and they read me my rights. The news media always attracted the tourists, who would elaborate to their family and friends at home how they had witnessed a bad guy getting busted and probably going down for the count. Vegas likes the squeaky clean image, but the tourists remember the old days when the mob ruled. Part of the thrill of being in Las Vegas.

I was taken downtown in the back of a patrol car. Can't say I enjoyed the experience. Somebody always tries to frame detectives. This was just going a little further than I'd anticipated. It was rare for a cop or a police detective to get arrested because there's a tendency to protect each another. Only when there is an investigation by Internal Affairs do you find major arrests. This just didn't feel right. If they wanted to talk to me, I would have met them at the station. I wanted to know what they had against me, but I knew I would find out in time.

Once at the station I was fingerprinted, booked, and taken to a holding cell. It was a long night. I made friends with a drunk named Tony Botello from the east Side. Dirty blue jeans and a three-day-old white tee shirt made up Tony's standard code of dress when he was broke. Tony told me when things were going right he dressed with the best. He was a hustler. Botello always had a little deal going on. Making a little money on the side. That's what it's all about when you work the streets. He moved with a downtown crowd who kept the police busy with apartment robberies, an occasional convenience store heist, and lots of back alley stick-ups. Why is it that so many of the tourists hang out on the rough part of Fremont Street? A young punk pool hustler comes to town and thinks he's big time in a big city. He's hustled into a couple of pool halls and led up the ladder for a big fall; but it goes the wrong way and he wins, then has the crap beat out of him in a back alley. Sometimes they get him owing a grand and set him up with a convenience store heist.

Tony also sold information to the cops. He liked being a source. The problem with sources is that they run out of good, solid information, so they start making it up. That's when you ditch one and wait for a new source to turn up. My lucky day. Tony brought me up to date on what the bar situation was now like. Seems like the really bad ones were still really bad. But he pointed out a few establishments where the local gossip could be had for a twenty. A hell of a way to gather information. Took my mind off the problem of why I was in jail. Not much you can do about it when you're locked up. Just sit back and wait. Try to get beauty sleep so you can look presentable for the judge at the arraignment.

Uncle Leo showed up bright and early Wednesday morning and posted bail. I also had Uncle Leo post bail for Botello. He might come in handy as a source, and besides, this meant Botello might do me a favor in the future. Leo had tried to free me in the middle of the night, but the D.A. wanted me to go before the court the following morning so the judge could set bail. I was formally charged with tampering with State's evidence and possession of stolen jewelry from the Desert Sage. Other charges were pending upon further investigation. The only comment Uncle Leo had was that the police had a good case on the surface.

Once we arrived at the office he waved me off so he could return phone calls. I found a stack of messages and mail that needed attention waiting for me on my desk. I wasn't up for it. Good thing Sheri took care of the important stuff. I stewed for a while and used this time to get my thoughts together on how I had gotten myself into this mess. More important, what was I going to do about it? Somebody was setting me up and doing a terrific job of it. But who? And why?

Sheri walked in and held out a steaming cup of coffee for me. "I hear brew in the slammer is really bad."

"I would have to agree with that rumor." I reached for the coffee. "Ahh, Starbucks...a long way from boiled coffee grounds and rats' tails." She smiled and was gone. Sheri knew I needed time to think.

I ran many possibilities through my mind and could not come up with a single good lead. It had to be something to do with the case. Pleasure dead, then alive. Then there is always Jody -- no one had ever seen her. And how did those diamonds get into the safe? I've also got Olsen on my back, but for him it's payback time. It wasn't worth his time to make life difficult for me, which would be too simple. True, we had professional differences, but that was part of the job. Part of being a cop was having a few guys you don't get along with. Just like one vice-president not liking another who had the better office. Then you get his office, and they move him into a corner office. Then you start thinking that the corner office was a better deal. It never ended. No, it wasn't Olsen. But it sure as hell was tied up with Pleasure, and her long-lost friend Jody, whoever she might be.

I knew I was going to have to investigate the Desert Sage robbery and find out how this tied into Pleasure, or at least Pleasure's room. From the few questions I'd been asked at the department I was able to learn the approximate time of the heist and to tell them where I had been and what I was doing. They didn't believe me for one minute, and I couldn't blame them. Even I didn't like the way my story sounded. I'm sure they thought it was phony as hell. That's why Uncle Leo has repeatedly said, don't say anything. He must have said a hundred times, "Tell me your story, and then I'll tell the police the truth, but only what I want to tell them." Good advice. It has to be remembered that lawyers are telling you the story they want you to hear, even if there's hardly a thread of evidence behind it. I used to do it all the time.

Uncle Leo stuck his gray head in the door. "They're not going to file murder charges."

"I appreciate the good news."

Uncle Leo entered and took his customary place in a chair directly in front of my desk. "That's because they haven't completed a test on the bullet found in McCaddy and the 9-mm found in the hotel safe."

"My fingerprints are all over that gun. Daily saw me pick it up in the hotel room."

"Of course. The police already know that. The fact that you handled the gun when Daily watched you pull it out of the safe has not fooled them a bit. They figure you put the weapon in the safe. You were just covering for the fact that your prints were already on it."

"At least that part is true. I was going after Pleasure's gun, which I had placed in the safe earlier. The one Pleasure had given me."

Uncle Leo's eyes strayed to my law library looking for books from his office, which I had a habit of stacking on my bookshelves. "Nice story. What can I say? It sounds like a story. It won't sound good in court, but who am I?"

"You're my lawyer."

Uncle Leo studied me. "I haven't taken the case yet. I hate losing cases."

"What about search-and-seizure procedures?"

"What about them?"

"Can't we attack them? Can't we build a timeline to show that procedure broke down leading to the evidence so it can't be used in court?"

"That's a possibility. There's always a problem someplace, and we can address it if we get that far. They'll have a problem with individual chronology reports, property reports, and chain-of-evidence. The usual. On top of that they usually make mistakes in the murder book."

The murder book, I thought. The step-by-step records the investigating officer puts together on each case. I started to feel better already.

"So, how much time do I have before they I.D. the bullet in McCaddy?"

"They've sent it to the FBI labs in D.C. Thank God they're backlogged. You should have about four days."

"Good. I've got to get to work." I stood and headed out of the office.

Uncle Leo just watched me. "Where are you going?"

"Time for some good old detective work."

Uncle Leo pointed to my desk chair. I knew he wanted me to sit back down. I'm perceptive in these kinds of situations. I sat down feeling like I just took the first bounce from a bungee cord. I had a couple more bounces to go. "Thanks for bailing me out."

"I'll only do it once," said Uncle Leo.

"I take it I'm in trouble."

"Not with me you're not. With the Las Vegas Metro you've got a lot of problems."

"I'll take care of the police."

"That's fine. But you got to start thinking a little bit. You always make the same mistakes. You go off like a firecracker with a short fuse. You should take on a partner. One who can talk some sense into you...try working with Sheri more."

"I work alone. Like to make my own decisions."

"I'm telling you, you need to slow down. Remember you had the problem when you first got to homicide? You made the arrests, all right. But the FBI came in and told you if you'd gone through procedure, you would have been told to lay off those hoods. They had them set up for a meet with their backer."

My phone flashed indicating a call was waiting for me, but I ignored it. "Yeah, I remember."

"Remember about a year later when you spotted the bank robbery over on the Strip?"

"Yeah, but...."

"Yeah, but...that's no answer. If you had taken a little more time you would not have arrested the wrong man. If you had requested backups, and then asked for an I.D., you would have learned it was a priest. A Catholic priest. You know how much embarrassment you caused the department because you didn't slow down? Sometimes you just move too fast."

"I move at my own pace," I said regretting the words as soon as I heard the sound of my own voice.

"You might have the wrong pace," said Uncle Leo, leaning forward. "If you want to learn about pace, study handicapping. That's the point. If you had talked over this break-in at the hotel with a partner, you might have been talked out of it. A regular room, I have no problem with. But a room taped off by the police! A crime scene! Doesn't that make for a problem?"

"Can I claim entrapment?"

"Sure, but it won't do a damn bit of good. They'll claim they were simply protecting a police crime scene and the number one suspect happened to break into the hotel room...and let me emphasize the word break-in...and then proceeded to remove the crime scene tape from the safe, which you just happened to know the combination to. Then you compounded the problem by removing an obvious weapon from the safe, destroying any possible fingerprints that could now help you."

"But my finger prints were already on the gun," I said in my defense.

"What if it wasn't the same gun? Whoever placed the diamonds in there might have switched the gun."

"Oh, I hadn't thought of that. Can I claim diminished capacity?"

"Better. Think about it next time. Crime scenes are traps. Police are looking for anybody who's not supposed to be there. That's basic. That's what a crime scene is all about. You weren't supposed to be there."

"Point well taken."

"Start planning ahead a little more. The police want to look good. Your helping them is making it easier. You are a regular P.R. agency for them."

"Got it."

"Think about it."

"Okay, okay."

Uncle Leo leaned back in his chair. "I've got to try and call in some favors. Don't beat anybody up in an alley. It won't look good to the D.A. downtown."

I nodded my head in agreement as I left Uncle Leo's office. I stopped by my office and picked up another Glock. Can't have to many of them around. I knew Uncle Leo wanted to look for his law books, so I left the office. I hated these rounds with Uncle Leo. Particularly when he was right. I always felt like the criminal. I had already tossed around the idea of working with Sheri more. She had her own cases and we could help each other out. I never wanted to admit to one of my fatal flaws, which was my sometimes moving too fast. Part of my style; I just liked working alone. I had already made all the contacts and knew all the players. It just felt wrong to bring somebody in whom I would have to clear everything with. It wasn't going to work.

I headed back to the MGM Grand late Wednesday to start to deal with the problems at hand. I swung into the parking lot and tossed my key to the valet. As I moved toward the elevator I picked up a package at the front desk left for me by Julie Fuller - Official Business, MGM Grand. I was tempted to open it as I moved into the elevator, but I restrained myself.

Happy people moved in along with some un-happy people. I blended in and listened to their stories. As I got off on the 30th floor, I suddenly remembered I hadn't played my daily slot and made a mental note to hit one on the way to dinner. A lot was on my mind. I felt that everybody was moving faster than I was and it was time to get rolling. First, a quick shower to rid myself of the grime of prison life, thankful I didn't have to shower with "the guys." I lingered under the two-headed shower probably a bit longer than I needed to. These suites were great. I found my dry-cleaning hanging in the closet. That was handy. At least I knew while I was in jail my clothes were being taken care of. It's the small things I like about being comped at a nice hotel. They take care of the details while you were out being arrested.

I moved to the desk where my computer was set up. Checking carefully, I determined that no one had touched my brief case or my computer. You never knew for sure these days, but I always played it like somebody could tamper with it. It was time, or past time, to add some notes to my file. Sitting with a towel wrapped around my waist and a view of the Strip below, I typed. All I needed now was a couple of shots, some cigs, and a hot babe knocking at my door. Detective day dreams, Vegas style.

I typed a few notes for my log and saved the file in my database. I got dressed, locked the suite and headed toward Lanning's office. Thought I would check in and see what he had to say. The basic problem as I saw it was the fact that I had broken into Pleasure's room and opened the safe. I felt I could explain that away, but I was left with the problem of the 9-mm and the diamonds. I was haunted by the fact that the bullet found in McCaddy could be fired from the 9-mm in the safe. I supposed the D.A. suspected the same thing. I could not determine if this was the same gun Pleasure had given me. I would of course deny it, and it would be backed up by Daily that I handled the gun when I opened the safe. Thank God Daily is an honest detective. But it still made me look like prime suspect number one.

Surprisingly, I was able to get right in to see Harry. I had decided that from now on I would give him only a verbal report. I still considered Pleasure to be my client. The Reports on Investigation were for my case notes. Harry was finishing a phone conversation when I entered. I waited until he put the phone down.

"Sorry I wasn't able to get you a written report like I promised. I was somewhat detained. I'm sure you understand."

"Jail has a peculiar way of slowing people down. It might even be good for you," said Lanning. He rose from his chair behind the desk and met me in the middle of his office.

"Well, if I had a choice between jail and that suite you comped me, I choose the suite."

"House guests in both cases."

Laughter. At least he had a sense of humor. "Let me get right down to the facts," I said. "There are two different problems the hotel is faced with right now. One, the murder of Pleasure, and two, the diamonds in Pleasure's hotel safe."

"These are not the hotel's problems, they're your problems," said Lanning with an edge in his voice. He moved a step closer to me. We were at a stand-off.

"You know what I mean," I said.

"Don't forget the gun," Lanning added.

"I haven't forgotten. It was placed in the safe for a reason. Probably to frame Pleasure." I held my position. I knew if I took a step back, Lanning would be all over me.

"But Pleasure's dead," said Lanning.

"Why frame me? Who could know that I would open the safe? What I'm concerned about is how the diamonds got from the safe in the Desert Sage to the smaller safe in Pleasure's hotel room."

"Why?"

"The perfect set-up to blame the Desert Sage robbery on Pleasure. Somebody got greedy and took Pleasure out."

"Why not blame you?"

"Nobody could know I was going to enter the hotel room and open up the safe."

"Why did you?"

"Part of my job," I answered. "I was hired by Pleasure. She entrusted me with the safe combination. I wanted to know if there were any clues in the safe. Something I might have missed."

"Why?"

"That's my job. That's what I do. I've got a client, and I work the case." I put an edge in my voice, just like a tough guy.

"True," said Lanning. "I have to tell you, I got a few calls this morning. Seems like some people believe you're bringing more attention to the hotel than trying to keep us out of the news." Lanning turned and walked back around his desk and sat down. I felt the worst was over.

"Yeah, I know. I feel that somebody is working against me. These things happen from time to time. We'll get past it."

"We'll get past it?" questioned Lanning with raised eyebrows.

"Right. I'll get past it. I stand corrected."

"You do that."

"I'm not pleased by the way Olsen jumped in and had me arrested. Doesn't make my job any easier."

"Yeah. He did a great job. What can I say? He's a bit of an over-achiever."

"He's a putz."

Harry laughed at that. "I think that pretty well sums him up. He can intimidate the tourists. But he knows all the crooks. We need him. We don't have to like him."

"I don't."

"Join the club."

I turned to leave. The conversation about Olsen was upsetting me.

"You've got a reputation in this town," said Harry. "Just go out and do the job. But remember, I have a hotel to run, and part of that is to make sure I have only the best of guests. If things get too hot, I will have to distance myself from you. Got it?"

"Got it."

"Good, go solve something."

"Consider it done." I turned and left Harry's office. I felt bad about not telling him I believed Pleasure was still alive. But when you are a P.I. you have to learn to keep some information to yourself. Information is power, so they say.

Eleven

I slipped into my suite and thought about grabbing a Carlsberg beer out of the small refrigerator. Just like a first class hotel to know that my favorite beer was a rice-based Denmark beer. It would have to wait as I was headed out to talk to some of the witnesses who were present at poolside. The Desert Sage Jewelry Company might present a problem since I was a possible suspect in the robbery and murder. I checked for messages and left. There was a lot to do.

I picked up my car and headed cross town to American Shooters Supply and Gun Club on Arville. I had used Shooters for supplies ever since I was a cop on the force. It had the best selection of handguns and rifles in Las Vegas. There shooting range was used by everybody, and they conducted CCW classes on a continual bases supporting firearms education. In fact, Shooters Supply is where I had met Abby. She was getting in a few practice rounds and we started talking. Next thing you know we're the best of friends.

The gun business in Vegas is a strange one. Try to bring a weapon in on a plane and you'd never get past security. Most of the illegal guns are brought in by car from Chicago, New York, or L.A. Safer for the bad guy. Some are clean, but most are dirty. Actually, most guns brought into the Las Vegas underground have a bad history. Too many drug deals and drive-bys to impress the girlfriends. Who wants a Blood or a Crips gun? Nobody. Even the dumbest thug doesn't want to pick up a piece and have it turn out a hot item connected to a murder.

Las Vegas still is a tough town. The Wild West had nothing on this place. Guns are right at home here. All part of the action. Tourists can even go to a firing range and take a few shots at a silhouetted target with a variety of weapons. The thing to do when bored with gambling. A new stress reliever. Blow away a target with an Uzi. I'm surprised they don't have them in the hotels.

I parked and entered Shooters Supply. Walking in was like walking into an Army supply depot. One thing for sure, they were not subtle. They thought if they could take your breath away when you walked in the door, you would never go anyplace else. It worked. Once you were in the store you were in an armory. Rifles, shotguns, and semi-automatic weapons lined the walls behind glass. Other glass cases housed AR-15's, AK-47's and SKS's. The people at Shooters know guns, and know how to use them. Every employee carried at least one handgun that you could see.

"Fargo!"

I turned to see Johnny Andrews. "Hey, Johnny. What's going on?"

"Oh, you know the usual. I'll be finished here in a little bit."

I gave him a wave, and his attention went back to his customer. Her short-cropped brown hair hovered above a face full of freckles. Probably a secretary on her day off. She was trying to pick out a comfortable revolver. People don't realize how many woman own handguns. I went over to look at the holsters designed for concealed carry. I was always after a new way to carry my weapons. Nothing struck me so I moved on. I walked along the cases until I found the pellet and dart section.

The pellet guns looked surprisingly like the real thing. The dart guns were used for animal control. I guess if you dipped the little sucker in the right mixture, it would become very deadly.

Andrews walked up and stuck out his hand. "So Fargo, what's going on? Are you here to use the range?"

"Nope. Not today. Just had some questions for you." "What's up?"

"I heard there was a lady at the MGM Grand killed with a dart on Monday."

"Where did you get that piece of information?" I asked.

"Well, you know, we get so many of the guys down here. And anything unusual finds its way to this place if it has to do with a weapon."

"Have the boys been here?"

"Oh, yeah. They hit this place early this morning and got the records of everyone who purchased a dart gun. Which is not many, by the way."

"Any name come up that might fit the crime?"

"Actually, they were hunting for your name. Seems like you finally made it to the top ten."

"Security at the MGM Grand thinks I did it."

"Olsen was right in here with them. He was mighty disappointed your name wasn't on the list."

"Olsen was here?"

"Yep. He's working with the police to get you locked up. Told me he was personally going to put you behind bars. Seemed to take a real interest in this case."

"I wonder why," I said.

"Didn't say. Who are you working for?"

"Well, for one, the victim was my client. So I'm sort of curious as to what kind of problem she ran into." Didn't need to tell him Pleasure might still be alive, I thought.

"Interesting. Olsen didn't tell me that part. He told me you were banging two ladies at the MGM Grand, and the situation got out of control."

"Two ladies?"

"Yeah, someone named Jody."

"Olsen's full of crap and spreading it all over this town."

"Olsen's always been full of crap. We all know that."

"Forget Olsen. Tell me about dart guns."

"Actually, it starts with blow guns. Not much to them. Long history. They were discovered hundreds of years ago in different parts of the world. First ones were made out of bamboo or hollowed-out wood. They're still used today by the pygmies in Africa for hunting."

"You're kidding. I thought they were more of a sport than anything else."

"Nothing further from the truth. Ninja spies used them prior to 1500 in Japan for silent assassinations with poison darts. They were really good."

"I bet they were. How about today's market?"

"Deadly. Take this Stealth blowgun here." Johnny picked up a dangerous-looking weapon. "All aircraft aluminum tubing. High quality with anti-inhale mouthpiece to ensure no dart inhalation and provide maximum airflow."

"What's the range?"

"You can expect ranges up to two hundred and fifty feet."

"You're kidding!" Andrews handed me the blowgun and I pulled it into position as if I was going to use it. I was impressed with how light it was, and that it had a built-in sight to help aim it.

"Not a bit. That's why they use them for hunting."

"Powerful?"

"With certain models you can put a dart through a quarter-inch piece of plywood. It'll get the job done."

"How about close distances?" I handed the blow-gun back to Andrews.

"We have different manufacturers that produce twenty-four-inch blowguns, but they don't have much of a range."

"What about a very short distance...say six or seven feet?"

"You could use just about anything."

"No special requirements?"

"None. Just a tube and the dart. Problem is to make sure you don't inhale the dart."

I grimaced at the thought. "What if it's a poison dart?"

"Bigger risk."

"How about a straw?"

"Sure. Kids do it all the time."

"Then five feet would be no problem?"

"None whatsoever."

"What about poisons?"

"That's one thing we don't sell. You have to contact a private source for poison darts."

"But you could take a dart, dunk it in some poison, and then use a straw to deliver it."

"Anything's possible."

"Well thanks," I said. "You've helped a lot. I've got a handle on this. I take it you don't have an index for people buying blowguns?"

"No. We're not required by law to register that kind of information. We have a catalog mailing list if that would help."

"No, I don't think that will be necessary."

"Call if you need anything."

"Thanks, I'll catch you later." I waved and made my way out of the place.

Andrews gave me the thumbs up and moved over to help someone else at the counter. I had some ideas to work with. Certainly finding the murder weapon would be next to impossible. But I was starting to get an idea of how it came down at the MGM Grand. One step at a time.

Twelve

I was Metro's focus of the crime. When there's pressure on the police to perform, they go after the most likely suspect. Guilt or innocence often has little to do with it. It is better to have someone behind bars than no one at all. Politics is everywhere. In this way the political types, including D.A.s and Homicide Inspectors, who don't have a conscience, can state that a suspect has been apprehended and is behind bars. Many cops rationalize that if they did send someone to jail who was innocent, the guy probably did something illegal in the past anyway, so it doesn't really matter. The Feds do the same thing, but they call it a squeeze play. They have other motives. Justice is sooner or later. This bothers me, especially when I'm the innocent victim. They always say the jails are filled with innocent people. The public would be shocked to learn the truth.

I headed back toward the Strip, getting more upset about my being the target and Metro's effort to put me behind bars. With that thought, I switched destinations and headed toward my home in Summerlin. Hadn't been there for a while, and I needed to get some additional clothes anyway. I turned onto Tropicana and took a right on Decatur, which I used when I wanted to avoid the Strip traffic. Three more turns and I'd be home.

As I drove my BMW effortlessly through mid-afternoon traffic, I started to map out my tactics. Obviously I was a target, but I initially thought this was an effort by Olsen to gain some personal respect back from the department. Everyone knew he needed it. Why would he be tagging along or even leading the police on a case like this? There were other problems to consider. Who really killed the Jane Doe that the Metro Police and the MGM Grand think is Pleasure? Is there any other forensic information that would help? How did the robbery tie in? How did the diamonds get into Pleasure's safe? And finally, where in the hell is Pleasure?

I needed to confer with Uncle Leo and Sheri to get them started on certain angles. I felt that after we covered the basics, two things needed to be done. One was to plant myself at the MGM Grand without being spotted and see if I could pick up on anything unusual. I might even spot Pleasure. Nobody else would be looking for her.

The second item on my agenda was going to be fun. After all, I was in Las Vegas, and besides, detecting was always fun. I picked up the car phone, hit the auto dial, and waited.

"Good afternoon, Law Offices."

"Hi Sheri, it's Fargo. Is Leo in?"

"Nope. He went down to Metro to check on what's happening. He's actually checking on another case, but the halls talk, as he says. He felt he might turn up something."

"Good. I've got something for you. I want you to get a copy of the coroner's report from the medical examiner. Call him. The number is in the file. Tell Herbie you're working with me on this one. Also ask him if he ever found out the name of the Jane Doe."

"Right, no problem."

"And second, can you get me Olsen's home address?"

"Olsen! Uncle Leo's going to kill you."

"No, no. I don't want to talk to the guy. I want to follow him."

"You guys will be driving in a circle."

"Detectives do that," I said, beginning to turn into the Summerlin subdivision where I lived. "Phone it into my voice mail and I'll pick it up on the run. Also, I want to get together with both of you tonight and discuss strategy and tactics."

"So you're getting back to normal."

"Yeah, you could say that...Wait a minute," I added, feeling anxious. As I pulled into my cul-de-sac I saw a mass of black-and-whites. Getting closer, I could see my front door opened. "I really needed this."

"What's going on?"

"Olsen's hit my home. Hell, the bastard's car is even in my driveway. Looks like they got a warrant and tossed my home."

"I'll page Uncle Leo right away."

"Right, and get him back to the office. If they hit here, you know the office will be next."

"Will do. I got you covered on this end."

"Still want to be a detective?"

"Yep. I like the action."

"Right now I'm not enjoying it. Bye." I shoved the cell phone into my pocket and jumped out of the car leaving it to block Olsen's. As I sprung up the steps Olsen stepped out and waved his hand at the two uniforms, who immediately jumped all over me.

"Frisk him," Olsen shouted.

"Am I being arrested?" I yelled at Olsen. "You're not even a cop. You don't have the authority," I screamed.

"But I do," said Peter Daily walking out of my front door.

"Besides, you're out on bail," yelled Olsen.

"He's carrying," one of the officers said. He pulled my Glock, sniffed it to see if it had been fired, then held it high.

"Let him go," Daily said. The other officer released me.

"Bag the gun," said Daily to the officer. "Fargo, you know you're not suppose to be carrying while out on bail."

"What are you doing working with a scumbag like Olsen?" I asked Daily ignoring his comment.

"He's a friend of the force. We've got a legal warrant, and Olsen just tagged along for the ride."

"Well, you should have called me," I said as I pushed my way past them and into my house. The entire place was torn apart. "Really good job, guys. Very nice. Your mothers would be proud."

"You should really take better care of your home." Olsen smirked. "I always thought you were a neater guy than this."

As I walked from room to room, it was easy to see they had gone through everything I had. The place was ransacked, drawers dumped on the floor. I made my way back to the front entrance and noticed the search warrant had been taped onto the door. My neighbors were gathering outside. The police were finishing up and moving out.

Daily took me aside. "Look, we've got to do our job. Olsen has given us some leads. You understand. There's some pressure on this one."

"Yeah, but you didn't have to go to this extent," I said as I motioned to my belongings thrown everywhere.

"The police were never tidy people," said Daily, and he headed down the driveway.

"What about my piece?"

Daily turned and faced me. "Got to keep it, Fargo. You know the rules. I'll overlook it this time, but not the next time." He turned away and left me standing there.

I entered my home and walked around my living room trying to cool down. I was amazed that the police had gone this far. I started to dial the office and Olsen came screaming into the room.

"Fargo, get your damn car out of the way!"

"You're in my driveway," I yelled back. "I could have you towed."

"Just try it."

"I might do that."

"You wouldn't dare."

"Listen Olsen, what gives? You know me better than that. You know I didn't kill Pleasure, and you know I'm a straight cop. So what's the deal?"

"What's the deal? I'll give it to you straight. I don't like you. You're a hack P.I. and you got caught in Pleasure's room, and it's your word against a dead victim's that you had the authority to be there. Then you get caught again putting diamonds into the safe along with a gun with your prints on it. That's why. You're dirty, and I've got you."

"Did the gun tie back to McCaddy?" I asked.

"I don't know, but it doesn't matter. You're dead meat. You're mine. You're going down. We'll have the bail pulled by the end of the day, and that's when we're going to come looking for you. The streets will be safer with you behind bars."

Daily stuck his head in the door. "All right now. That's it. Fargo, if you could get your car moved, I'll get Olsen out of the way."

"Thanks. He's starting to get on my nerves."

I departed, followed by Olsen and Daily. I could see two black-and-whites down the street apparently waiting for them. Ten to one they were on their way to my office. I moved my car and Olsen peeled out making a lot of noise. I grabbed my cell phone from my pocket and speed-dialed the office as I ran into my house.

Sheri answered. "Law offices."

"Sheri, Fargo. They're on their way. They just tossed my place."

"How bad?"

"Bad. My cleaning lady is going to put a contract out on me. If they catch her, she'll get off. No jury would convict her when they see this place. Did you get hold of Uncle Leo?"

"Yep, he just walked in. He said he'd take care of things on this end. He wants you to spend time trying to find Pleasure. He thinks they're going to revoke your bail."

"I already got that message. Tell him, okay. I'll be careful. They can't arrest you if they can't find you."

"Right."

"Let's go to plan B," I said."

"Right. That's what Uncle Leo thinks."

I hung up the phone and went to the bedroom to get some clothes. Now the problem was to find Pleasure before I was brought in again. I had a little time. I picked up the things I needed and left.

The last thing I did was to leave a note for the cleaning lady who took care of my place once a week. I left five one-hundred-dollar bills on the table with a note apologizing profusely. I tore the search warrant off the door and put it next to my note. I took one last look and was gone.

First things first. I headed directly back to the MGM Grand, where I buried my car in the parking lot. On the way to my room I hit a slot just for luck and found out I didn't have any. No surprise there the way my day was going. My real purpose was to pick up any tail that might be on me. Sure enough, I doubled back and picked up a security guard pretending to be a P.I. I moved to the elevator and took it straight to my floor. I packed a shoulder bag with my clothes, and put the computer and peripherals in their own bag. Time for a replacement weapon, I thought. I donned a shoulder holster and pulled out another Glock from my computer case that fit it perfectly. As I have said before, you can't have to many. For added protection I added another .38 caliber, which I wore in a waist holster behind my back.

I glanced up and down the hall. No one was in sight. Nice suite, I thought, as I closed the door.

Thirteen

RUBY ANN BARRE, even with the anger and frustration of revenge building inside her, was careful to observe the details of her surroundings. She arrived in a black Mustang rental car early Wednesday afternoon in front of a rundown apartment project on the south side of Las Vegas Boulevard. Every large city has these, some worse than others. Many of the casino's support people, from waitresses to dealers, use this nearby housing to cut expenses. They're usually the ones who figure all they need is one good run at the tables and they can move on to greener pastures. Even though the dealers work with thousands of dollars every day, they are paid small salaries. Above minimum wage for sure, but not much above. They count on the tips from tourists to make ends meet. But you have to work at the big-name casinos to get the big tips. Often the only greener pastures many of them would ever see were when the felt on the tables was changed.

Hustling had been Ruby Ann's passion for the last fifteen years. Using a multitude of aliases all backed up with appropriate I.D.s, she moved between one life and another. Montoya Martinez Colorado was deceased -- gone forever the moment McCaddy had died. He was foolish. Ruby Ann was smart. Every part of Colorado's existence was carefully eliminated within hours of the robbery.

As Ruby Ann entered the apartment complex driveway she studied the bland buildings that needed repair. Although stucco was good in the desert heat, without continued maintenance it looked tired and worn. Early Las Vegas construction was not a romance with modern design, but a romance based upon practicality and simplicity. These older units had been built in the fifties to provide cheap housing for the population of transient workers. Soon the landlords found they could make money with these units, particularly if they didn't spend a lot maintaining their appearance. Locals who viewed Las Vegas as their home, as opposed to a stepping stone to the better life, usually settled in one of the many residential neighborhoods away from the activity of the Strip where single family houses, town-houses, and condominiums clustered in better than average subdivisions. Condo's, for those who have made it, start at one million and go higher then I care to think about, were being built right on the Strip, or close to it. Small cities with fifty floors and fantastic views.

The apartments reminded Ruby Ann of her child-hood. Growing up in dwellings like these had motivated her to find a life of luxury and class. Ruby Ann drove her black Mustang until she saw the parking space one-one-seven. She checked the hand-written note she was holding and then carefully parked her car. She got out, locked the car, and took a careful look at her surround-ings. The parking space was east of the Sahara Hotel parking lot in an alley running between her and the famed Strip casino. Only one entrance led in and out of the apartment complex. This would work, she thought, as she turned and headed toward one of the apartments. The complex was painted in a light green that had faded badly under the relentless Las Vegas sun. There was evidence of many coats of paint, which probably did more to hold the building up than anything else. Structural paint, a new concept in engineering.

She approached a doorway at the front of the complex. Ruby Ann had carefully timed this appointment by running a series of errands designed to make her activity appear normal, and to also throw off any tail that might be keeping track of her movements. She was sure she had not been followed, but one could never take a chance in her line of work.

At only twenty-eight, Ruby Ann had seen the hard part of life, always on the run, not knowing where she would end up next. Her beauty had given her an advantage, but her heritage had been her fate. Her father, Dale "The Banker" Murphy, a bank robber and hustler by trade, had supported her and her alcoholic mother throughout her tentative teen years. Having a father who was in and out of jail was a common situation for the family, and they learned to cope with it. Part of doing business. If you're gonna do the crime, you gotta be willing to do the time -- an expression bantered around by kids, but reality to many who lived by the means of quick thinking, timing, and running for a living.

Complications arose when the "three times and you're out" law was passed. This put a damper on the bank robbery business for most criminals, but her father persisted in his trained profession. His reasoning was it took years to learn the trade.

Everybody thought robbing a bank was as simple as walking in, sticking a gun in the face of a teller, grabbing the money, and running out the door. Not true for the professional thief. First, there was the endless job of picking which bank you wanted to rob. Then came the time-consuming process of watching the rhythm of the bank; how it interacted with the public, and how it handled what it called security and invincibility. Because all banks have large walk-in safes, they start from the concept of being secure. Just believing you're invincible can set in motion a chain of events that will eventually lead to failure to protect a weakness in the system.

Once a professional bank robber knows what the weakness is, he goes to work to exploit that weakness into a successful robbery. Murphy had explained many times to Ruby Ann that there were three times to hit a bank. The first is when the bank is just opening for the day. The process of letting bank employees into the bank is always to be watched. The routine gets comfortable, and after it gets comfortable, it always gets slack. When this happens, you can bet the bank will be taken advantage of and hit.

The second is during the routine banking day when customers are allowed into the bank for financial transactions. This is the biggest window of opportunity, as the robber can enter through a predetermined entrance and at a time of his or her choice.

Finally, the third time was when the bank is getting ready to close. For the most part, banks feel most vulnerable during the last half-hour of business. The thinking is that at this time of day more money is in the teller cages than at any other time. Not exactly correct. People deposit checks, but want cash for spending. There is always more cash in the teller's cages at the beginning of the shift than near the end, Ruby Ann's father instructed. Large cash deposits are continually moved to the back. Something to consider. There was always something to consider.

Ruby Ann squinted at the apartments in the bright sun, thinking of her past conversations with her dad about his exploits. You spend a great deal of time watching the target bank. Routines, when you learn them, become weak points leading to vulnerability. When the odds seem to favor the thief, you go in and do the job. A thief views this as a business. You get up in the morning, shave and shower, drive to the bank, rob it; then go home, play with the kids, have a beer, and watch a cop movie you rented at the local video store. Sure, there are a lot of drug types who hit the first bank they see, but they're out to solve a drug problem, not make a living.

She thought about all her father had taught her, and realized she was in a field where only well-trained operators survived and lived to steal another day. Her father had taught her well. Many times Ruby Ann and her father spent the afternoon running all the different escape routes from a proposed target. This was actually one of the first steps. If you didn't have a secure escape route, with several alternatives and built-in diversions, you simply passed on the bank no matter how attractive it might look. Driving in traffic with her father also taught her how to avoid being tailed. How to double back. How to spot a tail. How to make a left-hand turn from the right lane, which will screw up anybody attempting a tail. All the years with her father had been paying off the last couple of weeks.

Ruby Ann had received a phone call from someone who referred to himself as "the voice." Ruby Ann had expressed her anger very clearly. The killing of McCaddy was an accident, the result of bad information she'd been given by her partner, "the voice." Because she was getting what she wanted, she broke some important rules. She didn't know who her partner was, nor did she like having a partner in the first place. It was a one-sided relationship in which she took all the risks. It bothered her. It made her stomach queasy. But she had no choice until she could learn enough to turn the tables. That's why she had demanded this meeting. She had her own plans, and no matter how smart her partner was, she was smarter.

The agreement had been simple. "The voice" would call in some favors to get her father out of prison. Ruby Ann was not given the details, but it followed a very basic plan. Someone who was out of favor would take the fall for the crime her father had pulled. There would be a confession, or there would be death. It happens all the time. She would be given instructions in detail for one major heist. In the end, she would be able to disappear without any possible connection and with enough money to retire in any part of the world with her father. Who could say no?

Because she had no knowledge of who her so-called benefactor was, if she were caught, she would not be able to turn state's evidence against her partner. This worked great for her partner, but gave her no cards to play if she found herself framed for the job. One of the biggest problems with committing a crime was having a partner. A partner always meant trouble. The court systems operated best when everybody was making deals. Including the court. If you talk, you walk. You've got an edge if you can hang someone bigger than yourself. One of the easiest deals to make was to give up your partner. And when you were looking at a possible twenty-year stretch, walking away always looked pretty good. Of course, there are situations where you end up in prison protecting someone, and then they turn on you. That's another story. When it came down to it, there weren't many stand-up guys any more.

Ruby Ann had her own plan. Her goal was to free her father. Her second goal was to burn her partner to protect herself down the road. Her partner was the only one who knew she killed McCaddy, who was the innocent one in this whole deal. Sometimes even an average citizen has to learn when to talk and when to walk. McCaddy had learned the lesson the hard way.

She spotted the apartment door she had been looking for. One knock on the door and she heard a buzz from inside. Ruby Ann remembered her instructions and slowly entered the apartment. In front of her was a darkened living room containing a stool, which had a small spotlight focused on it. On the stool lay a small headset with a microphone attached. She walked over, put on the headset, and sat on the stool. Instantly she was met with a blinding light. Ruby Ann shielded her eyes from strobe flashes that surrounded her completely. She started to reach for her sunglasses when a muffled, distorted voice burst through a loud speaker system behind her.

"Don't put on your sunglasses. Do not look right or left. The light is meant to make it difficult for you to see. Close your eyes."

Ruby Ann did so, and this made it easier for her to concentrate.

The distorted voice was a new twist, she thought. On the first phone call the voice was clear and crisp. The distorted voice continued. "You screwed up, Missy."

"I didn't screw up," Ruby Ann spit out in a flash of anger. "I reacted to bad information. You're an amateur and you gave me wrong information, and I had to burn McCaddy to get out of there."

"You did the job, you made the drop. So what's the problem?"

"I'm at risk."

"So am I."

"So why don't you just shoot me," said Ruby Ann.

"I wish I could, but that would draw even more attention. I can't. I don't trust you, but I need you. You're part of my plan. But you're a planner yourself. You wouldn't have come here without taking some precautions."

Ruby Ann smiled.

"Thought so. So here's the deal. Your father's papers are in order and he is to be released soon. He knows nothing of this arrangement. Do you understand?"

"Yes," said Ruby Ann speaking into the microphone. "How did you do it?"

"This is no concern of yours. If you persist in asking questions or trying to find out who I am, Murphy will be returned to prison for violation of parole. It's very, very easy to do. Murphy will be implicated in the killing of a guard. When he gets back, his life will be hell, all because of you. Remember this Missy, people at the top can pull strings one way or another, and it doesn't matter whether they're innocent or guilty. It doesn't matter to them. It's part of the job. It's the way it is on the inside. Do you understand?"

"Yes," said Ruby Ann. Her thoughts were racing as she tried to keep one step ahead of her "partner," who obviously had a plan. She needed to know how much information he really had. It might help piece the puzzle together. Normally she would have been long gone. Out of town and part of history. But this time she had to stay to keep track of loose ends. And her partner, "the voice," was the loose end.

"The next phase is the most important. You are to follow the directions to the letter, and you should apply all of your skills to the task at hand. It's almost impossible to fail, but you still must apply yourself."

"I understand. The newspapers claim they have a suspect and the police are closing in."

"The newspapers need a good story. Keeps pressure on the police department if the public thinks they are about to solve the crime. It makes for good copy. Nothing more."

"What is keeping you from turning me in as the killer?" asked Ruby Ann.

The distorted voice continued. "Because there's no evidence against you. Just my word. No fingerprints. No eyewitness. No tapes."

"How did you select me? Why am I the lucky one?" Ruby Ann asked sarcastically.

"Remember the San Francisco job four years ago?"

"You know about that?"

"And more. Much more. But I really chose you because you're good. You've had steady employment for the last year as a travel consultant. A nice cover if I do say so. Explains your travels. No, you don't make a good suspect. Besides, that's not our agreement. Our agreement protects both of us. Your father will be released from prison. I have my own agenda and my needs are being satisfied."

"Is this our last meeting?"

"Yes. We have to open up the second part of this operation. I see no reason to change course."

"What is the second part of the plan?" Ruby Ann asked.

"When you get back to your room at the MGM Grand this afternoon, please check with the hotel desk. There will be a package waiting for you. Take it to your room and study the contents thoroughly. When you have read the contents, destroy the package as we have talked about in the past. This is most important, as this package is the only item that can link you to the crimes. The package cannot link me to any crime. Do you understand?"

"Yes, I do."

"Good. After you read the contents, please commit the plan to memory and destroy it. We are both being protected by this action."

"I understand. Has the package been delivered already?"

"No."

"Can I ask you one question?"

Silence filled the room. An angry distorted voice filled the void. "No."

"I just wanted to know what you're getting out of this. I know you will make some money, but it would be nice...."

"Please! Don't bother me with questions concerning motive. Motive is what the police need to convict a suspect of a crime. Even if the suspect didn't commit the crime, the motive may be strong enough to convince a jury they really did do the deed."

"Do you have a partner?" asked Ruby Ann interrupting the voice. Silence filled the room. There was a slight buzz from the speakers, and some heavy breathing.

"You are not as bright as I first imagined...."

"I'm sorry...."

"Sorry. I don't think you know how long I have been setting this up. To ask questions only gives you more information. More information could make your life real short."

"I just thought...." stuttered Ruby Ann.

"Thinking is not what you have been hired for. I do the thinking. You do the listening. We have our agreement."

The lights went out all around Ruby Ann. She opened her eyes to total darkness but with a retention of flashing lights when she closed her eyes. Looking to her left she could see a small amount of light seeping in under the front door. She stumbled across the room, opened the door, and was met with blast of sunlight so bright she had to cover her eyes. Ruby Ann hastily dug her sunglasses out of her side pocket.

With distorted eyesight and pain from the glare of the sun, Ruby Ann found her car and sat for a few minutes to regain her composure. She tried to replay all the conversations back in her mind, but found it difficult to do so. She knew she would keep her end of the bargain. The criminal mind was a law of its own. Justice will always win out. She had no reason to go against "the voice." Not yet anyway. Timing was everything. But one worry remained; would her father be released from prison?

Ruby Ann was curious by nature, for being curious was part of self-preservation. After sitting for several minutes, she moved quickly from her car back to the apartment building. She entered and her hand sought the light switch on the wall. Finding it, Ruby Ann snapped on the lights. She saw that the stool she had been sitting on had been put back in an open bar area that separated the kitchen from the living room. The apartment was furnished, and the focal point of the living room was a stereo system and a Karaoke machine, no doubt used by her partner. She checked the kitchen once, noticed a large pile of mail on the kitchen counter. Vacation mail. Her partner had simply found an empty apartment and moved in for a few hours. She went to a wall calendar, which indicated that the tenants wouldn't be back for three days. The perfect set-up.

She left, having learned nothing about her partner other than the fact that he was meticulous, a planner. It was obvious that her partner knew the ropes, and knew how to put this kind of operation together. But was he going to cheat her? She didn't care; she was going to cheat him. Beat him at his own game. Ruby Ann didn't like having a partner who was in control, and she didn't like killing because someone else screwed up.

Ruby Ann arrived at the MGM Grand late Wednesday afternoon and checked in at the front desk. True to his word, whoever he was, a package had just arrived for her. As she moved through the casino she looked around. Ruby Ann felt as if she was being watched. With her looks, people were always staring, but this was different. She felt more vulnerable, more out of control than she had ever felt before. Working with a partner she didn't know gave Ruby Ann the creeps.

Gamblers worked the slots in a rhythm that would be the envy of any Motown group. The casino had a sound and a life of its own. Ruby Ann viewed these people as not understanding money. She had learned early in life that if you pulled a bigger handle, you could get bigger money.

She moved to the elevators, and took one to the tenth floor where she had a room. She felt flushed and decided to grab a Coke at the vending machine on the way. Usually she stayed in rooms more extravagant than this one, but she had to be part of the group that would pass in the night. It was best in her line of work not to stand out. Being part of the crowd was what her father had taught her at the age of eight. She had come home from school and complained about always being picked by the teacher to answer the questions for the entire class. Tough lessons for a kid to learn. For a nine-or-ten year old it meant not wearing the prettiest dress in the class. Or making sure she never locked eyes with the teacher when a question was being asked and a victim was being chosen. Ruby Ann learned her lessons well.

One of the first stings Ruby Ann had participated in was being the third hand-off person in a pick-pocket operation. As a child, she was never noticed. People would take one look at Ruby Ann and continue with their search for the culprit who had the wallet. Her reward was more spending money than you could possibly imagine. Other kids could only dream about money. Ruby Ann went out and earned it. It was a game, a daily game of survival.

Ruby Ann relaxed by the window of her room and enjoyed the view of the Strip north of the MGM Grand, and the desert and mountains beyond. The cool air from the air conditioning system blew gently on her. Some day very soon she would enjoy the world in a less plastic environment. The cool breeze would be coming from off shore, and she would have all the time in the world to lay back, to close her eyes without fear of being found, and to enjoy the fruits of her labors. A lifetime of work would finally be completed. Ruby Ann would be able to relax. She could almost hear the crashing waves hit the beach.

Fourteen

I left the MGM Grand Wednesday evening through the hotel guest registration area, noticing Julie waving at me as I passed. I changed direction and met her halfway. She was carrying another envelope.

"I have another report from Olsen," Julie said. Casually she brushed her hair behind her ears looking especially friendly. She was both direct and shy at the same time. Once she made eye contact, she never let go.

"Thanks." Julie was very attractive. I remembered I hadn't had a chance to open the first envelope. "I appreciate your help."

Julie glanced behind her as if someone was watching. She looked worried. Julie turned, grabbed my arm, and started walking with me out the swinging doors as if she was my best friend, talking non-stop until we got outside the door.

"Listen, I must be honest with you." She looked over her shoulder again, and I guided her to the left of the entrance with our backs to the parking garage. From this position we could see the front door and the cars moving in and out of the drop-off area, which was some sixteen lanes wide. "These reports I've been giving you...they've been changed. They're giving you false information. I don't know why. It's not like Mr. Lanning to do that."

"Thanks for being honest with me. Believe me it will help," I said.

Just then two macho Italian studs climbed out of a cab. They were carrying beer bottles from the previous casino. They strutted toward the entrance doors, and on seeing Julie gave a rude whistle. "Hey, baby, want to spend some time in Italy?" They laughed at the cleverness of their pickup line.

I put my arm around Julie protectively.

"It's okay, I'm used to it. The staff is very well protected. I can make one call and they're out of here."

I turned Julie so she faced me. "Julie, I want you to know that I didn't kill Pleasure although it may look that way. I know you may not believe me, but it's true. I was a cop too long to go bad now."

"You were a cop?"

"Yeah, here in Vegas. I worked over at Metro for a long time."

"You know, I do believe you...that you didn't kill that woman. It's that Olsen guy -- he's always trying to make himself look good." We moved toward the parking garage, getting nearer to Tropicana Avenue.

Julie looked at the bag I had slung over my shoulder. "What are you going to do? You look like you're leaving."

"Olsen and Peter Daily just tossed my home and are now headed over to my office. The rumor is they will either have my bail revoked or issue new charges, which means another warrant out for my arrest. But I don't know for sure yet."

"I can't believe they would do that. It doesn't make any sense."

"Just going by the book," I said. "But I can't wait to find out. The hardest thing to do is to solve a crime while you're doing time."

"I can help."

"How?"

"I'll check you out of your room, and I'll check you into a new one under another name."

"I can't let you do that. If they do put out an arrest warrant, you'll become an accessory to the crime."

"No, I want to help. It's just a room change to me." She indicated the new envelope she'd handed me. "Wait until you read that and then you'll believe me. I'd like to give you the real reports, but they'd hang me for it."

I hesitated. "I understand. You can really check me in again?"

"I work for the hotel manager. Of course I can. We check people in and out every day who need privacy. You wouldn't believe the stars who come here to gamble in the private high-roller casino in the MGM Grand. You never even hear about those people. You should see this place when they have a big heavyweight fight. It's unreal."

"I'm still concerned what happens if you get caught."

"Nonsense. Sometimes it seems as if half the people in town are using an assumed name. And besides, tomorrow starts my vacation and I will be out of town for two weeks. I leave on an evening flight. That gives you two weeks. If they ask me when I return I'll tell the truth. You're going undercover and I helped you get a new room."

"Okay. It might just work. It gives me two weeks, so let's do it."

"Fine. Here's what I want you to do. Walk down Tropicana for about ten minutes, then turn around and head back. Walk right back through these doors. Something will happen, and you'll get your room key. I won't know you."

"Okay."

"Who do you want to be?" she asked with a twinkle in her eye.

"Make it under George Arthur St. Clair. Any address."

"George Arthur St. Clair. Got it."

"I've got I.D. to cover the name. I really appreciate this. It's nice when the good guys get help, then the bad guys haven't got a chance. Thanks."

"Please, I wanted to help."

I squeezed Julie's hand and she turned and walked away. She stopped, came back and gave me a kiss on the cheek in a very tender embrace.

"Be careful, be really careful," and was gone.

As Julie walked away, I turned and walked for several minutes in the direction she indicated. Tropicana was backed up with traffic in both lanes. I then doubled back, made my way up to entrance passing several cabs and re-entered the MGM Grand.

I was puzzled by Julie's willingness to help. I wanted to check for a tail. Was this a clever way to keep tabs on me? It would be if Olsen and Lanning were that smart. But I didn't think they were. In fact, I was gambling on it - which is what it's all about. A detective becomes a quick judge of character, and my read on Julie was she was an honest person seeing something she could not justify. So she was taking a step, a gamble for sure, but a step.

I stopped and watched for any unusual activity. Convinced I was okay for the moment, and knowing that if I was being set up I was history anyway, I continued to cross the marble floor in the lobby and toward the casino floor. As in any town where large numbers of people come through on vacation, Las Vegas had its more populated spots. Where Tropicana Boulevard meets the Strip is one of those places. It was a heavily traveled intersection for people and cars.

I stopped for a minute and switched I.D.s. As a detective I find it handy to have an alias to work under. I had many. For the married bunch it keeps their families protected and out of the spotlight. I was ready to enter the MGM Grand as George Arthur St. Clair. I moved into the casino and was immediately engulfed by the sheer vastness of what the MGM Grand was all about. The biggest and the best. It was truly a spectacular casino.

I moved to the left to avoid the people behind me. On the right there was a large commotion. Like everyone else I stopped to see what was going on. Two large, tough-looking security guards were escorting two drunks out of the casino.

And wouldn't you know it, they were the two macho Italians who'd hit on Julie a little while ago.

Revenge can sometimes work into your plan. Casinos sometimes make examples of people, such as throwing them out on their ear. This gives the crowd a feeling of safety, as if someone is watching out for them. At the peak of the excitement as one of the guards physically took control over the most belligerent one, I felt something shoved into my hand. I looked down to see an envelope with the words MGM Grand on it. I turned and could just make out Julie as she moved through the crowd of tourists-turned-spectators. She turned, smiled, blew me a kiss, and was gone. Apparently I had just encountered the fast check-in service that everyone wishes for.

I glanced at the envelope and learned I was in the Diamond MGM Grand. Not making eye contact, I moved through a throng of Hawaiian-dressed tourists. I stopped and waited until no one was around and entered the elevator. Just as the door slid shut, a figure moved in and gave me a big smile.

"Fargo. Nice to see you again," said Pleasure.

Fifteen

RUBY ANN gave in to curiosity and temptation. She slipped on a pair of thin latex gloves commonly used in the medical community for protection against infection. For Ruby Ann, it was a matter of self-defense. Fingerprints were not something she liked leaving around. She carefully wiped the package to remove her prints, then opened it with a long-bladed stiletto knife that had been given to her by her father.

The stiletto, with the open web handle, had saved her a number of times. When she traveled she always checked it in her luggage, and then retrieved it after she arrived. No use setting off airport alarms. She pulled out a package similar to the one she had received the first time. The package contained one letter and two envelopes.

Ruby Ann,

Do not for a second believe you're not being watched. I follow your every move. You are the only person who can connect me to your misdeeds. Yes, your misdeeds. Granted, you have followed my instructions to the letter. You did well in pulling off the heist, and have split the money and jewels with me fairly and equitably. But you screwed up in killing McCaddy, and that's your problem. The problem I worry about is having a partner, and you are my partner. Like you, I work alone. You're only a tool to get what I really want. You must remember this. I will eliminate you whenever I want. Your only hope is to follow directions. I am fair, but not kind.

I know your past. I know your future. You must do exactly what I tell you to do. You are the agent of my success. If you screw up, you'll also take the fall. And there is always your father to consider. There is no way out.

In order for both of us to become free from the burden of your crime, we must provide a path for the police to follow that will lead them to a suspect. And as you well know, once the police have a suspect, they will prosecute even if they have some doubt that it's not the right person. A suspect is a suspect. Many times people get caught up in the politics of politics, only to be cast aside as a casualty. Innocent people are perfect targets because as soon as they're accused, they begin to act and look guilty. Being innocent just gives them something to think about when they're in jail.

You must trust me. I will destroy all of these photos and notes, as you must, if you follow my directions explicitly.

Ruby Ann's head snapped back at the mention of photos. Nobody had a current photograph of her. She could sense problems ahead, and was not happy. She continued to read.

Destroy this letter and the contents of the package by whatever means you like. Do not destroy this in the hotel room by burning or flushing down the toilet. Too many things can go wrong. Please open the smaller of the two envelopes.

Ruby Ann opened it up not knowing what to expect. Her hands actually begin to shake. Five photographs slipped out of the envelope. Each one showed her in various stages of entering or exiting Desert Sage Jewelry Company. The photos contained a time and date that corresponded with the time and date of McCaddy's death. Ruby Ann would have a lot of explaining to do if the police ever found these photos. She had underestimated her partner. Now she knew. She had no partner. She had a problem. Ruby Ann continued to read.

Our intended mark will be unknown to you. Take a handful of your diamonds and place them in an envelope. Take the remaining envelope you have in front of you, which is open, and place the envelope with the diamonds in it. Seal it and drop it in the MGM Grand mailbox located at the front registration desk. Do this tomorrow afternoon during the busy check-in period. Wear gloves, and also a wig, in case security has the mail drop covered on video.

Also, I'm trusting you not to examine the open envelope you are putting the diamonds in. If you do, it will only come back on you later. If you do look in the envelope you will not be able to pass a lie detector test. It's for your protection that you do not know who this individual is. I could have done this myself, but this is your role and will eliminate any connection to me.

Once you destroy the contents of this envelope, and deposit the envelope in the in-house mail system at the casino, you will be clear to leave. Within twenty-four hours your father will be released. If I see you in Vegas, I will cancel your father's freedom. I'm firm about this. It's up to you.

Your Partner, Forever.

Ruby Ann placed the package on the bed and thought about what was being asked of her. The instructions were more explicit, and this time, more threatening and frightening than before. Certainly her partner, if she could call him a partner, had everything worked out. But every plan has a weak spot. In every strength, there is a weakness, and for every weakness, there is a strength. You just have to find it. That's what her father had taught her. He had also taught her that you don't know where the weak spot is until you execute the plan. That's why you have back-up plans.

The decision she must make is to either follow the advice she had been given, or to plot another course of action. She had to admire the plan. If it worked, she would have a chance of not being blamed for the robbery of Desert Sage and the murder of McCaddy. But she also knew it would be hanging over her head forever. Ruby Ann knew the history of partners. They always gave each other up. The problem was that it was a one-sided deal. She could be looking at life in prison if those photos ever got into the wrong hands. The worst part is that somebody would always have something on her. Even twenty years from now. He could ask her anything with the promise of getting the photos back. Rob a bank, make a hit. Her partner had a get-out-of-jail-free card for sure. She had nothing on her partner. Nothing yet, anyway.

Sixteen

PLEASURE gave me a kiss lightly on the cheek. Another couple got on the elevator on floor five, and we rode in silence to the eleventh floor.

I closed the door to my new suite, turned around, and looked at Pleasure. "So far, I have to say, this is the most interesting assignment I've had in long time."

"I'm glad you feel that way," said Pleasure as she walked across the suite checking out the accommodations. She took off a black silk jacket that matched her cocktail dress. She had my attention, and I watched her carefully as she seated herself by a small table that overlooked the Vegas Strip. She studied the view with a steady gaze.

"I don't know if you've heard, but I've had several problems since I left you at poolside," I said.

"Life does present problems doesn't it?"

"Well, you might say that," I replied. I thought about how she had appeared in my life from nowhere. I was always careful in selecting my clients, but I felt that this time Pleasure had selected me. I was not sure I knew who she really was, or what she was up to.

"First of all, do you know, for the record, that you are listed by the Las Vegas Metro Police department as dead?"

Pleasure turned and looked me in the eye. "Really?"

"Did you know that? Yes or no?"

"My, my, my. We are direct, aren't we?"

"Yes or no?"

"No," Pleasure responded. "But it could have its advantages."

"I'm sure it could. But it's causing me a lot of problems."

"I can't imagine why."

"I'll get to that part. Who is the girl in the morgue right now?"

"Don't know," said Pleasure.

"The D.A. thinks it's you."

"Not possible. I'm alive and well." Pleasure stood and twirled around to illustrate the point. She sat down and crossed her legs.

I walked over to her, stood above Pleasure, and marveled at her beauty. She was as sly as a fox. Never before had I been faced with a client who caused me so much trouble, but at the same time intrigued me so much. True, she was a hustler, but then again, who wasn't? I knew I had to get to the bottom of what was happening before she disappeared again.

"Would you care to tell me exactly what is going on?" I asked as I sat down.

"Well, for the last few days I've been hanging out at the Rio, getting a little sun, enjoying the fine food. I've really just been taking it easy." Pleasure turned away and studied the view.

"I'm happy for you."

"Thanks."

"You are aware that I've been brought up on charges of robbery at the Desert Sage Jewelry Company?"

"No." Pleasure turned toward me quite surprised.

"They also think I might have whacked its owner, McCaddy."

"Why would they think that?"

"Seems like the jewelry from the robbery turned up in your safe."

"My safe?"

"The one in your hotel room. The one you gave me the combination to."

"Oh, and how are you connected?"

"I happened to be examining some diamonds that mysteriously appeared in the safe when the cops busted me. And now I'm in a whole load of trouble."

"I didn't have any diamonds in my safe. Just money!"

"Well, there were easily a hundred or so diamonds in your safe."

"When did this happen?"

"Within twenty-four hours of the robbery. Day before yesterday."

"That's impossible," said Pleasure. She rose from her chair, walked across the suite and opened a small refrigerator, which had a key hanging from the lock.

"But that's what happened," I said.

"You want anything?" asked Pleasure, still bent over the refrigerator. If she was teasing me, she was doing a great job.

"I'll pass."

Pleasure pulled out a sparkling water, twisted the cap off, and poured it into a crystal glass from the shelf above the refrigerator. I watched her. She was an unconcerned citizen. She seemed to have no concept of time, or any understanding of other people's problems.

"Umm...this is good."

"Listen, I just want you to sit down here for a few minutes and explain to me what happened after I left you for your hotel safe."

"It's that important?" Pleasure strolled across the suite and sat down.

"Yes, it is."

"Okay, I'm ready." Pleasure stared directly into my eyes.

"What happened?"

"After a few minutes I decided to leave the pool area."

"Why didn't you go back up to your hotel room?"

"Didn't feel it was necessary. I had an appointment at the Rio. I changed at the pool, and then left."

"Who did you go and see?"

"Private business."

"I'm your P.I. How about sharing?"

"Not right now," Pleasure said as she took a sip of the sparkling water.

"Do you know who took your place on the lounge at the swimming pool?" I asked.

"No. I didn't pay any attention."

"Did you check out of your hotel?"

"No," said Pleasure, unconcerned with the questions I was asking.

"Why not?"

"I was planning on coming back."

"You had left quite a bit of money in the safe."

"It was a safe. That's what it's for."

"But you checked in at the Rio?"

"Not at first. I thought about the money when I was at the Rio, but I figured it would be secure."

"You had plans to come back to the MGM Grand?"

"Certainly. At least I did when I left, but after I got to the Rio I decided to stay overnight. One night led to a couple of days."

"You just forgot about the money in your safe?"

"Fargo, I never forget about money."

"What about hiring me?"

Pleasure reached over and put her hand on my knee. "I would never forget about you. You know that." I was disappointed when she removed her hand. It was a subtle gesture, but it had a great effect.

"But you vanished."

"And I found you again. I knew you were working on my case while I was at the Rio."

"Can you prove you were at the Rio?"

"I was in the casino before that. I have markers that can be verified."

"Markers? That sounds serious. You're a gambler?"

"That's what I am."

"What game?" I asked.

"Hold'Em."

"You play poker?"

"Down to the last card."

"And you know what the last card is?"

"Every time," said Pleasure smiling.

"I admire a woman who plays poker. Even more if the play Hold'Em."

"That's good. We'll have to get a game together sometime."

"I'm not sure we're not playing right now."

"I can assure you we're not," said Pleasure.

"I might just lose on purpose," I replied.

"Not with me you wouldn't."

"Why?"

"I tend to tease."

I shifted my eyes at the obvious sexual overtones. She never moved a muscle. "So you play poker," I repeated.

"That's why I left the MGM Grand. Had a poker game I didn't want to miss."

"Big time?"

"I'm either up or down several thousand dollars a night. I usually sit in a game for about four to five hours."

"That much?"

"Yep."

"That long?"

"Like to see how the tables are running. Find out the weakness and strong points of the other players."

"Makes sense."

"That's how I make my living."

"You're kidding?"

"Not at all."

"What about the money in the safe? If that's poker winnings, wouldn't you want to go back there and retrieve it?"

"Sure I did. But remember, I was checked in for a week. There's no reason I should have had to worry about my room. You, Jody, and the maid were the only ones who had keys."

"Not any more. Now it's evidence."

"Then you're just the guy I need to help me get it back."

"Besides the Desert Sage problems I have, they also think I whacked you at poolside to get your money."

"You're kidding?"

"Nope. I expect to be arrested shortly. I'm undercover right now, or on the run, depending on who you talk to."

"I don't need the money right now. I also have money in a safe at the Rio." Pleasure turned and studied the view of Las Vegas. No matter what time of day, it's an impressive sight.

"And what about the money that Jody was carrying?"

"She and I were partners in a private game in Monte Carlo. I should never have gotten involved, but I did. We won, I left, and she was bringing our money in."

"How much?" I asked.

"About a hundred thousand dollars."

"You're kidding!"

"I bet the farm and won."

"Well," I said, getting up and pacing the room. "I still have a problem. I'm involved in legal actions that involve you. I'm not sure how you fit in yet."

"I don't fit in at all other than the fact that I left the MGM Grand and moved over to the Rio. I was going to send for my bags and have the contents of my safe removed and held for me, but I wasn't able to get it done." Pleasure ran one hand through her hair arranging it perfectly.

"Have you heard from Jody?"

"No. I can't imagine where she is. I would like to get money from the MGM Grand and move it over to the Rio."

"I don't think that's possible right now."

"Why not?"

"Well, for one thing, the police have you listed as dead. The second is your room has been taped off as part of a crime scene, and third, as I said, everything in the safe is considered evidence."

"Now that's going to be a problem. I'm sure I'll have another game here, and I like to have a room at the casino I'm playing in."

"I can't help you check in here. I'm sort of sneaking in-and-out of the hotel myself."

"I know the feeling," said Pleasure.

"Tell you what, why don't you use my room?"

"What about you?"

"I'll be in and out a lot."

"What happens if we both want to sleep here?" asked Pleasure teasingly.

"We're adults. I'm sure we can work out something. Right now I don't want certain people in the hotel to know you're alive, if that's all right with you?"

"Won't bother me any. I just wanted to check in with you, which is why I came back to the MGM Grand. To tell you the truth, I did walk by my old room, saw that it was taped off as a crime scene, and returned to the lobby. That's when I spotted you."

"Must have been a shock?"

"I don't need surprises."

"Where to now?" I asked.

"I'm headed back to the Rio for another Hold'Em poker game." Pleasure adjusted her chair away from the table.

"You're a serious poker player."

"A girl has to have her fun."

"I'm all for fun," I said.

"Not until you find Jody. That's why I hired you."

"You are aware that the robbery and murder at the Desert Sage Jewelry could have been committed by a woman?"

"You think it was Jody?"

"It came to mind once or twice," I said, watching Pleasure carefully. I had no idea if the killer was a woman, but I thought by throwing it out I might get a reading from Pleasure.

"Jody? No, it can't be Jody."

"Why not?"

"Jody is a mystery. She's one hell of a poker player, and as I told you already, she makes me look homely. She's not a thief. Couldn't be Jody, I just know it. It's not the way Jody would go about solving a problem."

"Still, it could be her. She was supposed to have her luggage in your room. Somebody came along and put the jewels in your safe."

"Why would they do that?"

"Trying to pin the murder and robbery of the Desert Sage on you."

"Maybe they were going to pin it on you," said Pleasure.

"No, that's no good. They had no idea you were going to hire me. Plus the fact, they had no idea you were going to move to the Rio. It's unusual you just picked up and left. When you did that, you threw somebody a curve."

"I do it all the time."

"Throw curves?"

"No, move to wherever I want to be."

"That's throwing curves."

Pleasure thought about this for a few seconds. "Point well taken," she said with a slight smile and a nod of her lovely head. She stood up and moved closer to the windows, which showed a neon kaleidoscope of colors that portrayed Las Vegas as everybody likes to see it. Dazzling colors that promise untold tales of entertainment and fun. Her reflection bounced back from the window at me. She was quite a picture against the neon glow of the Vegas lights.

"You come here often?" I asked as I stood and moved closer to the window. I studied the view of Vegas as well as that of Pleasure.

"I love this city. Look at it. Thousands of twinkling lights promising everyone an adventure. Who could not come to this city and find something they would remember forever? Maybe even a lifetime of memories. Each one of those lights has a story. A history. This place has been carved out of the desert and has turned into one of the most successful gambling resorts and vacation centers in the world. Everybody wants to come here, and everybody wants to return."

"So what's your story?"

"Just out for some fun," she said. "What's a girl going to do? What are we going to do?"

"What are we going to do? I don't follow."

"The night is young."

"But the night has problems, and the police are tying loose ends together as we speak. When they find me they are going to arrest me for something I didn't do."

"Every night needs an element of danger," said Pleasure.

"I could've bet you would have said that." I stared into Pleasure's dark eyes.

"How about going dancing?"

"What? Dancing?"

"Yeah, dancing. Ever hear of it?" Pleasure put her arms around me and kissed me deeply. I responded.

"Sure, but...."

"A few spins for old times. A late night dinner, just the two of us."

"I think with the problems at hand, I should decline."

"You could be in jail by tomorrow. Just think of all the wonderful memories you could take with you."

"I'm sure they'd be wonderful memories, but just the same, I've got to find out why those jewels ended up in your safe."

Pleasure picked up and flung her jacket over her shoulder. "Never say I didn't ask you out."

"I'm honored at the request, but I've got serious problems."

"Maybe the next time we meet we'll be able to dance till dawn."

"I hope so," I said as Pleasure walked toward the door. She turned around and glanced back. She was alluring. I was starting to kick myself. "If I need you, can I find you playing poker at the Rio?"

"Most of the time," said Pleasure studying me. "I'll see you there." She turned and walked out of the room.

I have to admit I was as impressed with her the second time as I was the first. If I didn't have the problems at hand, I would have jumped at the chance for a night out with her. I had to keep reminding myself that Pleasure was the cause of all my problems, even though she hadn't done anything. Or at least I think she hadn't done anything.

I knew that I was dealing with someone who not only interested me, but seemed to have an interest in me. I also knew it could be part of a huge charade put on for my benefit. If she was telling the truth, at least I could find her at the Rio playing poker when I needed her. I kept thinking she represented some kind of problem, but when I thought through the situation, I realized the only thing Pleasure had done was to leave a hotel and not tell anyone. Of course she did hand me a gun that had been recently fired, but I would deal with that when it became a problem.

She had hired me to find Jody, which was the extent of our professional relationship. If she was behind the murder of McCaddy, that would be different, but other than the diamonds in her safe, there was no indication that was a possibility. The diamonds were circumstantial, and wouldn't fly in the courts. Even more important, there appeared to be no physical evidence linking her to the crime. It wasn't comforting that everything seemed to be pointing to me, and I know I didn't do it. More and more I felt that Pleasure was a free spirit who played Hold'Em poker, big-time poker, and I bet she was very good at bluffing.

Seventeen

I left my hotel room early Thursday morning dressed in casual clothes of a tourist. To me it was a costume because most people never wore this stuff at home: shorts, Hawaiian shirt, and dark-tinted sunglasses. This way I could move in and out of the casino without Olsen's security guards following my every move. I stuffed the two envelopes from Julie in my back pocket and went to my favorite place – one of the private booths facing the huge electronic tote board for tracking the ponies.

I had to laugh. I looked over to where I usually sat and there was Uncle Leo, wrapped up in the daily races. Behind him were two house dicks watching every move he made. They probably figured if they stayed with Uncle Leo, they would find me. I found a seat in one of the private booths. I could glance over my shoulder toward the entrance to the casino from the Strip, or to the poker room, which was behind me. It was perfect. I could see the electronic boards, plus I had a monitor right in front of me so I could view the races in private, or watch on the large screen up front. From the booths it was easier to observe the telltale signs of a horse in trouble, running wide on a turn, or maybe with a slight limp in the warm-up. A horse with a braided mane might indicate an inside belief of a win and a photo session. Anything that helped in handicapping the race and placing winning bets.

I had picked up a Racing Form at the newsstand on my way to the sports area and went about the task of getting a couple of bets lined up. Might as well play the part of the tourist losing all his money for awhile. As I did so, I pulled out from my back pocket two envelopes from Julie and opened the first one. I know I should have opened them sooner, but it didn't happen.

The first was a one-page sheet with one paragraph.

To: Fargo Blue
From: H. Lanning

Olsen is staying away from your operation inside the hotel, but I would take odds that he is working with the police to try and bust you. I told him that if he comes up with the facts he can place you under arrest for murder. If Olsen has any other suspects in mind, which I don't think he has, he is keeping this to himself. Olsen is convinced that you are guilty.

H. Lanning

I tore the note into small pieces and placed them in my left front pocket. So Olsen was keeping an eye on me in the hotel, but telling Harry I was being left alone.

On my way to the Sports Bar I did what I could to find out if I was being followed or not. I didn't pick up anything unusual. I checked out some of the regular entrances and I thought I was able to pick up a couple of hotel security men watching for somebody. Possibly they were watching for my entrance into the casino area.

I tore open the second envelope.

To: Fargo Blue
From: H. Lanning

Olsen is now working at tying you into the McCaddy killing. His goal is to put you away for a long time. The police are working closely with him. He said he has enough information to arrest you in two days. Let's end this charade, because it looks like you're it.

H. Lanning

I folded the note and put it in my breast pocket. When I filed my case notes, I would include this information. Olsen would probably go for an arrest in about twenty-four hours. That was certain. No way was he going to let Harry know exactly what he was doing. I watched the next race and continued to study the racing forms while also watching the monitors on the giant screen. What the hell did Olsen get for busting me? If I were convicted of the McCaddy murder it would be good for his career. He would be able to impress the police with his detective abilities and use it to get a pay increase from the MGM Grand, plus more money for his security budget. Olsen was a snake. That's about all I really knew. My main problem was that Olsen was after me for what appeared to be his own personal satisfaction for what I had done to him years ago on Fremont Street.

I'd caught Olsen with cash he wasn't suppose to have. He said he was going to turn it in. That's what everyone says, I thought.

I pulled out my portable cellular and hoped like hell that the ears in the sky were not monitoring this channel right now.

"MGM Grand. May I help you?"

"Yes. This is St. Clair. Could you connect me to Harry's office? I'm looking for Julie."

"I'm sorry, sir. Ms. Fuller is on vacation for a couple of weeks. Could somebody else help you in her office?"

"No thanks. I'll call when she returns."

"Thank you for calling the MGM Grand."

I quickly dialed Julie's cellular and hoped she was in the area. I waited for the connection. I probably was taking a chance on using this phone, but chances were that Olsen would not be able to tap into it even though it was a radio frequency that a cub scout and Mr. Wizard could track down. I had the advantage that Olsen did not think I was in the hotel.

"Hello."

"Julie, it's St. Clair."

"Mr. St. Clair. How are you today?"

"Just fine," I said softly so I would not be overheard. "Thanks for the notes and advice. I was hoping I could reach you before you left Las Vegas."

"I'm at the airport."

"Hope you have a great trip. I was wondering if you might help me with one problem?"

"I'll try," said Julie. "You'll have to hurry though, they're calling my plane." I could hear the roar of a jet engine in the background.

"Do you have any contacts here at the MGM Grand I could work with?"

"No...no I don't. Why, may I ask?"

"Just thought if I needed something while you're gone...that's all."

"No one I could trust, if you know what I mean?"

"I understand. No problem."

"How about this. I'll give you a call every other day around noon. I can probably help you just as easily as if I were right there."

"That should work out fine. You'll call day after tomorrow?"

"Right," Julie said. "What's the phone number?"

"You have it. Use my cell phone.

"Good. Where are you?"

"Sports Bar."

"Good, try and win something. It will take your mind off your troubles."

"I will, and I appreciate your help. There's a late-night dinner in this for you when I figure out what the hell is going on."

"Are you hustling me?" I could tell Julie's eyes were twinkling.

"Not yet," I said. "Not yet."

I hung up the phone. I decided to take one more chance on using my cellular. I hope that Uncle Leo had his turned on. I turned around and glanced over my shoulder and saw Uncle Leo reach in his coat pocket.

"Hello," Uncle Leo answered over my phone.

"Fargo here. I'm checking in."

"About time," said Uncle Leo. "Did you find Pleasure?"

"She found me."

"What did Pleasure have to say for herself?"

"She left the pool area right after I did. I won't say where she went or what she's doing, but the feeling that I get is that she's not involved in the McCaddy robbery or murder. However, somebody is pissed off at her and that's the connection."

"Any leads?" asked Uncle Leo.

"Not really. I know where Pleasure gets her money, and I know what she does for a living. She is owed some money, but in her business that is not hard to understand. It could be that simple. But why would they plant the jewels from McCaddy in her safe?"

"To either frame Pleasure, or somebody else, like you."

"Somebody else. That's interesting. But why me?" I had to think about that for awhile. If the killer was trying to frame Pleasure, why weren't the police after her? After all, they found the jewels in Pleasure's safe. Of course -- they still think Pleasure is dead. It's me they seem to want.

"Couldn't Pleasure have knocked off Desert Sage and placed the jewels in her safe?" asked Uncle Leo.

"Why would she do that? But could she? She would have had to go through a crime scene ribbon and open up an extra lock, which the police had attached. No, I really don't think Pleasure would have done that. Somebody else did it."

"The only people who had access were the police."

"Funny you should mention that, but you're right. The only real access was by the police. It was a police lock, not a hotel lock."

"What about Jody? Have you found her yet?"

"Nope. No sign of her," I said.

"Could she have done the heist?"

"Not according to Pleasure, but I haven't ruled her out yet. You have to admit that it fits, though. Jody becomes pissed off at Pleasure and decides to send her up the river."

"How much was Jody delivering to Pleasure?" asked Uncle Leo.

"About a hundred thousand according to Pleasure."

"That's motive. What's your next move?"

"I'm going to check on exactly where Pleasure was during the robbery of the Desert Sage. That will rule her out. Then, I'll try and follow her, but I don't figure that will be easy. She's slippery, in a nice sort of way. But where Pleasure is, Jody might be close by."

"What about the pool area and the Desert Sage?"

"I'll get to it real soon. I might have Sheri help me."

"How are you going to get around? Olsen has been looking for your car."

"Working on it."

"Good. Got to get going. I've got to make a bet on a pony."

"Take the long shot. Run-with-It just changed on the Golden Gate board and it looks like stable money," I said, then clicked my cell phone shut. I turned around to see Uncle Leo glance up at the board and then turn and look around him slowly. He knew I was nearby, or sitting in another Sports Bar somewhere. He spotted the two security men watching him, and I knew he would keep them busy for the rest of the afternoon.

Next I got out my computer and set it up. I connected via Wi FI and went online to one of my email accounts and sent a quick message. It took a matter of seconds. I knew Sheri would be checking in on a regular basis. Part of the routine with an operation going on. I had no new messages waiting for me.

I then signed off and brought up some handicapping software. It was not unusual to see computers in the Sports Bar. Many betters are starting to use small laptops to handicap the horses. Casinos love it because the losers feel more justified when they lose. With my back to the crowd, and my eyes on the monitors, I settled in to an afternoon of betting. It would take a while for my plan to work.

After three races I connected to my e-mail account again and downloaded one message. Everything was set and ready to go. Right on schedule. I dumped the e-mail and deleted it from the drive. I then ran a utility program that wrote over the used disk space. Now it was permanently gone.

After the next race I rose with two or three other bettors so we could make early bets on the next race. I went to the front of the Sports Bar and then to the left. I would not start to make my way out of the casino until I knew whether anybody was following me. It's sometimes harder to act natural when you think you are being observed. I stopped and watched some baseball on the sports monitors adjacent to the Sports Bar. I became part of the crowd.

I walked through the slot-area and didn't pay any attention to hotel personnel. I just watched the tourists playing the slots. That's what all the tourists do: they either play slots, or they watch other people play them. One lady hit a winner, and I stood with a small crowd while she squealed with delight as the coins poured forth. Too bad it wasn't a five-dollar machine. This one was a quarter machine, and she had hit it for three hundred dollars. It coughed up quite a few coins, which made a racket all by themselves. The more noise of coins hitting the trays, the more people think they are winning.

The crowd began to break up and I headed for the main entrance directly across the street from the New York, New York. I was there in a matter of minutes. To the left was the old reliable Tropicana, where Abby danced nightly. The Excalibur stood majestically on its own corner. I walked to the right and rode the escalator up to the pedestrian overpass. At this intersection people are not allowed to cross the street directly into the casinos. You have to travel above ground, getting a great view and allowing traffic to move swiftly through the intersection.

As I walked across I was treated to an overwhelming sight of the skyline of New York City -- compliments of the New York, New York Hotel and Casino. The Cab drivers all over town joke that the NY NY was bringing in muggers from Central Park to give the place some atmosphere. Lavish in detail, giving an incredible feeling of being in New York. Yet structurally, it was only one building. I entered New York, New York and proceeded to a point where I overlooked the main gambling floor. Just like in New York, various neon signs flashed their messages to a New York audience. I gave the post next to me a slap for good luck, and turned and walked past

Houdini's Magic Shop and Coyote Ugly exiting outside on another overpass, which led me directly to the Excalibur.

The Excalibur was a hotel that had an atmosphere all its own. Knights of the Round Table. The kids love it. They have a floor all their own with games of chance and skill. There was even an arena where Knights dueled against each other to win the hearts of the princess. The Excalibur had one of the largest gambling floors in town.

As I approached its entrance I stepped onto the moving sidewalk that carries people effortlessly into the hotel. I reached the top and moved to the side to watch the people behind me, looking to see if I had been followed. If my pursuers were on the people-mover they were trapped. My gut told me I was being followed.

I then worked my way across the casino floor to where Tower One was located and headed for the parking lot. I crossed the parking lot and walked straight into the covered parking area, then up the nearest rows of cars. Half way up the ramp I found it -- a blue Neon. I walked around to the driver's door, opened it, and reached under the seat to find the waiting set of keys. Within seconds the Neon was in traffic and headed down the Strip. Just another rental car.

I had e-mailed Sheri that I needed a new car. She had e-mailed me back that she'd arranged for the Neon to be at this location. Simple solution to an old problem. With the Internet, operators can communicate with coded files over the Net to little-known e-mail boxes or even temporary web sites. Information of all kinds, plus diagrams and maps, are a keystroke away. Unlike with cell phones, a pursuer can't pick up your modem calls, and to hack into the system requires a starting point. Although I knew there was a good chance my conversation with Uncle Leo could have been picked up, I felt secure no one had picked up the e-mail message.

It was time to get down and get dirty. It was time

to kick some butt. All I had to do was find one to kick. I turned onto Las Vegas Boulevard and headed for the parking lot of Caesar's Palace.

Eighteen

VINCE OLSEN walked into the security complex of the MGM Grand, which was well hidden from the gaming tables and mobs of tourists. A vast complex of cameras surveyed the entire casino. This was the backbone of the security system. Any pit boss could call security and have an individual watched if they suspected foul play at the tables. That was just for openers. As soon as an individual was identified a coordinated, a well-rehearsed campaign is launched to determine if the suspect is a card man or dice man working the casino. In blackjack, a new dealer is brought in or a new set of cards is introduced. Nothing illegal about it -- just a new deck. Security would set up spotters to see if signals were being passed from another accomplice. If there was a seat available, a new player would enter the game -- who was another card expert working for the casino. Sometimes the shill would be a beautiful woman or a handsome stud. The rule was, do whatever was necessary to break a gambler's winning streak. If the house determined it was being scammed, the individuals would be photographed and asked to leave the casino. Cheats of any kind were documented and their files passed on to other casinos.

At the dice table similar techniques were brought into play. They brought in new stickmen. They changed the dice, sometimes after every roll. Sometimes the shills were used as a means of distraction. I mean, ask yourself, how many times have you seen a woman drunk making foolish bets at a craps table while everyone drooled over her body? The goal is to do whatever it takes to get the dice to produce for the casino, and not for the artist who is working the tables.

Tables do have their streaks, and one out of a hundred people knows how to bet to take advantage of a hot roll. These streak-bettors are just as dangerous as a cheater. Streaks help the public perception of the fortunes that can be won. Streaks are marketed in the casino; the money is counted in the back room. There's an old story told about a craps table that started to "pass" and hotel executives from other casinos arrived by cab to get in on the wild ride. The hotel executives knew how to bet, and they loved a good run of the dice. Money management is what it's all about on both sides of the table.

"I got here as soon as I could," said Olsen walking up to an old-timer in the security area. Olsen pulled out a chair and sat down in front of a bank of monitors. The modern casino security system is a maze of cameras capable of documenting all the moves of a professional cheat. Modern technology at it's best.

"We've got everything on tape," said the Troll. The Troll was a legend himself. He had started thirty years earlier when his father was just retiring. His father was in the business from the very beginning. He had lived above the casino gaming tables in the rafters. They had bunks and hot plates hidden away and so they would not have to leave. They walked on gangplanks, which were linked together over the entire floor of the casino peering down through mirrors watching suspected cheats. The crews, which worked the ceiling, knew every trick in the book. If dealers tried to pocket a chip in any manner whatso- ever, they were caught. Dealers sometimes just disap- peared.

The Troll was a consultant to the security forces at the MGM Grand. He assisted Olsen on special assignments.

"Let's play the tape," said Olsen. "How did you find Fargo in the casino?"

"Just picked him up in the Sports Bar. Sheer luck." A technician hit the play button and the Sports Bar appeared.

"I don't see him," said Olsen.

"Hang on a minute," said the Troll. "There he is just walking in."

"That's Fargo. Nah...you guys are pulling my leg. When are you going to be able to tell the difference between a tourist and our hot-shot detective?"

"Just hang in there. Roll the other tape. We've got him on two different cameras at the same time." Another monitor came to life showing a different angle of Fargo walking in. "All right, freeze it and let's blow it up," said the Troll. A medium shot of Fargo appeared on the screen and then it was enlarged.

"I'll be damned."

"Yeah, he thinks he's got us fooled. Move the tape ahead, boys."

"What's next?" asked Olsen.

"He hangs around the Sports Bar, makes a couple of bets, and then exits the casino. We were on him all the time. Stop it here." The tape squeals to a stop. "Here he's talking on his cellular. Our guy on the floor had a scanner hooked up to a tape. Fargo appeared to be talking to someone called Julie who was with the hotel. We didn't get everything as everyone and his grandmother has a cell phone out here.

"Damn cell phones. They either help or they're a pain in the ass."

"We nailed him on the second call. Watch." The camera pans over and we see Uncle Leo. "Fargo is talking to his lawyer, the famous Uncle Leo. This guy is hooked on the ponies. Never spends any time in his office. Jump ahead." Again the tape is speeded up and we see Fargo playing the horses with the laptop.

"Move it forward." The tape accelerates and eventually they pick up Fargo watching the lady hit her three hundred-dollar slot machine. Then it shows Fargo walking toward the front entrance.

"What happened outside?" asked Olsen.

"I had three two-man teams ready to work the street. Fargo is really worried about being followed, so we did a front tail. A little more difficult to pull off, but we got him. He even tried to catch us at the entrance at the Excalibur. He stopped at the end of the people mover, but he didn't fool us. We weren't behind him, we were just ahead of him. Since he figured we didn't know where he was going, we wouldn't be able to follow. We had teams set up all over the place. He could have gone in any direction."

"I'm impressed. Thanks for all the hard work. All of you guys, a fine piece of work. Where is he now?"

"We've got him driving the Strip in a rental car."

"I want to know where he's going. I want to know whom he's going to see. I also want to know who this Julie is and where she works. We're going to arrest him as soon as I get word from Vegas Metro."

"It'll be a little tricky since we're now stuck doing a normal tail, but we should have an idea," said the Troll. "Not our normal operation, you understand, but we'll try and do the job."

"Thanks, I appreciate it," said Olsen getting up. He shook hands with a couple of the security members of his team and then left the office complex.

"That guy is out to get Fargo Blue," said the Troll. "He's been after him since he got burned down on Fremont Street."

"We've all heard that story," said Randy, one of the technicians.

"Yeah. Haven't we all," said the Troll.

"He's still one of the biggest jerks around," added Randy.

"You've got that one right." The Troll smiled. "That's why he's head of security and you're just watching television monitors all day.

"True, but he's still a jerk," said Randy. Everyone nodded in agreement.

The blue Neon went through the Caesar's Forum parking lot with a security car from the MGM Grand a few cars back. They had lost sight of it a couple of times but now they had Fargo in view. The tail car was being driven by Jason "Shooter" Schulman, also a former cop who liked the Strip beat better than hauling drunks to the overnight tank on Fremont. Shooter took a lot of ribbing at the station as "Shooter" was slang for a mob hit man. He was called Shooter ever since the time he'd declared he was going out to make an arrest and ended up in a three-hour shoot out. When asked how he felt about it, he said it felt just like being in Nam. Shooter liked Nam. Over there, the rules were simple. Kill or be killed. The story was he did two-plus tours before they finally put him on a plane to the States. They had to tie him to his seat. The war ended before he could get back. Said he missed it. He had a hard time adjusting. He was a sniper.

Shooter had more respect working at the MGM Grand than any other casino because people thought it was a class operation. He knew it was just like the others, but this one had a better coat of paint. Even with all the paint and decor, the casino still raked in the cash based on a steady percentage everybody knew it was going to make.

Riding shotgun was Perkins, part-time hustler and private detective who had answered the ads for a full-time position as a security officer with the MGM Grand. When off duty, his specialty was photographing husbands with hookers and then busting them. He sometimes got carried away with the photos and used them as the basis for a small-time blackmail operation. Nothing makes a guy sweat more than having a half dozen eight-by-tens of a long-forgotten night show up in the morning mail.

The car phone broke the silence.

"Hello," answered Shooter.

"This is Olsen. You guys on Fargo?"

"Yeah, we got him. He's not going no place."

"Where are you now?"

"We just went through the Forum parking lot. We thought he was going to stop here, but he went right through it. I think he's using it as a short cut to work his way over toward Sahara Boulevard instead of driving down the Strip. Taxi cabs do it all the time."

"You've definitely got him behind the wheel?"

"Oh yeah. We got a clear shot of him after he passed us on the way out of the Excalibur parking lot. We got his license number; GA2880, which is one of those standard rental cars. We slide up on his blind side once in awhile, and Perkins puts a glass on the plates and the back of his head. He ain't going nowhere. Trust me."

"Well, just don't lose him. I want to know what Fargo is thinking and where he's going."

"Gotcha, boss."

"Call me." Olsen hung up the phone.

"What the hell was that all about?" asked Perkins changing lanes one more time.

"Olsen, he's trying to trap Fargo into something. Some game he's playing."

"I hear Fargo is an all-right guy."

"Yeah, but he made some mistakes along the way. When's the last time you heard about a private eye being straight as an arrow?"

"I don't know anybody straight as an arrow," Perkins said.

"See, that's just the point."

Perkins straightened up. "I see him. Fargo's making a turn that's going to take him toward Sahara Boulevard."

"Keep on him. There's no telling where he's going now."

"He's turning."

"I got him," said Shooter. "We've got to be careful. We're kind of low on gas."

"If he hits the Interstate, or heads toward Boulder Highway, we're in trouble," Perkins said.

"With what's going on, why would he head out there?"

"Beats me.

Nineteen

I walked through the Forum Shopping Arcade after enjoying a pastrami sandwich and one-too-many pickles at the Stage Deli. A favorite place of mine, as it's long and narrow. You could sit in the rear with your back to the front and no one would ever see you. I usually sat toward the back on the left side facing front. I could see everyone, but it would be tough to see me.

I had to smile. Behind the wheel of the blue Neon was a friend of Sheri's who was taking the tail for a spin out into the desert. We had made the switch as I drove through the Forum valet parking area. All I had to do was open the door, grab my bag, and slide out. Sheri's friend Angel, slid in and took the wheel. A nice day for a drive. I was betting that the tail had not seen the switch. The tail was betting that I was still in the Neon. That's Las Vegas. Make a bet, and take your chances. I always said, assume you always have a tail.

MGM Grand security. Probably not as sophisticated as I thought, I mused to myself as I walked by Planet Hollywood. But the MGM Grand were better than most. With Uncle Leo making it difficult for the cops and buying us some time, I proceeded on the course I was most comfortable with, detecting. Some have described detective work as the relentless pursuit of inconsequential details that mold the framework of the crime and point the direction toward motive and opportunity. There is a thread of truth in this, but the real problem is to look at all the details and figure out which one is actually a clue. That's usually found in your gut and your instinct. All the details must be checked, but it's your gut that tells you where to go looking.

However, on this one, I felt as if my hands were tied. It was a sick, nauseated ache I had in my gut. I was not at all pleased how this case was developing.

I was determined to find out the real story, and sometimes the real story is not the obvious one. Police are not likely to change direction once they have narrowed down their suspects to one good possibility. After all, they have to eventually face their political constituents. They had me fingered for the crime, so my work was cut out for me.

I stopped and studied the cascading water over roman sculptures of horses, which appeared to be carved out of marble. To the right was a new wing to the Forum that captivated many shoppers for an entire afternoon. I sat on one of the benches and studied the statues.

The situation was getting serious. Particularly after that long conversation with Pleasure, which had set me straight on a lot of issues. I felt I might be a little less conspicuous if I were two, instead of one, so I gave Sheri a call. I had a slight advantage in that Sheri was a bit more attractive than I am. Actually, Sheri was a lot more attractive then I am, and more then most women, for that matter. At first, women didn't exactly love her for her looks, but after they got to know her, they warmed up to a real hard-working, honest, let's 'get it done by this afternoon' P.I.

It was somewhat intimidating when Sheri started to tell stories about her past adventures that easily topped most stories men tell, real or made up. Like the time she went out on a Coast Guard cutter in search of a couple who had been sailing the northern route to Hawaii. They had hit heavy seas that broke their mast. Then their rudder broke, and they were at the sea's mercy. The last radio message received was that they had abandoned ship. Air and sea rescue was already in operation, but it took a while for the Coast Guard to arrive on the scene. Sheri had spent the better part of three days working a rescue grid at their last-known location. With a little bit of women's intuition, she had found them alive, clinging to what remained of their vessel. The sharks were circling, but Sheri had arrived in time. Sharks were always circling around Sheri.

I cautiously moved out of the Forum and into Caesar's casino. I took the back elevator and moved up to the second level of parking. Even though for all practical purposes I was George Arthur St. Clair, I still looked like Fargo Blue. Worse yet, I felt like Fargo Blue. I hoped my tourist outfit would outwit any hotel security guy I might have met in the past. As soon as I entered the parking area Sheri pulled up; I got into the back seat and lowered myself to the floor. We were off.

"How long did it take you to shake them?" Sheri asked as she maneuvered her Lexus down the ramp and out toward Industrial Boulevard.

"I don't know, but they were all over me. Hopefully we can get some work done now. Did you bring my clothes?"

"Yep. They're in the trunk. Everything you wanted. Where're we headed?"

"First thing we do is head back to the MGM Grand and check out the pool. They'll never expect us to show up there. Then I want to check out the Desert Sage Jewelry Company and try to figure out how those jewels got in Pleasure's safe."

"Sounds good to me. It will be nice to start getting some answers."

"That's the plan," I said. I still kept out of sight below the seats just in case a second or third tail spotted us.

Sheri pulled a hard right and moved across the Strip toward the MGM Grand. We made our way back and parked in the back lot, checked to see if we were being followed, and then moved into the casino. "Are you ready for some fun and work?" I asked.

"Yep, I'm a working girl." She gave me a look. "Not that kind. You got to be careful in these places."

I grabbed my Hartman carry-on bag from the trunk that Sheri had packed for me, and we headed toward the pool. A happy couple. "A man and wife today. Did you bring your suit?"

"Yep, just like you asked. It's on underneath. What are we going to do?"

"Well, we're going to combine a little pleasure with some work. Asking questions has the tendency to shut some people up. Especially tourists, if we're lucky enough to find one who was there at the time of the hit. But if we pretend we're someone else, a curious couple, then sometimes you can get answers. You always have the option of telling them who you are and trying to pull some weight the tough way."

I stopped next to a slot and dumped three dollars into the waiting machine. "Pull it for luck?"

Sheri gave it a pull. "I thought you gave up on these bandits." The slot spun and one by one came up a loser. "See, I told you so."

We continued our walk through the casino. "Old habit, hard to break."

"Why?"

"Did you ever hear the story about the guy who sold aircraft carriers for a living?"

"No," Sheri said, not understanding what I was getting at.

"Well, somebody asked him if he had sold any, and he said, 'No, I haven't, but I only have to sell one.'"

"Well, that makes a little more sense. One good pull or one sale of an aircraft carry wraps up the financial problems."

"That it does. You just have to keep on trying, and of course the casinos are counting on it."

"Anyone in particular we want to talk to?" asked Sheri.

"Yeah, a Mr. Williams. He was on duty during the time period that Pleasure was murdered."

"But you really don't know who it was?"

"We have no positive I.D's. But remember, nobody knows."

"Do you think it was Jody?"

"No. But I don't know for sure."

"Why don't you take Pleasure to the morgue and have her try and I.D. the body?"

"That's always an option. But I'm guessing that Jody is not the murdered woman. Just a feeling I have."

"Why?"

"Because Jody's luggage was in Pleasure's hotel room. If she had changed and gone to the pool, Pleasure would of known. There is no sign that she removed anything from the luggage when she dropped her suitcases. If she changed into a bathing suit for the pool, she should have gone back to Pleasure's room, and right now there is no sign of that."

"We need to check her luggage," said Sheri.

"Right."

After checking in using the new key card I'd received from Julie, we moved over to two lounge chairs. We found spots in an area near where Pleasure had sat on the day of the murder. We dropped our stuff and I took off my shirt. I had already stashed my weapon in my bag.

"Are you sure you didn't get me down here so you can see me in my bikini?"

"You're a sharp kid. I've been trying to figure out an angle for months," I said as I looked around. I gave her a wink. "Go ahead, make them jealous."

And she did.

She sort of slid out of her shorts and revealed a very bright yellow and very brief bikini bottom. This created a dilemma. The yellow was so bright you almost had to close your eyes, but you just couldn't. I was so thankful it wasn't a string bikini. I did have work to do. Sheri then stripped off her top, which I swear she removed in slow motion. Anything slower would have put the world off its axis, spinning it out of orbit through the universe forever. She was one of those women who never really looked that big up front, but when you got down to the bare essentials, she had it all in the right places. I prayed I wouldn't drool noticeably. She was a P.I. and I was going to treat her with all the respect in the world. Or at least I would try. Points for trying, I always say.

"Do you need some help with the sun-tan lotion?" I asked with as much respect as I could muster.

"Nope."

"Just thought I'd ask. Realism, you know goes a long way."

"Eat your heart out," said Sheri as she laughed and threw her shirt at me. We both sat down. "How did I do? Do we look like a happily married couple from Detroit on a two-day vacation?"

"I don't know. But there's not one guy out here who has even looked at me."

A young, tanned pool attendant approached. His shoulders and chest were the kind you see in weight magazines, tapering down to a washboard stomach and a narrow waist. Sheri licked her lips to make me jealous. I wasn't the jealous type, but I hated the guy just the same.

"Good afternoon," said the pool attendant. He carried two sets of towels with him. "Anything I can get you?" His eyes swept over Sheri. At his age I probably would have paid to work here. Sheri was putting on sun-tan lotion, very much aware of the attention.

"No thanks. Oh, by the way, is Williams working today?" I said.

He reluctantly looked at me. "No, he's off today. He works the food end. Could I get you a poolside menu from the snack bar?"

"Sure."

"Yes, sir."

"What's your name?"

"Scott. Scott Monroe."

"Thanks, Scott, for your help."

He bent over, placed the towels next to us, and took another quick peek at Sheri. It was then that my memory clicked in. He was the one who had delivered the towels to Pleasure.

"Scott, were you here a few days ago when that lady had the problem at the poolside?"

"Yes, sir, I was. The bee sting."

"Yes, that's the one," I said.

Scott leaned over in a very confidential manner. Either that or he was getting a better angle on Sheri. "It wasn't a bee sting. Someone killed her. Someone nailed her with a poison dart. Right in the butt."

"Oh really! That's not what we were told," I said.

"Yeah, but the hotel doesn't want anyone to know."

"Can I tell you something in confidence?"

"Sure." Scott sat down next to Sheri. Took some sun-tan lotion, squirted it in his hand, and turned toward her indicating her legs. "May I?"

Sheri smiled. "What a gentleman. Sure, be my guest." She glanced at me and smirked.

We all sort of leaned together. "Scott, I'm a private detective, and Sheri is my associate."

"Really? P.I.s! Interesting. Are you working the case?"

"Yes, but we can't tell you who our client is."

Scott nodded as he worked farther up Sheri's legs. "Scott, this is very confidential, do you understand?"

"Yes, sir. I do."

"Good. What did you observe that day?"

"Well, let's see. The lady was sitting in this area. She caused quite a bit of a commotion among the workers."

"How so?" I asked.

"She was very pretty. I mean...well...we get a lot of pretty women here at the pool. Like you, ma'am."

"Call me Sheri."

"Yes, ma'am, I mean, Sheri." Scott had worked his way far enough up Sheri's legs that anything farther would be a medical exam. He awkwardly put the sun-tan lotion down. "Well, she was quite the knockout."

"How so?" I asked.

"Ahhaaaa, well, she was quite well developed...you might say."

"You mean she had a nice set on her," Sheri said. Sometimes you could tell Sheri had been in the Coast Guard.

Scott blushed, and then looked away. "Yes, ma'am...I mean, Sheri. She caused quite an attraction. We flipped a coin in the poolroom, and I won. So I brought the towels out to her."

"What was she doing then?" I asked.

"She was talking to some guy that had come out to visit her. They talked some, and then he left. I sort of remember him putting some suntan lotion on her back. He almost had her top off. He...he sort of looked like you, sir."

Sheri rolled her eyes at me. "You don't say."

"Oh yeah, we were watching from the poolroom with a telescope."

"A telescope?" I shifted position and looked toward the poolroom. It had a window next to the entrance.

"Yes, sir. I shouldn't really be telling a guest that. Sorry."

"That's okay. Remember we're P.I.s on a case and this is confidential."

"Oh right." Scott seemed relieved.

"Then what happened?" Sheri shifted her bikini top, conscious now that someone might be focusing on a close up.

"Well, this guy leaves. I can remember because it gave us a better shot of her. So we were taking turns checking her...out...sorry ma'am...when she just got up and left. But we really lucked out because another women walked up and took her place. She was...ahhhh, also built. We nicknamed her the GB lady."

"The GB lady. What does that mean, the GB lady?" Sheri asked.

"Ah, it means...promise you won't tell anyone?"

"Your secret's safe with us, Scott."

"It means 'Great Breasts'."

"Scott!" exclaimed Sheri.

"Sorry, ma'am." Scott twisted awkwardly. "We nickname a lot of the people out here every day as sort of a game and as a way to quickly identify someone or a group. There's 'Great Breasts,' 'Small Tits,' 'Big Ass,' 'Hooker Lady,' 'Stud,' 'Fatso,' 'Not-a-Chance,' 'The Goober Family,' you know. It's sort of a game the pool guys play. It helps pass the time and we have some fun. Easier to get through the day."

"I see," Sheri said. "You should be ashamed of yourselves."

"Yes, ma'am."

"Go on with your story, Scott," I said.

"Just a second," Sheri said. Do you have a name for me?"

151

"Ahaaa, no ma'am. I mean Sheri."

"Come on, Scott, what's it going to be?" said Sheri in her best pleading voice.

Scott looked a bit awkward, and somewhat embarrassed. "I think it's going to be, Felt Legs."

"Felt Legs! Oh my God. I bet you're a real hero among your peers today, aren't you Scott?"

Scott looked away, embarrassed.

"I see. I see. What about the old guy here?" She indicated me with a shrug of her shoulder.

"I'll name him Mr. Lucky."

Sheri laughed. I didn't. "Great, great," I said. "A critic in the group."

"He's got you pegged all right," Sheri said.

"Go on with your story Scott. The lady you brought the towels, what happened then?"

"She gets up, takes her stuff, and leaves. The new lady sits down in her place. She strips down to her suit and lays back to get some sun on her back. She had undone her top."

"You would know," said Sheri.

"Yes, ma'am, I mean Sheri."

"Then what?"

"Well, that's when it happened. Everything's sort of normal and then all of a sudden someone starts screaming, so we all come running to the pool area thinking that someone is drowning. It turns out this lady has had a convulsion of some sort, and we go over to her and there is this bee on her butt, which I guess turned out to be a dart."

"Did you see anything else unusual?"

"No, no one did."

"Scott, can I have a look through the telescope? I want to see what kind of detail you saw on that day."

"I don't know, sir."

"It will help."

"Well, okay."

Scott and I headed off to the poolroom, and Sheri lay back to catch some sun. We went past the counter where the towels are handed out, and sure enough, a nice looking telescope was set up looking out over the pool area. One lifeguard was hunkered over the scope checking out the view. He stood up, looked at Scott, and then backed away.

"Help yourself," said Scott.

I lowered my head and took a look. With a slight adjustment of the focus lens, I had a clear and rather close up view of anything I wanted.

"You're right, you can just about see anything you want in here. Where's today's hot number?" I asked.

"She's over by the green umbrella in back of the three palm trees."

I looked up, took aim, went back to the scope, and moved into position. Yep, Scott was right. In front of me was a topless babe. She was wearing a red string bikini that should be illegal. Also helping was that fact that she was almost naked. Being a detective and principal investigator of Fargo Blue Investigations, I could only say one thing. "Something Naked This Way Comes."

Scott laughed. "You read Bradbury."

"Doesn't everybody?" I swung the scope over toward Sheri, and there she was. All laid out tanning herself. She raised her left hand to her brow, scratched her forehead with her middle finger and then flipped me off. She had guessed I was checking her out. I then focused on some of the gates behind the palm trees. It looked like they might be easy to open. If that one was easy, they all would be. I reluctantly left the poolroom, and we walked back toward Sheri.

As we approached, Sheri propped herself up. "Did you see me?"

"Ahhhhhh, yes, I did take a look," I admitted.

"How's the detail?"

153

"Good detail. Bad manners"

Sheri smiled. "How about you, Scott?"

"No ma'am, I mean Sheri."

"Good boy. What a gentleman." Sheri made a face at me.

"Scott, can you give me some details about the pool area?" I said as I thought about the situation.

"Yes, sir."

"Can you get into the pool area without signing in?"

"No, it's impossible. You can't get in here unless you're connected to some room. They run the key card against the computer on everyone. It would be too easy for the locals or other people from the other hotels to decide to come and spend the day here. All the hotels have some security and precautions set up around their pools. But we're really very careful. This is one of the better pools in Vegas, and we want to protect our guest's privacy."

"With the exception of the telescope," Sheri said.

"Oh God, I knew I shouldn't have told you that. Don't tell anyone. I would get into all kinds of trouble."

"Don't worry, Scott. We're on your side," I said. "I'm all for ingenuity. Believe me, there isn't enough of it in the world today. But there is one way you could help us out." It's always nice to have something on your sources of information.

"How's that?"

"Let my office know if anybody else besides the police come around asking questions."

"Easy enough," Scott said.

Sheri was quick on the draw. She handed Scott one of her cards. "Call me, anytime."

"Right ma'am...I mean Sheri." Sheri smiles.

Scott made sure we had everything we needed, and then he trotted off towards the snack bar.

An hour is sometimes short, or sometimes long, depending on where you are, and what you're doing. If you're at the dentist, an hour is just short of an eternity in real time. If you're on vacation, an hour takes about a second. If you're lying in the Vegas sun, an hour goes by fast, but you'll remember every second of it because you'll turn into a crispy critter mighty fast. We had ordered from The Cabana Grill and they delivered within a few minutes right by the pool. Sort of a burger layered with pastrami and served with spicy mustard. Included was a Kosher dill pickle that had more than its share of garlic which I was not able to pass up. Different and tasty. I'll be drinking water for the next thirty days.

Before we left I grabbed my bag and headed to the men's spa by the pool area by the Cabana Grill. I wanted to change into street clothes. I also wanted to make sure there was no outside entrance. A gate by the tennis courts attracted my attention. I walked up and could make out delivery trucks in an area behind the casino. I gave the gate a gentle shove. I was right. It was just like the one behind the palm trees. Easy in, easy out. So much for security. Even though the MGM Grand tried, it would be easy to either walk in near the deli entrance, or come in or exit through the rear delivery area. I walked into the men's room and looked around. There was no sign of an outside entrance. I changed into a pair of slacks, shirt, and a sports coat that I had carried with me. My .38 went into the hip holster. I left to meet Sheri by the pool area. She had already changed.

"This place is a sieve," I said as we walked toward the casino. "When I came out to meet with Pleasure the first day, I used a key card from my own collection. I wonder if Metro knows how easy it is to get into the pool area. They never talked with Scott, or anyone else from what I can tell."

"Yep. That's what I think," said Sheri. "Anybody with half a brain could get in here. And if brains don't work, a bikini and some skin would probably do the trick."

"Guys like Scott would be hard pressed to kick out anything in a bikini," I said as I watched another blonde make her entrance into the pool area. I was thinking about coming back and spending the afternoon. I looked around. No security in sight. "I bet they came in through the front and right back out again."

"You're probably right," said Sheri. We were almost out of the pool area. "Check out the red topless number over on the right," Sheri said.

I smiled, and glanced back for one more look.

I didn't think you would miss something like that," Sheri said.

"Always working," I commented.

Twenty

SHERI and I left the pool area and headed toward the casino. The Desert Sage was located at the beginning of the Studio Walk next to the casino floor. The mall also contained a food court, trendy restaurants to satisfy every taste, and a video arcade to keep the young ones busy while the parents spent their time looking for the big win to pay for the trip.

The Desert Sage Jewelry Company was conveniently located right off the gambling floor, being one of the first store fronts high rollers would see when they entered the Studio Walk. We strolled by casually and tried to case the place. As expected, it was open for business. A service corridor appeared to be located off to the right and ran down behind the shops.

"I'm going to check the rear of the shop. You take a look out here."

"What am I looking for?"

"Clues." I disappeared behind a door marked "service entrance."

I was right. The Desert Sage had a rear door, and it appeared to be a very secure metal-cased door with a complex alarm system. I found the exterior entrance in back and it was also secure. I joined Sheri back in the mall area.

"Anything?"

Sheri scrunched up her nose. "No. You can't really see anything from out here. How about you?"

"Just as I suspected. A rear entrance but very secure." We were standing to the side of the Desert Sage, observing it.

"Looks like an expensive shop," said Sheri. "Why here?"

"For the winners. It's a convenient way to spend your winnings. Impress the women, or for some, a young man -- a patron of the casino for the evening."

"What do you think about them being open?" said Sheri.

"Business as usual, grief in private. Everyone still has to make a living."

"How do we approach this one?"

"I think here we're going in as Fargo Blue and colleague. I'll think we should flip our P.I. badges and appeal to their sense of decency. I want to take a look at the scene of the crime and talk to the owners about McCaddy."

"Was he married?"

"That's what I hear, but I have no knowledge of the relationship. Makes you wonder why he let someone in at such an hour and took them in the back with the safe open."

We walked into a very impressive and elegant showroom. Glass cases circled the outer room and were framed in a dark rosewood casing. The floor was thick with a rich, dark emerald green carpet. Behind the glass cases hung mirrors, which gave the room a larger appearance and enhanced the lighting, which was recessed. In the center of the store stood another glass case that looked like solid gold. As we moved around the case a tone sounded announcing our arrival. I looked up and noticed that two different security monitors had focused in on us. A beautiful woman with thick dark hair approached from the back of the store. She wore an expensively tailored suit that seemed to tie in nicely with the rosewood cases and the emerald green rug. She strode forward with her hand outstretched to greet us.

"Good afternoon. My name is Rachel. And yours is...?" She gripped my hand, made eye contact. She was all smiles and sales.

"Fargo, Fargo Blue."

"Good afternoon Mr. Blue."

"You can call me Fargo."

"And Fargo it is." She let go of my hand and moved to shake hands with Sheri. Sheri met her halfway.

"Hello, my name is Sheri." She absently pushed a strand of her hair back behind her ear.

This was definitely for the rich and glamorous. Sheri fit the glamorous part. But one valuable lesson these boutique store owners have learned is that you generally can't tell the rich from the poor. The rich are the ones who sometimes dressed eccentric. It's the working guy from the corporate world who comes in with a business suit. The rich have time, and with time and money, who cares. Till anyone knew anything different, we were millionaires. They couldn't take the chance we weren't, because businesses don't gamble -- people do.

Rachel smoothed her dark wine-colored suit that appeared to be glued to her body. She was deeply tanned, very self-confident, and used to dealing with people. As she stepped aside a private viewing area could be seen in the back of the store. It was richly furnished in expensive antique furniture, with just the right lighting and accouterments to make it a very important place. And yet, it still was very observable from several positions in the store. Looking up, I noted two more security cameras focused on this area.

"What a wonderful selection you have, Rachel," I said.

"Have you been here before? Did one of our customers recommend you to our little place here?"

"Well, actually, we're not here right now to look at any of your jewelry. We're detectives working for a client who has some questions regarding the murder and theft that occurred here several days ago."

Rachel's face changed to one of disappointment. Commissioned sales. You can tell every time.

"Oh my, that was tragic. You'll want to talk with Wayne Luperstein." Rachel moved to the back and was immediately replaced by a double-breasted suit of a sobering dark color. The only thing that made it work was a very bright tie. You wondered who dressed this guy in the morning. It was then I noticed the mirror adjacent to the viewing room. A one-way mirror was my guess.

"Good afternoon. My name is Wayne Luperstein. Please call me Wayne. I understand you have some questions regarding the unfortunate incident several days ago."

I pulled out my I.D. wallet and flashed my P.I. badge, and then took out a business card and handed it to him. "My name is Fargo Blue, and this is my associate Sheri Austin. We're here on business. We're private detectives. Our client is interested in finding out more details on what happened in the jewelry theft and murder you experienced a couple of days ago."

Looking up from the card, he said, "Oh my, yes. The police did mention your name. You're a suspect. Said I should notify them if you came back here."

"Back here? That's interesting."

"Well, yes. . .they believe you were involved. Oh my, I really need to call them, and our attorney. This is so upsetting." Luperstein took a step back as if he were about to be assaulted.

"Oh really? Who said you should call the police if I should appear?"

"It was a police officer named Vince something?"

"Vince Olsen," I said.

"Let's see...I have his card right here. That's right, it's Olsen...Vince Olsen."

"He's not with the police. He's with casino security." I gestured to the casino. There was something about this guy that made me want to know more about him. If he believed what Olsen had said, he would have called the police right away. He was stalling.

"Yes, that's it. Same thing. Badge and a gun."

"Not the same...I can assure you. I am not part of this and I'm no longer a suspect."

Sheri gave me a quick look.

"I...I don't know how I can help you, sir. We have experienced a terrible loss here, and we're just now getting back to some sense of normalcy. The funeral was quick and simple. Red McCaddy had no real family here in Las Vegas other than his wife, Darlene. How can I possibly help you?"

Sheri turned on the charm. "How about answering just a few short questions and we'll be on our way?"

"Fine. But please, this has been very difficult, and the police did say that they were ready to make an arrest any day now."

Sheri pointed to a glass jewelry case cabinet. "My, my, that is one of the nicer looking tennis bracelets I have seen in a long time. Usually you just see the cheaper looking ones in the mall windows."

"This is not a mall," said Luperstein defensively.

"This one looks like it's entirely made of one-quarter carat stones. And brilliant too. May I have a look?" said Sheri.

"Oh, most certainly. You have a good eye, young lady." Sheri was winning his confidence. Good cop, bad cop. Luperstein now had something to do, and that simple trick had eased his tension immediately. I was impressed. Sheri was going to be a better-than-average detective, if not great.

"The police file said that Mr. McCaddy had stayed late, and had received a visitor on that evening. Is that correct?" Sheri asked.

Luperstein pulled out the bracelet and laid it on a black velvet pad, which displayed diamonds in the best way possible. The bracelet sparkled with brilliance. Sheri started to examine it as if I were going to buy it for her. I hoped she wouldn't be too disappointed.

"Yes, that's true. Red had his usual quarterly appointment to purchase stones."

"Don't you usually buy stones from New York, or from Antwerp directly?" Sheri continued. She held out her wrist, and Luperstein gently laid the bracelet across it, admiring the bracelet almost more than Sheri did.

"Yes, but we're a small jewelry company, and we don't have the family connections to buy at the right price to allow us to become competitive. Red had come up with a contact about a year ago that gave us a price edge. But he kept it very quiet."

"Were the stones hot? The ones he bought?" Luperstien was securing the bracelet to her wrist. "That's what we thought initially, but we checked it out and everything came up clean. The lady had a good source."

"It was a lady."

"Yes."

"What's the name?"

"I don't know."

"Anything you found in Red's business papers that would give you a clue?"

"Nothing. Not a thing."

"Have you been contacted by this lady's company wanting to keep you as an account?"

"Not that I know of. I suspect I won't hear from her until next quarter when she makes her rounds." Luperstein stopped cold and glanced at me.

I'd remained silent, admiring Sheri's manner of eliciting the necessary information.

"You don't think McCaddy was murdered by our wholesaler, do you? I never heard of this happening in the diamond business," Luperstein said in somewhat of a worried manner. He glanced back at Sheri, who was still examining the bracelet. He continued to watch her every move.

I stepped in. "We don't know who this woman is. She has to be included in the suspect list until she is ruled out."

"Do you work for her?" asked Luperstein."

"No, I don't."

Sheri glanced at me.

"Tell me more about your wholesaler," I continued.

"She was very secretive in her dealings. I think she was an independent with good connections. Not uncommon in the diamond business."

"I expect it is," I said.

"The bracelet looks marvelous on you, ma'am," Luperstein commented.

"Thanks. Call me Sheri."

"Sheri it is. Could I show you another bracelet that you might find very interesting?"

"Why yes, that would be nice."

Luperstein extended his arm to point the way. "We'll have to use the private showroom just off to the side here. It also has the proper lighting to display the diamonds. Right this way."

We followed him to a small room. I noticed that another salesman came out of the office door to take Luperstein's place in greeting the customers.

"The lighting in this room was specially designed for the proper viewing of gems -- diamonds in particular," Luperstein said. "Many of the Strip's dealers, particularly in malls, use special spotlights that can make bad stones look fantastic. And fluorescent lights are terrible. So, as any reputable dealer would, we imitate natural sunlight."

Luperstein laid the tennis bracelet out on the velvet pad. Then, from a tray he had brought in, he removed another tennis bracelet that was even more spectacular.

"This is what I wanted to show you. The tennis bracelet you were examining was made up of quarter-carat stones. Nice, but not sensational. This tennis bracelet is made from all one-carat stones."

"Look at this, Fargo."

I glanced at the bracelet and was struck by it's beauty, and especially when it was being admired by Sheri. Looks like it's perfect for you Sheri.

"Sheri smiled. Thanks, Fargo."

Mr. Luperstein beamed from ear to ear.

"Mr. Luperstein, how long have you been at this location?"

"For several years. It's very much of a marketing strategy. We have nothing but upscale clients who come to the MGM Grand once or twice a year. They call ahead and tell us what they want, and we make the selection available to them when they come in. They're, let's say, very comfortable here."

"I see. How about the winners and the losers?"

"We get those on a daily basis. Either the guy lost a lot of money and buys something for the wife to ease the tension, or we get a real winner. Usually we make a sale to everyone who comes into the showroom. Without exception."

Sheri looks up.

"Without exception?" I repeated.

"Yes."

Boy, is this guy going to be disappointed when we leave, I thought. "Mr. Luperstein, where do you usually take a diamond wholesaler when they visit you? Like the young lady Mr. McCaddy saw the other evening?"

"Oh, the diamond business is very honorable. This room, usually, because of the lighting." Luperstein kept his eye on Sheri as she examined the bracelet.

"Fargo, I always wanted one of these."

The only thing I could think of was how glad I was she hadn't wanted two of them.

"Now, I do want to comment on one item," interjected the jeweler. "These stones are all considered 'VS1's' with an 'H' color rating, American cut with standard proportions. Since these are investment-grade diamonds, we also offer you the choice of selecting the individual stones before mounting to better assure you that there are no hidden flaws covered up by the mounting." Luperstien took out a small velvet bag from a small locked drawer, and with a dramatic flare poured out approximately fifty one-carat diamonds onto the table.

"Oh my goodness!" exclaimed Sheri. She started to poke through the pile, and Luperstein handed her a 10x loupe.

"Let me show you how to examine these, my dear."

"I understand that you have an elaborate security system here built around the opening and closing of the safe," I said.

"That's true, but we have just modified it now that McCaddy is no longer part of us."

"Would it be normal for McCaddy to take the buyer into the back room?"

"Yes and no. The best place to observe the diamonds is here. But if she was bringing in an unusually large purchase, McCaddy might have taken her into the back so they could be secured in the safe."

"Where did he live?"

"He had a place outside of town – small, exclusive area. They liked their privacy. We're assisting his wife, Darlene, with the settlement of the estate. This is a small company, but we take care of all our legal affairs through the corporation. Darlene will be well taken care of and will remain a silent partner."

"Do they have children?"

"Yes, two. Both grown and married with their own lives. They live out of state."

"You said he had no real family?"

"Just the two, Mary Ann and Keith. But they had a falling out with the family over some of McCaddy's indiscretions."

"Indiscretions?"

"Let's say that they're like any family with internal disputes better left alone."

"Who is your legal counsel?"

"Westmont, Howard and Glasstone. We work with Glenn Howard."

"Local?"

Sheri pulled her head back from the loupe she was looking through. "Yeah, they're local all right. Their name came through the office on a case Uncle Leo was working on."

"That's true," said Luperstein confirming. "They also have an office in Beverly Hills."

"Could I see the rear of the store?" I asked.

"Fargo, I want to keep looking at these beautiful stones. I need to know pricing."

"If you have to ask the price, you can't afford it. Right, Mr. Luperstein?"

"Well, normally, price is never an issue when acquiring diamonds of this investment quality. But we must all watch our pocketbook."

"So how about the tour?"

"I don't know if I really should. Hotel Security thinks you're involved in some way. And then there is the police."

"Well. How about this? You phone the police and let them know I'm here, and then you take me on the tour. By the time they arrive, Sheri will have made up her mind. What do you say?"

166

Luperstein picked up a phone and spoke quickly into it. "Rachel, could you assist the young lady while I escort Mr. Fargo Blue on a tour of the facility?" Luperstein paused, never taking his eyes off Sheri. "Yes, thank you."

The door opened and Rachel entered all smiles. I was escorted to the rear of the store leaving Sheri to examine the stones.

I followed Luperstein around the corner and came immediately into the back.

"Why didn't you call the police?"

"I'm in sales. What can I say?"

"What about the surveillance tapes?" I inquired.

"The intruder took the tapes."

"Really," I said. This was a pro job, I thought. "What about the exterior camera?"

"Just a blur as someone walked in. That's what they tell me."

We arrived at the safe, and it was open. "I understand there was a lot of damage to the safe."

"Yes, there was. It cost us a fortune. Super glue was used in the various openings so it was almost impossible to open. A real mess."

"When did you find out about McCaddy?"

"I was called down here when Darlene, McCaddy's wife, got suspicious about his absence. There was no question that something was wrong."

"How many store owners are there?"

"Three."

"Is Rachel the third partner?"

"No, Rachel is an employee. A trusted one at that. She used to have her own shop, but decided she liked working with more exclusive clients. It takes money to capitalize a store like this. It's hard to get diamonds out of your life, so she works here as an employee assisting us on some of the more expensive products."

"Do you suspect Rachel?" I watched Luperstein very carefully.

"No, no, not at all. The police took a statement from her, and that was it. Why?"

"Sometimes it's the one you least expect."

I walked into the safe and looked around. Various shelves were empty where the different display trays were deposited at night. A series of drawers had different markings on the front panel, indicating different grades and sizes of diamonds.

"How about the third partner?"

"The third partner is Jack F. Green. He's a silent partner."

"I thought it took two keys to open the safe?"

"No, only one key at the right time. Two keys if it's not the right time."

"Who opens the safe now?"

"I open the safe. We changed the lock since the entire door lock system was ruined. We have two keys plus a combination lock. I'm the only one who has the combination."

"What if something happens to you?"

"Our attorney has a copy locked in his safe."

"So you always buy your diamonds from this lady?"

"No, not exactly. For the last year we bought a lot. In fact, Red canceled his trip to Antwerp this year because he was getting such good deals. We still buy from the regular wholesalers who come through. But she was an independent who had extraordinary prices that allowed us to compete. It was a remarkable find."

"How did McCaddy find her?"

"She approached him, as I understand it. She came in the store one day when McCaddy was here. Placed a jewelry case down and opened it up. She had over a million dollars in stones right there. They talked, and struck a deal."

"Is it normal procedure for a buyer to meet with a wholesaler by himself?"

"It's not uncommon," said Luperstein.

"Do you think McCaddy was attracted to this lady?"

Luperstein looked around as if being watched. He leaned over in confidentiality. "Between you and me, McCaddy could hardly wait to meet with her. He was quite taken by her. She came in only once every three months, and McCaddy always looked forward to her visits."

"He told you that?"

"Oh yes, but I can't let that get out. His wife, you know."

"What was the attraction?"

"He told me that Montoya..."

"Montoya! You said you didn't know her name?"

"Oh, her first name was Montoya. We never knew her last name."

"Did you tell that to the police?"

"Yes, everything I've told you."

"Then why do you think they suspect me?"

"Vince Olsen told me they caught you with the diamonds in the room of a young woman who was murdered."

"And what do you think?"

"I...I don't know what to think."

"That's to be expected." I took a good look around. I noticed plenty of security. Luperstein was uncomfortable and awkward.

"You were saying that McCaddy told you something?"

"Oh, yes. That Montoya was the most beautiful woman he had ever met. And she actually knew more about diamonds than many people in the business for years. He felt that she flirted with him. Really led him on. I told him to be careful."

"Was he sexually attracted to her?"

"Yes, I do believe so. He was quite taken with her."

"Do you think...how do I say this...did he have a sexual thing going with her?"

"No, I don't think so. He was always very discreet. But he did have a reputation with the ladies," the jeweler said, lowering his voice.

"Really."

"He made one comment that I found revealing. He said he would give her anything if she ever asked for it."

"And that he may have done," I replied.

I met Sheri in the lobby. We had left Desert Sage with the usual "...we'll be in touch with you if we need anything." We fell behind a group of tourists and headed straight for our car. Hotel security was not in sight. If spotted, I knew Olsen would be contacted and a net put out to pick us up.

"Well, did you learn anything boss?"

Our pace increased and we moved briskly through the casino.

"Yes, I think so. The wholesaler's name was Montoya. The police may not even know that much. She never gave her last name. She was an independent with deep family connections in Africa. This was approximately her fourth visit."

"How did the jewels get into Pleasure's safe?"

"That's still the mystery. I don't know. I think Montoya set up McCaddy. Now all we have to do is connect her to Pleasure."

"It doesn't make any sense," said Sheri.

"How's that?"

"Why would a respected diamond dealer commit a theft and murder for only two million dollars?"

"We don't know if Montoya is a diamond dealer. She could just be working a scam."

"What makes you think that?"

"She got away without a trace. But, one thing for sure, no one leaves cleanly. They only think they do."

Twenty-One

SHERI and I circled the block where the McCaddy house was located in a nice area of Henderson. I was driving. We knew this was a devastating event in Darlene McCaddy's life. I wondered how much of what Luperstein knew had been told to Darlene. It was not my position to be the bearer of bad news. If it was meant to come out, it would. What I wanted to find out was what sort of man McCaddy was. Was he a family man? How did he spend his time on weekends? What sort of life and interests did he have that allowed him to get set up for murder? We parked, walked up to the door, and rang the bell, not knowing what to expect.

The door opened, and a woman of middle age, who was somewhat reserved, clutched her robe while her eyes darted back between Sheri and myself. She had dark circles under her eyes.

"Mrs. McCaddy?"

"Yes. Can I help you?"

"Yes. Mrs. McCaddy, my name is Fargo Blue and I'm a private detective interested in background information regarding the murder of your husband." I stuck my hand out. Mrs. McCaddy glanced at my hand but did not return the gesture.

"This is my associate Sheri Austin. Could we come in for a second?"

"I don't know. I'm not really seeing people right now."

Sheri grabbed Darlene's hands and held them. "Mrs. McCaddy, we are truly sorry for your loss, and although we can't even come close to the feelings you have right now, you have to understand we are very concerned."

Mrs. McCaddy smiled weakly. "Call me Darlene."

"Perhaps our interest will even help you in some way," Sheri continued.

Darlene stepped aside and we entered a pleasant foyer tiled in marble. The skylights allowed enough light for the thriving plants in the planter adjacent to the entryway. This led to a living room carefully designed and well furnished. The narrow planked oak hardwood floor gleamed brightly. It was covered with a colorful Oriental rug that brought the room together in a splash of color. I could see a large dining room at the end of the living room, and a china cabinet filled with mysterious looking pieces. Probably Chinese Rose Medallion porcelain produced before 1850. I had only seen them one time before during a case, and I never forgot their beauty and workmanship.

Sheri and I sat down while Darlene took the seat opposite us. Her burnt-orange terry cloth robe complimented the casual elegance of her home. Sheri spoke first. "Darlene, we are interested in finding out about your husband and anything that might help us find his killer. It's a very tragic crime, but we need to get information as soon as possible."

"Yes, yes, I understand."

"Have the police been here...?"

"I'm sorry," Darlene said interrupting Sheri. "Who are you, and what is your interest in my husband?"

Sheri glanced at me. I started in without missing a beat. I wondered if she knew I was the police's target. I envied Sheri's ability to relate empathy so quickly after meeting someone.

"Ma'am, I'm Fargo Blue. As I mentioned, I am a private detective who has been hired to investigate...certain situations...surrounding a series of events. One of those events was the murder of your husband."

"Oh my."

"So, even though these incidents are most likely unrelated, it is important to find out if there are any threads connecting them." I stretched the truth a bit.

"What incidents?"

"We are not at liberty to explain at this point. Client confidentiality."

Darlene nodded, expressing her understanding and grief at the same time.

Sheri continued. "Have the police interviewed you?"

"Yes, the same day they found Red. They have called since then, and said they had already collected some of the diamonds. They busted some guy placing them in a room safe at the MGM Grand. Said they would be making an arrest shortly."

"Yes, we heard that too," commented Sheri. "But we're still interested in anything that you might be able to tell us about Mr. McCaddy's last day. We understand he had a late appointment?"

"Red spent many late nights at the store. I think his partners took advantage of him. They certainly are taking advantage of me. Those hotel shop hours are terrible. But he did say he had a wholesaler coming in, and he would be late that night."

"Mrs. McCaddy, did Mr. McCaddy have an office here at the house? Did he do much work here, or even store any gems here?" I asked.

"Please call me Darlene, and you can call my husband Red. Everyone did."

"Thank you, Darlene," I said. "Now, did Red have an office here?"

"Yes. He has a study."

Darlene looked down to break eye contact. She was still getting used to the fact that her husband was dead. I felt sorry for her. "What did he use his study for?" I asked.

"Red's whole life was diamonds. He has an extensive library where he continued to learn his craft. He has a couple of scopes, and some other equipment. He would often bring gems home and spend the evening preparing GIA certifications. It was the way he unwound after a long day's work."

"What a loss," I said.

"Yes, Red used to say that each diamond had a story, and he tried to imagine the path each one took."

"Sort of like people," said Sheri.

"Yes, yes you're right. Just like people. You're welcome to look. I brought his briefcase home with me when I went down to identify him." A tear rolled down her face that she ignored. "I can't bear the thought of going through it."

"Did the police examine the briefcase?"

"Yes."

"Do you think we could take a look?"

"Sure, if you think it will help." Darlene rose and we followed her into a study located right off the living room. Bookshelves lined two of the walls, framing a window that looked out on distant foothills. The light, cherry-wood bookcases matched a huge desk, which supported an impressive scope with a plastic cover. It looked expensive.

Darlene reached under the desk and pulled out a briefcase. "Here it is. There is no lock. Red felt if there was ever a robbery he didn't want any of us to risk life or limb when everything was totally insured."

"Did he have a safe?" I looked around the room and could see no obvious signs of one.

"Yes, there is a small one under the desk. I do have a combination someplace. I'll have to look and see if I can find it."

"Darlene, this is going to be very helpful. Could Sheri and I take a few minutes to look at his briefcase? It may seem like we're prying into your business, but we want to make certain that the police have the right man."

"I don't see why not."

"As I said, we're interested in finding out some background info. It might help us, and it might help you."

"Who hired you?"

"The MGM Grand."

"Okay. That would be fine. Could I get you something cold to drink?"

"Yes, that would be great." The pastrami burgers had made both Sheri and I thirsty. Darlene left, and Sheri and I got down to business.

About an hour had come and gone since Darlene had brought us the pitcher of lemonade. She had changed from her robe into some light casual clothes and looked better. The briefcase's contents were what I had expected. It was amazing what people carried. Inside a purse or a briefcase was a window on a private world.

We looked at each item in the briefcase one by one. We set aside anything we wanted to examine in more detail in one pile, and put the other stuff in another pile. As we did so, we took a complete inventory of each item, both for our protection and for Darlene's use if there were any questions regarding Red's estate.

Down at the bottom I found an appointment calendar tucked away among a raft of diamond appraisals. I turned to the date of Red's last appointment and read: Meet M. at 9.3 for buy and D.

"Well, let's see," Sheri said. "Could the 'M' stand for Montoya? And '9.3' could stand for 9:30. Perhaps an appointment. And 'buy' probably means purchase. What does the 'D' stand for?"

"A mystery within a mystery."

"It could stand for...." and Sheri stopped as Darlene entered the room.

"I found the combination to the safe written on the bottom of a dresser drawer upstairs in Red's closet. I'm sure this is it."

"How did you know where to look?" I asked.

"Many years ago when the safe was installed, Red told me where to look for the combination if something happened to him. This is the first time I've checked."

"Let's give it a try," I said. I took the combination and got down on my hands and knees and reached under the desk. I gave the dial the appropriate spins, and sure enough I heard that silent "click," which all burglars know and love. The door creaked open, and we peered in, not knowing what to expect.

The safe had two shelves on top and a larger space below. Both contained assorted wrapped packages and bundles of papers. I pulled out a bundle.

"That looks like our will. Something I need."

I handed it to Darlene. The second package looked like a diamond pouch. In fact, it looked exactly like the ones I'd found in Pleasure's safe. The diamonds did come from the Desert Sage. I stood up, undid the straps and rolled it out. In front of us was probably half-a-million dollars' worth of diamonds.

"Diamonds were part of our retirement plan," Darlene said. "We had been purchasing stones at cost for the last twenty years and securing them here, and in a safety deposit box downtown. Red felt if anything ever happened I would have enough assets in these stones to be okay in the future."

"Were they part of your estate?"

"Yes and no. I...I wish you hadn't seen these."

"Never saw a thing," I said. I pushed the bags back into the safe. "Did you see anything, Sheri?"

"Nope. I didn't see anything."

It was typical in the diamond world. Immigrants had come through Ellis Island with only the clothes on their backs and often thousands of dollars worth of stones in their shirt pocket. Likewise, many Germans had made their way to South America with similar fortunes tucked away.

"Darlene, when we got here you mentioned that you felt your husband's partners were taking advantage of you. In what way?" asked Sheri.

"Everything is such a mess. Red's partners, my partners now, are starting to give me a bad feeling."

"You mean there is question as to your ownership in the store?" Sheri asked looking at me. I knew that look. The problem's in my court.

"Yes, that Luperstein. He's going to give me trouble. I just know it."

"Perhaps you need to get this will down to your attorney, Mrs. McCaddy," I said.

"That's the problem." A couple more tears. "My attorney is the store's attorney. I don't know what to do."

After years of being on the beat, and then a detective, I had learned to sense trouble. And Darlene was in trouble. It is not unusual for partners to take advantage of the surviving spouse. Greed does strange things even to the most honest businessman.

"Darlene, I would like to suggest something to help you. As I said, I'm a private detective. I have for a long time now shared an office with a very honest trial attorney who knows his way around this town. I would like to introduce you to him. An introductory meeting, if you will. If you're being taken advantage of by your partners, it's important to take action right now. Don't wait. There are papers that need to be filed, and they should, under the present circumstances, be filed by your personal attorney. Can I set it up?"

"That is nice of you. But I don't want to trouble you."

"Let me assure you it's not any trouble. And it will make you feel good by taking control of the situation. It will give you something to focus on."

"Yes, I think that will be good."

"Here's what we'll do. Sheri will come by tomorrow morning at eleven to pick you up. She will take you to meet Uncle Leo, he's the attorney, and you and he will have a nice long chat over lunch."

"He's your uncle?"

"No, just old," I said. "He's everybody's uncle. You'll see when you meet him."

"Thank you so very much. I appreciate it."

"It's the least we can do," said Sheri patting Darlene on her shoulder and giving me a smile.

When we left the house I backed out of the driveway and entered traffic. Keeping my eyes on the rear-view mirror, I spun the car around and started back toward Darlene's house. No car made a following move.

"Fargo, why are we going back?" asked Sheri, mystified by my actions.

"Just checking for a tail."

"You're always thinking, aren't you Fargo?"

"Yep."

"Fargo, that was a nice thing you did back there. Helping out Darlene."

"If I hadn't offered, I know you would have."

"He's my uncle too."

"Everybody needs an uncle."

Twenty-Two

SHERI and I entered Uncle Leo's private office. You could always tell how important a phone call was by the position of his chair. If he faced the desk, it was a routine call. If he turned away from the desk and faced the wall, we all knew it was important. I slouched down in a chair as I listened. Uncle Leo was all business.

"You don't have the evidence to make the charges stick," said Uncle Leo. "You know that. Why don't you go out and find the real killer?" Uncle Leo turned his chair around and faced his desk. He put his fingers to his lips in the universal gesture of silence.

"Multiple charges. So what. It's all circumstantial."

More listening. "Look, I'm Fargo's attorney. If you're going to make an arrest, call me. We'll meet you at the station. I don't want any of this grandstand stuff that Olsen is so famous for."

Getting angry. "Yeah, I know he's not with the department. But you better tell him that, not me. It's like Olsen's your boss."

Uncle Leo held the phone away from his ear. It's obvious that someone is yelling his head off. Uncle Leo is all smiles. Back to the phone.

"I can't hear you when you're out of control."

More yelling. "Either make the arrest, or give it up. In either case, I'm going to make you look so bad your boss will never be re-elected."

Uncle Leo slammed down the receiver. "That will give them something to think about."

"Who was that?"

"That was Daily trying to shake us up."

"Daily? That doesn't sound like Daily," I responded.

"Everybody's got a career to make. This case is a career maker."

Sheri pulled up a chair and handed us both a fresh mug of coffee.

"Thanks," I said. Uncle Leo nodded in agreement as he took a sip of the rich Guatemalan brew. Starbucks, of course. One of the office's vices, the best coffee in town.

I leaned back and put my feet up on the desk. It was conference time. "So tell me, what happened? I assume that Peter Daily and his sidekick Tonto were here?"

"Yep." Uncle Leo just stared at my shoes.

I quickly removed my feet from the desk remembering that I wasn't at home. I didn't get a thank you, but that was expected.

"They both came by to pay their respects," said Uncle Leo finishing his thought.

"Search warrant?"

"Yep. Just as you thought when you left your place. I aggravated the hell out of them, as the warrant only said your office."

"But isn't this my office," I said motioning to the room.

"What does the sign say out front?"

"Law Offices."

"Who owns the building?"

"You do."

"Do you want me to go on with the finer legal points of a lease arrangement?"

"But I still don't understand. Everything's in my office."

"I did some remodeling." He pointed over to Sheri's domain just outside his office. I leaned back and looked outside the door, and sure enough there were my two four-drawer filing cabinets neatly stacked next to Sheri's desk.

"Isn't that obstruction of justice?"

"Nope. They didn't tell me they were coming."

"What about my computer, and my investigation notes?"

"They got that."

"That's fine. Won't help them a bit."

"What about your other files, other cases, your contacts?" asked Leo.

"I keep them out on the Net. They don't have the password and have no idea it's there. There is nothing in my computer except processing software."

"It's on the Net?" Uncle Leo queried.

"Yep, on the Net. I'm using a site on the Net as a server for backup. Sheri taught me." I glanced over at my back-up partner. "Give Uncle the basics." I felt a sense of relief that I had taken the time to protect my files.

"You can store documents, information, databases, anything you want at various places on the Internet. I thought it would be good idea because then Fargo's office goes with him anywhere. If he lost a computer, his data is protected."

"What about hackers?"

"A hacker can get in anywhere. But first you have to know where, and then you have to be really good to figure out the encryption program we're using."

"How about my stuff?"

"Some here, and some out there."

"How about tax stuff or financials?" Uncle Leo asked.

"Protected."

"Good."

"What does Daily want?" I asked.

"He wants you. He's convinced you're guilty of killing Pleasure and robbing the Desert Sage and killing McCaddy."

"On what evidence?"

"That you broke into Pleasure's safe twice, and that you were caught with diamonds that came from the Desert Sage."

"Circumstantial? I didn't break in."

"That's not what they'll say in court," Uncle Leo countered. "Breaking into Pleasure's safe we can argue, but being caught with the diamonds is pretty much a cold hard fact. Can't dispute that in court. It's a key fact linking you to both crime scenes and to Pleasure. It's for a judge to decide. Everything else is circumstantial."

"I can't afford to wait in prison. You know what will happen. As soon as they get me busted they will stop looking for the real killer."

"Worse than that," Uncle Leo said as he pulled a file from his desk. "They will tend to bring forward only this information that will make you look bad. Suppression of exculpatory evidence. It happens all the time."

"They can't do that," Sheri said.

"Happens all the time," Uncle Leo repeated sounding tired and disgusted. "Figure two completely innocent people per one hundred."

"Wow," Sheri said, bewildered.

"So now, what do we do?" I got up and strolled over to the window deep in thought. It was a bright and beautiful afternoon. I didn't want to let this interfere with what I had to do. Detectives are always finding themselves in conflicting situations. Par for the course.

"It's a matter of positioning," said Uncle Leo. "Positioning will lead to strength. Daily indicated that they would not make any arrest for approximately three days. I think they want to watch you."

"What for?"

"As you know, innocent people tend to look guilty when they know they're being watched. When they find you again, they'll tail you so you can lead them to more evidence that they can use against you."

"And what's my strategy?"

"You tell me. You're the detective."

"You're my lawyer. I asked you first."

Sheri smiled at the exchange.

"I don't know where you're staying," said Uncle Leo. "And I don't want to know. If you have an alias, I don't want to know that either. I don't want to know what you're doing. Just don't do anything illegal. It looks bad in court."

"But I thought you said that if they put out a warrant, they will call you and we'll all report to the station together."

"Right."

"But...."

"You can't report to the station if Uncle Leo can't find you," said Sheri.

"Oh, I see. A little delayed action."

"Right, but if we delay it to long, Daily will pick you up. I can probably get you two extra days. No more."

"So I've got maybe four, maybe five days to work with?"

"Right, but I will suggest one thing. If I were you I would put Olsen under surveillance."

"Olsen! Why him?"

"It's a start. Ask yourself this. Why is he so fired up that you're guilty? He's even convinced Daily this is going to jump-start his career too. On the surface it looks like it goes back to your past relationship with Olsen, but it has to be something deeper than that."

"Think he's part of it?"

"He's part of something, that's for sure. We need to know more about Mr. Olsen."

"What else?"

"I think you should file another report for the record. In these kinds of cases you're best to develop a paper trail."

"Anything I can do to help?" asked Sheri.

"You've already been a great deal of help," I said. "I'm going to dictate a report for you to transcribe and to file. You know the usual. While I do that, will you fill in Uncle Leo about his new client that he is having lunch with tomorrow at eleven thirty?"

Uncle Leo looked at his desk calendar. "Since when do you make appointments for me?"

"Never, except this time. Sheri, fill Uncle Leo in on Darlene McCaddy. I think we can help her, and at the same time we might be able to dig up new information about McCaddy."

"I'll take care of that," said Sheri, "but there is one thing I have to ask."

"And, that is...?"

"Darlene McCaddy doesn't know, or didn't know at the time we interviewed her, that you're the prime suspect. What do we say when she finds out?"

"We're going to take the aggressive position. That's what I'm going to have Uncle Leo do. Bring her up to date, and then sort of go under-cover for us. I don't think she's being told everything by either Luperstein or Peter Daily."

"Now I'm confused," said Uncle Leo.

"That's what makes a case interesting," I said as I stood, and headed for the door to my office. The one without the files.

I dictated the report using my notes and the previous reports as a base. I kept it straightforward and to the point. I didn't sway it to one side or the other, as I knew this would eventually become a matter of record if I ever ended up that far. I tossed the tape to Sheri as I prepared to leave.

"You know what to do with it."

"Are you headed out?"

"Yeah. But I've got one stop to make on the way. I'm going to try and get some more info from the street."

"Be careful," Sheri said.

"Don't worry. I'm well aware of the situation. I'll be in touch by cell phone."

Sheri reached in her drawer and pulled out a pager. "Here, keep this with you. It's an unlisted pager. Only I have access to the number. I will dial you only if we hear that Daily is going to arrest you and has a warrant out on the street."

"I hope I never hear from you."

"I've checked the number carefully. In case someone accidentally dials this number, the only one you should be concerned with is if it comes up seven-eleven."

"How appropriate...."

Twenty-Three

I kept Sheri's car, and headed toward the Fremont area, thinking and driving. It was time for a little deductive reasoning. Everything kept leading back to the MGM Grand where this all started: Pleasure, the safe, and the jewels. Because I knew I did not murder McCaddy, someone else did, no matter what the police wanted to think. But Olsen was trying to pin the murder of Pleasure and the robbery of the Desert Sage and McCaddy's murder on me. Just because they found me taking the diamonds out of Pleasure's safe doesn't mean I put them in there, even if they were traced to the jewel heist. Circumstantial.

But a good argument could be made that if I had access to take the diamonds out of the safe, I also had access to put them in there. I didn't like the argument at all. I could make the standard plea to take a lie detector's test but the D.A.s office would say it was not reliable. Olsen would then announce to the press that I had lied throughout my entire career, so a lie detector test was ineffective with someone like me. He wouldn't want me to take it because he knew I would pass.

I parked on Lawrence and walked over to Fremont Street. The arcade-like atmosphere of the overhead light show had been a hit with everybody. The casinos liked it as it brought in fresh money for the tables, and the pickpockets loved the crowds. I started to bar hop. A lot of problems on Fremont Street were a direct result of its being a local hangout for criminals, plain and simple. This is where you went for information when you wanted to know what was happening on the street. After all, these were the bad guys, who created not only the crimes, but also the information.

They hung out in the bars, hustled pool, and planned daring deeds in the night. A few drinks and the concept of a lifetime of drop-dead money is what they talked about. Early retirement to the beaches of the Caribbean or Mexico. One small heist that could take a bar fly into the realms of the super rich. They all dreamed about it, but rarely ever accomplished it. Which, strangely enough, was about the same as a young businessman out to make a score for himself. One good deal and the young Harvard graduate thought he could be on easy street. It was one and the same. It was just a matter of perspective.

When two or more guys scored, one of them would blow their cover by driving new cars to impress jeweled woman. Even a rookie detective could put two and two together and make a bust. What a bar offered was information for a price. It was here that I was going to find Tony Botello, my jail mate buddy who I knew always needed cash. But then, who doesn't in this town? The good part was that Botello owed me for bailing him out.

Tony Botello did not let me down. He was sitting at the end of the third bar I hit. He had a half-drained beer in front of him and was watching the TV monitor hanging overhead at the opposite end of the bar. Soaps. Who would figure Tony Botello for the soaps? I caught his eye and rubbed my thumb and finger together, indicating money. He nodded and went back to his soaps oblivious to me. He was talking to another old timer down on his luck. I always wondered, when you got down to your last dollar, do you spend it on a beer, or one more roll at the dice? I hoped I never found out.

Tony drained his beer, got up and said his good byes. He had things to do, people to see, and deals to make. I followed very shortly afterwards and caught him wandering down Fremont Street and into a strip joint. It was clear that Tony had no taste. Amanda's was one of the down-and-dirty strip joints in this part of town. Tony ambled in. I followed shortly afterward.

The first thing that hits you is the odor of perfumed air covering stale cigarette smoke, sweat, and booze. The next thing you notice is that the whole place pulsates with the beat of the music commonly found in strip joints. With today's stereo CD systems and oversized amps, there was no pause for the weak at heart. It was an endless pulsating vibration that literally moved the drink on your table. A buxom blonde with enough cleavage for everyone greeted me.

"My, aren't you handsome. Care for a more private booth in back? You can see the stage just fine from there and we can arrange for some special performances."

"Nope, sorry ma'am. I'm hunting for Ralph. Oh, there he is over there." I gave a short wave and moved toward the left-hand side of the elevated bar catwalk where the girls did their line dances. As I did so, a petite brunette managed to swing her entire body upside down on a chrome pole commonly used as a dance partner, among other things. As I rounded the other side I realized that she wasn't petite. I could tell even when she was upside down. I had an overwhelming desire to turn my head to check things out, but overcame the urge, as I was a professional. If they taught Physics this way I might have paid more attention. I should have been a teacher.

Tony and I did high fives as I sat down next to him. I had a beer while we chewed the fat for a while. Tony's eyes never left the stage where the girls were grinding away to the music.

"Thanks for the bail."

"Not a problem."

"And thanks for not hitting on me in the bar. Don't look too good with my friends." Tony spoke as his head bobbed to the music.

"I understand the game." Everyone passed info down here, but you never did it in front of your peers. Rules of the game. If you did you were quickly on the outs and you had to move on to a new city and a new street of thugs while you waited for that dream job. The one with the white sandy beaches and jeweled naked women. "You're looking pretty good, Tony." Slick, but good, I thought.

"You think so?" He ran his fingers over the white linen sports jacket, made more brilliant by the flamingo pink shirt underneath. He was a proud man with no taste.

"Going out on the town tonight?" I asked.

"Always going out. That's why people move to Vegas. Best going-out town in the world."

"Been back in the slammer lately?"

"Nah. They got me on a bum rap. Just picked me up. You know how it goes."

A topless dancer stopped and checked on our drinks. Tony couldn't take his eyes off of her rather obvious features. I had somewhat of the same problem.

"Four Samuel Adams." She scribbled down the order, gave me a wink, and brushed near my face. I never moved. I had nerves of steel.

"Man, you lucky dog you. What a set of knockers, huh?" Tony went back to the dancers.

A minute later the topless one appeared again and dropped off four Samuel Adams, ice cold. So was the barmaid. She had long passed the point where she was interested in her customers. The tease was all part of the job. I dropped a twenty on her tray.

"Keep the change, honey. And keep the chin up, it will all get better."

"It's not the chin I have to keep up." She shoved her chest out, and was gone. The dregs of work, bad relationships, gambling, or worse, have taken their toll.

I grabbed the beer by its slender neck, imitating the way Tony was drinking, and took a hit. It soothed away a little of the afternoon's heat. "You working?"

"You mean a job?"

"Yeah."

"I do a little work here and there. I sell some gambling supplies. Just clerking. Nothing fancy."

"Glad to hear you're going straight."

"I wouldn't say that. But I don't talk much about the fun side."

"The fun side? I don't think I've ever heard your line of work being described as the fun side."

"All depends on your point of view," Tony said.

"How true."

"Why the meeting? I don't talk to just anybody. You're making the news lately."

"Trying to stay important."

"Being arrested and thrown in jail is starting to give you some credibility."

"Thanks. You meet the most interesting people in jail."

"What do you want, and how much you paying?" Tony grabbed his next beer and swallowed deeply.

"I want to know what's happening on the street."

"Help me out. There is a lot happening on the street. Give me some direction."

"McCaddy. The murder and robbery."

"We're talking big money here," Tony said, as he tracked the rear end of the new dancer. I took out a hundred and slid it across the table. A hundred always made the conversation serious. That's why they invented the one hundred-dollar bill. To make it important. Put a whole bunch of hundreds together and it would be really important, bordering on impressive.

Tony signaled for two more beers. V for victory. "We're talking murder here."

I slid another hundred across the table.

Tony pocketed the two bills, and looked around, making sure no one was watching. "Word has it that Olsen is behind the diamond heist."

"Olsen. Doesn't fit. Not Olsen. Doesn't make any sense."

"You wanted to know what is happening, what the word is. The word is that a cop performed the magic trick at McCaddy's."

"Why Olsen?"

"Why not?"

"He's not a cop."

"He used to be a cop," Tony said.

"Because he's a cop?"

"Sure. I mean the public perception of cops helping people and protecting then from crime...I mean, let's be honest here. Don't get me wrong -- ninety-five percent of the cops serve and protect. They arrest the criminals. But that other five-percent are the ones you got to watch out for. They know most of the tricks and they got friends on the inside."

"Olsen's got a great job at the MGM Grand."

"That's called having an alibi, or cover. You can't imagine it's Olsen because you're too close to what's happening. Olsen has good cover. What can I say?"

I took a long pull on my beer. Another new dancer appeared on stage and started by removing her top. No tease here I thought. I wondered what was in store for the next ten minutes. Tony was making some points but I didn't like what I was hearing. Olsen certainly fit the picture, but I thought he was smarter than that.

"Look," Tony said leaning forward. "The job at the Desert Sage was perfect. Well planned. A pro job all the way."

"How do you know?"

"You wanted the word on the street, right?"

I nodded.

Tony continued. "There's not that many guys in Vegas that can plan that kind of an operation. A cop can. They know all the tricks."

"That's true," I said. "What about the diamonds? Have any turned up on the street?"

"I should be asking you."

"Meaning?"

"Meaning you got your hands on those stones before anyone did."

"I was framed," I said, amazed at what this little guy knew.

"The jails are full of innocent people, what can I say?"

"Forget those. Any others show up?"

"Not a one. I'm telling you. This was pro all the way. If it had been just a normal score, there would be neon lights advertising who did the heist all the way up and down the Strip. No jewels. Nothing. A pro job."

"But why does the street think it's Olsen?"

"I'm just telling you what I heard," Tony said. "The street has its own view of the world. What can I tell you?"

"What about McCaddy?"

"Cover your tracks. All part of the job."

"You think Olsen would risk a murder charge for diamonds?"

"You're not hearing me. It's just a part of the job."

"Murder, really?"

"Don't know. Don't care. It was a great heist. That's all I care about."

"Olsen seems to be targeting me as the guy who did the diamond heist. Any thoughts?"

"You think he's going to turn himself in?"

"No, of course not...."

"Think it through. As long as they can pin it on someone, the D.A.s happy. You know that."

"Yeah, right, but...."

"So who better than the guy who also knocked off that dame at the pool."

"You heard that too?"

"That's what the street says. Says you were at the wrong place at the right time. Says Olsen lucked out. Found himself a patsy."

"Feels like it." I thought about what Tony was telling me. Olsen was not liked on the street, that was for sure. He had busted many of the thieves who made their living in Vegas. Memories don't die easy. It was possible that the street was out to get Olsen. On the other hand, it would not benefit Tony to lie about what the rumor mill on the street was grinding out. What can be counted on was that there is always some fact behind the rumors. You just don't know which part is true. This is how the street communicates. This is how they knew what was going down. It's like the Dow Jones Average for crooks. In the next couple of weeks there will be more crime in-and-around the MGM Grand because of the rumors about the head of security at the MGM Grand. It stands to reason. When you hear that the security is weak at a seven-eleven, it's going to be hit.

"Thanks Tony." I pulled another hundred out of my wallet. "This is just a little extra in case you come up with any more news."

"I'll do my part...." Tony grabbed the money, his eyes never leaving the short blonde who had wound herself around the chrome pole.

"Anything I can do for you?" I asked.

"I'm in good shape. Nothing much going down. I keep to myself. Work the streets. You know how it is."

"Thanks," I said, standing. "You know how to find me."

"Later," Tony said. "Hope you work things out. The street's watching. If you get in over your head, we'll take care of you on the inside."

"Thanks. I appreciate it." Great I thought. Just what I need, friends on the inside. I left Tony at the bar and knew he was in for a long evening.

Twenty-Four

RUBY ANN BARRE took a deep breath as her taxi pulled into the Porte Cochere entrance to the MGM Grand off Tropicana Avenue. It was Friday morning and time to go to work -- if you could call it that, she thought.

"Welcome to the MGM Grand." A smiling young valet opened the cab door. He eyed the long legs of Ruby Ann as she emerged, and made no attempt to hide his approval. Dressed in a simple short skirt and high heels, she easily brought a few glances from homeward-bound husbands gazing at what they could only dream about. After all the tourists who come through Las Vegas, a nice set of legs was refreshing.

"Thanks." Ruby Ann smiled at the valet.

"Thank you, ma'am." He turned and gave high signs to the other check-in associates working the front. Ruby Ann walked into the lobby, crossed it, and enter the casino. When she was almost through the lobby she entered the restroom on her left. It was very busy, as the Keno area and the Hollywood Theater were close by. This was good. The busier the restroom, the better for Ruby Ann. Nobody would give her a second glance.

Ruby Ann moved inside one of the stalls and quickly went through a complete makeover. Through the years she had learned to become a quick-change artist, and even she had to admire the simplicity of what she could accomplish in a short period of time. Having entered the MGM Grand wearing a short dress and high heels, she attracted attention. The valet attendant would remember her. They always do. Most criminals enter wearing their disguise, but Ruby Ann was not part of this group. She was clever in her approach, and had the ability to size up a situation and make do with what she had to work with. The hotel, with its many cameras and security, would have been able to track her entrance into the MGM Grand and her departure. Ruby Ann quickly slipped out of her dress. She was almost naked. She never wore a bra, and nylons were rarely needed for her long tan legs. Yes, they would remember her entrance.

Next, Ruby Ann opened her bag and pulled out a pair of black slacks and a white silk blouse. They had been carefully folded to look freshly ironed. She pulled out a red wig and tucked her blonde curls under it completing the effect. Slipping on her black heels again, she folded her dress and placed it in her bag, which she had inverted to produce a completely different style of handbag -- flaming red. She was set to go.

Ruby Ann exited the stall. Nobody paid her the slightest attention. She checked her makeup in the mirror, then quickly joined several women who were leaving the restroom together. She quickly moved in the direction of the newsstand close to the lobby.

Looking more like a tourist, she actually enjoyed being somebody else for a short time. She was careful not to appear like a hooker. These women watched closely monitored even though they were an integral part of Las Vegas business. Where there is money, there is sex. Ruby Ann looked like she was on vacation and married. She blended into the crowd perfectly. No one gave her a second look. All part of the plan.

As Ruby Ann entered the MGM Grand' news stand. From there, she watched the elevator until she was able to secure one for herself. She departed at the second floor, moved into the business offices, and headed straight for the receptionist.

"May I help you?" smiled Brenda Frost, a young, dishwater blonde who was definitely in charge. Brenda was a little on the pudgy side, which never really bothered her. She had her share of men, and could get more if she wanted. But sometimes, attractive women irritated her. It was all too easy for them.

Ruby Ann pulled an I.D. out of her purse. "I'm Marilee Phillips from the Department of Employee Relations. I would like to take a quick run through your facilities this afternoon."

"Employee Relations?" questioned Brenda.

"Yes," said Marilee, smiling and putting her I.D. away.

"Were we expecting you?" Brenda was a little bit flustered.

"Are you new here?" questioned Marilee.

"I've been on the front desk for about six months, and we...."

"That explains it," interrupted Marilee, checking a clipboard she had pulled from the side of her red handbag. "I was here about...let's see...about seven months ago. We make unannounced stops to go through the management offices and security division."

"All areas?"

"No...Nothing to do with the counting rooms. We're from a different division."

"Oh."

"We work with the State Department of Labor in the Gaming Division making sure the necessary signs for employee protection and notification of employee rights are not violated."

"I see...I think...."

"You know the posters in the lunch room concerning Worker's Compensation?"

"Yes," Brenda said.

"Well, I just make sure they're properly posted. It works well for both sides. If anyone ever has a complaint, the casino can use the State's records to show that the proper forms were in place on such-and-such a date. Sometimes it stops a lawsuit. You know how belligerent some employees can get." Marilee laughed. "All I need from you is a floor pass. It takes me about four minutes to make my sweep and then I'll be gone."

"Is that all the time you'll need?" Brenda opened her desk.

"Well, sometimes a bit longer if I have to record a missing poster. But I'm generally done pretty fast. I have a lot of sites to do every day. It never stops. Inspections, reports and filing. And with all of these new casinos, it's never going to end."

Brenda eyed her suspiciously. "Here is the pass. If I can be of any more help, please just come back and I'll try and answer your questions."

"That would be great. I'll be out of here in no time." Marilee signed her name and walked to the right door leading into the maze of offices.

Twenty-Five

I tried calling Uncle Leo on my cellular early Friday morning as I pulled into the Las Vegas Metro headquarters. I wanted to know if he had already arrived at the police station. Uncle Leo had called me and said that the D.A. wanted to talk. It was going to be an informal discussion and I would not get arrested. If I were to be arrested they promised that Uncle Leo would be notified, and I would be allowed to turn myself in at a pre-arranged time. Sure. Even though they had said earlier in the day it would be at least three days, they had changed their minds and wanted to set up a meeting. I'm a cool guy in these situations. I wouldn't meet with them if my life depended on it. They want free information; they can pay for it. Uncle Leo said to get my butt down to the station. I said I would be there by high noon. It was show down time, Las Vegas style.

I felt like running. I could have made the Mexican border in an hour and a half. From there I could have winged my way into any of the fabulous South American vacation spots. I mean, think about it. Jail, or white sandy beaches, jail, or tanned beautiful women, jail, or tequila sunrises any hour of the day. Any idiot could figure this out, and here I was pulling into the D.A.s parking lot. I sure hoped I wouldn't be kicking myself in a couple of hours.

I approached the back entrance with some hesitation. Ever since I had first gone to work in this department chasing the Las Vegas' least-wanted element -- crooks, thieves, and assorted street life -- I had called this place my home. I was a one-man show. The top dog of the detective pool. I looked for the element in places other detectives feared to walk. Making the big busts got me promoted faster than anybody else at Las Vegas Metro.

Not that I didn't like the fringe benefits of the job. I won't lie to anybody about the fact that I was eating free in several of the casinos around town. They were happy to have me amongst their family, and it kept the general street life element from hanging around. Seems they don't like dining with somebody who can arrest them and haul their butts off for an overnight downtown. Another benefit in the casinos were the women who were freely offered, but I had never really had a problem in this department. I always had my choice of the young women who were police groupies and hung out at a couple of the more popular police bars, although not my type. These women were all the same. They wanted a good meal, loving, and fantastic stories of my famous exploits. I told lots of stories. That was a long time ago. Now I was mature and responsible. At least I hoped so.

I hesitated outside Las Vegas Metro where I had hung my hat for ten years. Most detectives would have a few drinks at the Down Under after their shifts and then head home to the wife or take the girlfriend to her place. Not me. I headed back to this building for midnight work. I would study my case files, going through all the pending cases on my desk every night in order to glean some shred of evidence that would bust a case wide open. Several times I was sitting with my feet up thinking about certain interesting cases when a clue would drop from the sky onto my desk. I routinely went through the open cases looking for a clue that everybody had overlooked.

One night I had just gone through the murder book on a year-old homicide when it occurred to me that the next-door neighbor, Sam Middleton, had never been interviewed. He had been on vacation and nobody had bothered to follow up. I woke up the apartment manager at two A.M. and asked for the forwarding address of the neighbor. Sam had left his address because he was told he would get a refund check for his security deposit. Everybody thinks they're going to get their security deposits back only to learn that the owners keep the entire amount for "wear and tear" on the apartment. Of course, the managers usually skim a little for extra cash.

I drove by Sam's apartment complex off Valley View Boulevard and found him renting apartment 2-C. I ran his file, and came up with a series of parking tickets, unpaid. One of them was for the night of the murder. I arrested him the next day, held him on suspicion of leaving the crime scene, and drew some blood. Surprise. It matched up with blood taken off the victim that had not come from the victim. Thank you, DNA.

The apartment manager was convinced the suspect had gone to Hawaii for the week. He had even driven him to the airport, watched him board an outbound 727, and then departed. The only problem was that Sam Middletown flew back into town to take out the neighbor. Probably a drug dispute. It got him life without possibility of parole. He should have flown on to South America. I remembered the case clearly. Not a bad night's work and some follow-up for just leaning back and letting things fall where they may.

As I entered the Police Department I knew that Olsen was working real hard to give me a bum rap. Why he was still pissed off after all these years, I had no idea. But the street information had been good. I was going to start taking a closer look at Olsen. Uncle Leo and Tony

Botello couldn't both be wrong. I thought Olsen was a stand-up guy. Kind of a thug with a crew cut, but a stand-up guy. Maybe Vegas was getting to him. Maybe he needed the big bucks. I would find out. I always did.

I signed in at the back entrance and smiled at Bernie who handled security for this area of the department. When I was a young detective he was one of the climbers in the department, but he had shot two innocent people during a bank robbery almost twenty years ago. He gave up the badge for a position as a guard. I couldn't blame him. It was an accident, but that's the way it was. Everybody thought he would get back on his feet, but he never did. Yet he probably had the best job of all. Worked for the police department and didn't have to shoot anybody. But then, there are cops who shoot and ask questions later. Way of life. Wrong, but a way of life. I slapped Bernie on the back.

"How ya' doing, Bernie?" I asked.

"Not too bad, Fargo. Hear you got some kind of beef with Olsen over at the MGM Grand."

"Word does travel, doesn't it?"

"Can't believe anything you hear though...."

"That's the truth," I laughed. "Just another day with somebody trying to screw somebody."

"Ain't that the truth," said Bernie. "Hope you got a real big screw driver when you get done with this one."

We both laughed. Bernie always knew who was right and who was wrong. Watching the entire department walk in and out day after day through the years had given him a sixth sense. He knew when somebody was on the take or downright dirty. He just knew.

Bernie gave me my pass and I worked my way up to the D.A.s office. It was currently being held by Robert Thorner, who had aggressive political ambitions in the State. He fancied himself as a future Governor, then Senator, and then a move into the big game. But the D.A. and I had almost grown up in the department together, and I thought I knew him well. My one fear was that I was going to be his stepping stone to a nicer office right down the street in the Governor's mansion.

I walked the long green hallways and thought about the troops. D.A. Thorner was a short, linebacker kind of guy, who used to lead raids in his early years as a detective. His favorite stunt was to crash though a doorway in the middle of the night. This always shook up the occupants and gave Thorner a reputation as the department's linebacker. You could compare him with a tank.

"Hi Robert," I said as I entered his office.

"Hi, Fargo. Understand that you and Olsen still aren't getting along."

"No problem. Olsen's still being an eager beaver. He always was short on facts."

"Not this time, Fargo."

I turned around and saw Olsen storming through the doorway. He walked over to the D.A.s desk and threw down a pair of handcuffs. "Just thought I would bring these along. I've been dreaming every night about putting you in shackles, Fargo."

"We all knew you only arrested criminals in your dreams," I commented. Olsen went for me on that one.

The D.A. yelled for Olsen to sit down. "Just take it easy, guys. We all used to work together." I backed off and sat down in a chair in front of Thorner's desk. Olsen steamed a bit and sat down on the chair to the side of me.

"Fargo never worked with anybody," spat Olsen as he slumped down into the chair.

Thorner as he started to leave the room. "I'll be back in a couple of minutes. I expect you to both act professional. As soon as Leo gets here we'll get started." He glanced at us, shook is head, and closed the door behind him.

I whistled a little tune that I picked up when I was a surfed the Pacific Ocean. I always wanted to try the big waves in Hawaii, but I never took the plunge. I figured this would drive Olsen over the edge.

"You know, Mr. Big Guy," said Olsen, "you're not getting away with this. One thing for sure is we've got you in the hotel room putting diamonds in a dead woman's safe."

"What makes you so sure that I was putting them in the safe?" I responded. "You know, you could take a look at all my statements and realize that everything I've told you is the truth."

"Your whole career was based on lies. Why would you know anything about the truth?"

"That's only your opinion. If we took a good look at your career, I'm sure we could find a couple of items that were not on the up and up."

"Maybe, maybe not."

"Tell me this, Mr. Hotel Detective. Have you found out who murdered my client down by the pool? And how about the McCaddy murder? Figure that one out yet? That's your real problem."

Olsen leapt up. "Why you son-of-a-bitch. I ought to...."

"Just sit down, Olsen," said Thorner as he walked back into his office. Uncle Leo was right behind him.

"Good morning, Uncle," I said.

"Good morning, Fargo. I hope you have not been spilling your guts to Las Vegas's finest."

"Nothing to tell them." It felt good to have Uncle Leo around.

"Please take a seat," said the D.A. Uncle Leo pulled a chair up between Olsen and me.

Uncle Leo started to get things going. "What I would like to do is set the record straight as far as Detective Blue and...."

"He's no longer a detective with this department," spit out Olsen.

"Neither are you," said Thorner.

"May I continue?" asked Uncle Leo.

Thorner waved his hand in approval. Olsen sat back.

"I would like to add," said Uncle Leo, "that Mr. Vince Olsen is an employee of the MGM Grand. It's also understood that Mr. Olsen is not a member of the Las Vegas police department."

"I don't think...." Olsen began.

"Leo is correct," said Thorner. "It is important, Olsen, that you remember you have no official power in the State of Nevada. That you're only an employee of the MGM Grand with an investigative and security role."

"Yes, sir," said Olsen, again sitting back in his chair.

"I would also like to add," said Uncle Leo, "that my client is a registered detective with the State of Nevada. He is bonded, and has sworn to uphold all the laws of the State of Nevada. He has formally retired from the Las Vegas police department and left the department in good standing. If fact, he still sits on two advisory councils here at the police department. At this time we would like the department to understand that we are not interested in hearing anything Mr. Vince Olsen has to say. He has no power of authority of any kind at Las Vegas Metro. For that matter he has no power of any kind in the State of Nevada. The only power he has is that of a security manager with the MGM Grand hotel. He's basically an employee."

Olsen shot out of his chair. "Sit back down," Thorner said.

Uncle Leo continued. "We would like to have him dismissed from this meeting, and we would also like to notify him that he is now under a formal court order to stop harassing my client." Uncle Leo tossed out what appeared to be a court-recorded document.

Olsen was up and yelling. "I am doing my job as the head of security for the MGM Grand to have arrested the thief who was found in possession of the diamonds from the McCaddy robbery-killing. I have to be here. It's my case," screamed Olsen.

"He holds no power in this office," said Uncle Leo.

"The detectives on this case know exactly...." stammered Olsen.

"The detectives on this case are not available at this time," said D.A. Thorner.

"But the facts of the case point to Fargo," yelled Olsen.

"What facts?" said Uncle Leo.

"The fact that he was caught with the stolen property in his possession. The McCaddy diamonds at my hotel."

Uncle Leo turned to me. "Did you have the McCaddy diamonds at the MGM Grand?"

"Yes, sir," I answered.

"What were you doing with them?"

"Taking them out of the safe located in room 2438 on the twenty-fourth floor," I responded.

"Why were you doing that?" asked Uncle Leo.

I leaned forward in my chair. Uncle Leo and I had gone through this questioning a couple of different times. I had learned in the past to answer only the question and not to give my opinion on the matter. As Uncle Leo had told me many times, my opinion wasn't worth anything. I tended to disagree with him, but Uncle Leo's the one keeping me out of jail.

"I was examining the safe for my client, Ms. Kimberly Weber."

"Had Ms. Weber given you the combination to the safe?"

"Yes, she had."

"This is not what this meeting was about," stormed Olsen. "Fargo was caught with the diamonds from the McCaddy robbery."

"That may be true," said Thorner. "But we have no evidence he was involved with the crime."

"He was in the room," said Olsen, standing up. "He was caught with the diamonds."

"Who caught him?" asked Uncle Leo.

"Peter Daily. He was on assignment to watch the room to see if anybody would come back to the scene of the crime."

"So it was Peter Daily, not Olsen, who observed my client. Not Olsen. At this time, I would like to renew my request that Olsen be removed from this meeting. We already have a representative of the MGM Grand in the room."

"Who?" asked Olsen.

"My client, Mr. Fargo Blue, is working personally with Mr. Lanning, Director of Operations for the MGM Grand Hotel."

"Bull," said Olsen.

"Mr. Blue, what is your position at the MGM Grand Hotel?" asked Uncle Leo.

"I am employed by the MGM Grand as the detective in charge of finding out who murdered my client, Kimberly Weber."

"And who employed you?" asked Uncle Leo.

"Mr. Lanning."

"Lanning," screamed Olsen. "This is all bull."

"And does your position supersede Vince Olsen, manager of security of the MGM Grand?"

"Yes, it does," I replied. "Olsen's in charge of the tourists. I take care of the investigation."

Olsen jumped up. "This is a bunch of crap." The veins in his neck bulged.

"I think under the circumstances, Vince, I will have to ask you to leave this meeting," said Thorner.

"I will personally call the MGM Grand this afternoon," said Uncle Leo. "I will ask Mr. Lanning if he could have Mr. Olsen concern himself with just the problems in the hotel and not with any official investigations that the police department is conducting."

"This is absurd," said Olsen as he got up and stormed out of the room.

"I want to thank you for coming down...." began Thorner, but the door slammed in the middle of his sentence. I turned to Uncle Leo and smiled, but he was studying Thorner.

"Exactly why did you bring us down here?" asked Uncle Leo.

"I was really interested in what Fargo has turned up. I will have to say that we do have some grounds for action against your client, but we don't think we would get very far."

"What action can you take?"

"He was found with the diamonds from the McCaddy robbery. Being an accessory to the crime, for openers."

"I guess what's important here," said Uncle Leo, "is that there are always two sides of the story. Why don't we agree to do this? As soon as Fargo can verify certain information we have in our possession, we will make that information available to the D.A.s office for your use."

"We can ask right now, or file obstruction of justice charges and haul Fargo into court."

"True, you can do that. However, my client has a very good record in Vegas as a police officer, as a detective on your staff, and as a private detective. He has contacts you don't have. Why not use this, harness this energy if you will, and work together toward finding who really did this thing?"

"Okay, that's good for now. But sooner or later I'll need that information."

"Let's set a date," I said. "Today is Friday...how about within the next two days?"

"Fine. One thing is for sure," said Thorner. "If I need Fargo, I know how to find him."

"How?"

"I'll just find Olsen." He laughed at his own joke. So did we.

Twenty-Six

RUBY ANN, posing as Marilee, entered the lunchroom where a number of employees were killing time. Marilee first checked her clipboard, and then walked over and studied the poster on the wall.

"Excuse me, Marilee."

Marilee turned around to see the receptionist, Brenda, standing in the doorway.

"Yes?" said Marilee, taken completely off guard.

"You have a phone call in the lobby. I couldn't find you right away and was concerned."

"No problem," said Marilee recovering her composure. "I was just finishing up here. Who's the call from?"

"He said it was from your office." The women both walked back toward the receptionist area.

"I appreciate your finding me. I left my cellular at home and I've been at a loss without it."

"It happens," said Brenda. "My boss gave me one and said I can't go anywhere without it."

As they reached the receptionist area, Brenda indicated where Marilee could take the phone call.

"Hello," said Marilee after clicking off the hold button.

"I'm glad to see you're doing your part of our agreement."

"Who is this, please?"

"Your partner."

Ruby Ann was shocked but held her composure. She looked up, wondering how close her partner was to her activities. She had told no one she was coming to the MGM Grand today. She had told no one what her name was and who she was working for.

"How did you know I was going to be here today?" asked Ruby Ann.

"I know everything," said the mystery partner.

"How could you know that?"

"I just know. Have you taken care of what I asked you to do?"

"I'm working on it," said Ruby Ann. "What about my father?"

"What about him?"

"He's supposed to be released soon."

"No, that's not correct. He's supposed to be released when you complete your assignment."

"I'm completing the assignment now."

"See that you do. And listen, your little stunt at our last meeting to try and find out who I am almost backfired. Remember that you're just a cutout. If you had found me, your father would have spent the rest of his life in prison, and you would've been dead."

"Just like to know who my partner is."

"Not possible. Not in this lifetime."

"Listen, I'm doing...."

"Marilee?" said Brenda, who had moved next to the redhead with a mixture of confusion and anxiety.

"Just a minute," said Ruby Ann into the receiver and looked up at Brenda. "Yes? Can I help you with something?" Her voice was on the edge of being agitated.

"Yes. I checked with the Department of Labor and they have no record of you. They said they never heard of anyone coming around. They told me to call security."

"I'm sorry. What did you say?"

"Who are you? I'll need some kind of identification before you can leave the building."

"I'm talking to my office now," said Ruby Ann, trying to remain calm. "Perhaps you should talk to them yourself?" She offered the phone to Brenda.

"No, I don't think so...."

"Maybe you should check again. Excuse me for a second." Ruby Ann turned her attention to the phone. "I'll have to get back to you. I have a problem here."

"I'm sure you do." The phone went dead.

Ruby Ann hung up and stood to face Brenda.

"They say you don't exist. They told me that those posters which you might be replacing are mailed to each employer when they need to be updated."

"They did, did they?"

"Yes, they did. I will need your I.D. and also your driver's license. I'm afraid I will have to call security."

"And what do you think you would do with those?"

"Turn them over to security when they get here," said Brenda.

"Well, I have to inform you that you're very good at your job," said Ruby Ann.

She reached into her purse and pulled out an I.D. "I'm with Internal Security with the MGM Grand." She flashed Brenda a very good looking security badge.

"My goodness."

"You have been under investigation on a number of points."

"Under investigation?" echoed Brenda, taken aback. "Me! Under investigation?"

"Yes, that's right," said Ruby Ann.

"I didn't know I was under investigation." Brenda's pudgy face was turning white.

"Well, you are," said Ruby Ann. "Please sit down."

"Right here? In the lobby?"

"Yes."

Brenda sat down a little bit apprehensive in the change of events. Ruby Ann stood, towering over Brenda.

"Weren't you told in your training that you were not to let anyone into the inner sanctum if they didn't have proper clearance?"

"Yes, they did, but I...."

"Then why did you let me in?"

"You said you were with the Department of...."

"But I didn't have an I.D."

"That's true...but...."

"But you let me into the offices. Isn't that correct?"

"Yes, it is. Am I going to lose my job?"

At that moment Vince Olsen walked in the front door and Brenda jumped up.

"Mr. Olsen. Can I help you?"

"Nah...just passing through." He strode across the entire length of the receptionist area, glanced at Ruby Ann, and then continued toward the massive wooden doors that led to his inner offices. He was obviously upset. His face was beet red, and he looked like he had been roughed up. If Brenda had turned and watched Ruby Ann, she would have seen a huge sigh of relief. Instead, Brenda stared at the door closing behind Olsen.

"I don't think you're going to lose your job, Brenda. I just want you to be more careful in the future. You know the casino deals in millions of dollars a year in business. We have to be very protective of all our departments."

"Yes, I know," said Brenda, her round cheeks sagging.

"I will write a memo today about this, but at this time I will not place it in your file. None of the staff will know you have been under investigation, so you need not worry about that."

"Oh, thank you."

"I'm also going to write in the memo that you took the necessary precautions and called the Department of Labor. You took the right steps."

"Thanks. I really appreciate you giving me a break like this. I mean...I did screw up just a bit. You were so...."

"Convincing," said Ruby Ann.

"Yeah, that's it. Convincing. I would never have guessed you were not from the employment department."

Ruby Ann prepared to leave. "Well, you know. That's why we go undercover a lot when we have to check out new employees. All part of the job, I guess."

"Thanks anyway." Brenda extended her hand. "I really appreciate you understanding my position."

"No problem," said Ruby Ann, shaking her hand. "Just one more thing, though."

"Sure."

"Please don't tell anybody that I was in, no matter what happens. I might have to come back here sometime, and it would help if you were on my side. Who knows, maybe there is a job in security for you one of these days."

"Oh, I'd like that."

"Good. I can count on you." Ruby Ann turned and walked to the wide set of double doors, smiled once, then made her exit. The secretary was a sly one. Simple, but sly. Ruby Ann had accomplished her assignment as planned, but what bothered her was the fact that her partner knew where she was. Had he known all the time? How could he have known that she was coming to the hotel today? He also had all the details.

Ruby Ann left the elevator at the ground floor and entered the restrooms, which were located to the right by the Mexican Cafe. Within two minutes she had switched her appearance from a redhead wearing black slacks and white top to a blonde with a short dress and tanned legs.

She exited the restroom, walked past the slot machines, blackjack tables, around the open bar, and left the casino through the famed MGM Grand entrance. The fresh air was invigorating. But a nagging thought kept coming back to her. How was she being watched? Would he be the one to end the partnership -- and with her death? For the first time she felt vulnerable and fearful. She didn't like not being in control. She needed to move quickly, to be slippery like a cat and to pounce on her victim before he knew something was wrong.

Twenty-Seven

PLEASURE sipped a glass of Chardonnay in an isolated corner of the Rio, but not far from the on-going festival of light, color and sound. The jubilant and party-like atmosphere attributed to the casinos immense popularity. The light played with the slight effervescent bubbles of the wine, making them sparkle. The light also complemented Pleasure, who was dressed in what she referred to as her "killer" outfit. It started with a black dress, cut low in front. With this she could distract a player with a shift of her shoulders or a slight movement of her body. It worked well when she needed just a bit of an edge on certain hands. To this she added black hose with a splash of gold glitter. Men were always attracted to her legs, and the glitter of gold heightened the effect. Black spiked high heels, which she removed during play, added to the overall effect. For rings she wore simple emeralds surrounded by diamonds, and her solitaire diamond necklace floated daringly at her cleavage.

Pleasure had a direct view of the poker gaming area. She was studying the various players. Even though she was not planning on entering a game until the evening, she knew that many professional poker players played a few hands in the afternoon to get their feet wet. This gave them time to study the other players who might be involved in that evening's action. Pleasure was doing her studying from a distance. She could evaluate players by watching their body movements and how they handled themselves between hands. She could determine the wealth of players by the way they carried themselves. Pleasure was able to observe the facial expressions of some of the winners and losers. Her ability to read a face during a poker game was one of the keys to her success. Many times she was able to read the cards of opponents because she had spent hours studying the players. This was her homework. Friday afternoon was the time for studying and planning her attack on tonight's tables.

The popularity of no limit Hold'Em Poker is because it's fun to bet. It is not a game of just deal the cards, and see who's got the best hand. It is much more a psychological game of who can outmaneuver whom. The whole game is built around the idea of having good cards, and bluffing with bad cards. It comes down to the basic "shootout' at high noon.

Pleasure's cellular rang. She reached into her handbag and retrieved it. "Yes?"

"This is Jody. Sorry I haven't been able to contact you."

Pleasure's interest immediately piqued. She shifted her cellular from one ear to the other while watching a group of Japanese businessmen enter the dark secluded lounge. She had not heard from Jody since her friend had arrived in Vegas. Like herself, Jody was a professional poker player who lived on the edge, traveling the world with the skill of knowing when to bet and when to hold. They had teamed up in Los Angeles, and since Jody had gotten Pleasure into a poker game, she was responsible for collecting the winnings.

"Where have you been? I've been worried sick."

"I'm okay. I was delayed after dropping my bags in our room."

"I've been waiting for your call. Were you successful in bringing in the cash to Las Vegas?"

"No. There have been problems," said Jody.

"What kind of problems?"

"Nothing that can't be solved."

"What kind of problems?" repeated Pleasure with a tone that required Jody to answer. Pleasure did not like losing money. A problem in and around poker circles always involved money. Jody was to have collected their winnings from a scalawag of a poker player who called himself the Governor. Seems his great-grandfather had once been governor of an eastern state.

"The Governor never showed up."

"He never showed...."

"That's right," said Jody.

"Not good...."

"I waited three days for him to make an appearance. It never happened."

"Did you try and track him down?"

"Yes. The phone numbers and addresses he gave us were no good. All false leads."

"I don't like losing money," said Pleasure. "The winnings represented over four months' work. Neither of us can afford to lose that kind of money. How he got into that game without table stakes is something we'll have to deal with. It won't happen again."

"It's entirely my fault," said Jody.

"No. It's mine for not staying in Los Angeles and helping you collect the money," said Pleasure. "Where are you now?"

"I'm in Las Vegas."

"Why haven't you contacted me sooner? You checked in two days ago."

"I've got a lead on the Governor."

"What is it?"

"Remember that Texan who kept inviting us down to his ranch for a barbecue and a little late-night poker with his buddies?"

"Ol' slow-dealing Cliff Barley," Pleasure said.

"Well, I contacted him. Seems he's known our Governor for quite a few years. The scum has done this sort of thing before."

"Seems like somebody ought to put a stop to this. Not good for the business," said Pleasure sipping her wine.

"We're not the only ones who feel that way. The Governor doesn't have the money, which is why he skipped town. Slow-dealing Cliff lent him the necessary funds for another game."

"Where's the game?"

"Right here in Vegas."

"A hotel game, or is it private?"

"Hotel game."

"How interesting. Which hotel?"

"He plays only at the MGM Grand. Comes here when he needs to make a stake for his private games. He's evidently got the casino bluffed that he's got money behind him because they always cover his markers."

"Why Vegas?"

"Lots of amateur gamblers. He waits for the right game and then starts bringing down a thousand an hour. Two or three weeks here and he's back in business."

"Does he know that I left for Las Vegas from Los Angeles?" Pleasure asked as she watched two Japanese tourists enter the poker game she had been studying.

"He's got no idea that either of us is here."

"This could be interesting. Are you able to find out when he's going to start playing?"

"Better than that. He's got a game planned for to-morrow night. That's the word from Cliff."

"At the MGM Grand?"

"Yep!"

"How convenient." Pleasure smiled.

"Everybody is going to be there," Jody said. "Cliff is going to fly up here and participate in the fleecing of some tourists along with the Governor, who also owes money to Cliff. Cliff is going to make sure he collects."

"Will the Governor stay in the game if we show up?"

"If Cliff is there, he can't get up and walk away. We'll be all over him. He won't be able to get out of the hotel. He picks up his chips and starts to check out, it'll be me, you, and ol' Cliff following his every move. Besides, if he's losing, the hotel is not going to let him walk out the front door."

"Sounds good to me," said Pleasure.

"Same stakes as last time. I think we have a way of recovering our money back from the Governor."

"How?" asked Pleasure.

"In diamonds."

"Diamonds?"

"You know how you always see him with long-sleeved shirts?"

"Yes, I remember that. He even wears them when he's by a pool."

"Ever see him in the pool?" Jody asked.

"Can't say I have, now that you mention it."

"He's got over one-hundred-thousand dollars of diamonds in his arm."

"What?"

"Under his skin he carries diamonds. He's had them there for years. That's why he doesn't wear a hustler's ring. He has his diamonds stashed under his skin. They were sewn in there a number of years ago."

"How are we going to get them out?"

"Sharp knife," answered Jody.

"How do you know all this?"

"The Governor talked a little too much about the old days when he was down to Cliff's ranch a couple of years ago. He actually showed everybody in the poker game his arm and what the bumps were."

"Sounds a little messy," Pleasure said.

"Ever hear of blood money?"

"Yeah...."

"Well, get ready. This is going to be it."

"Tough way to get diamonds." Pleasure rubbed her arm.

"That's for sure. Hear about the jewelry store that got knocked over?"

"Unfortunately I have. Seems like some of the diamonds ended up in my hotel safe."

"You're kidding," said Jody.

"No, I'm not. The day after I arrived here in Vegas. Some kind of terrible mix up."

"What did you tell the police?"

"The police think I'm dead," said Pleasure.

"Dead," reacted Jody.

Pleasure continued. "Long story. I'll tell you about it after we even the score with the Governor."

"That's a deal. I'm always looking for a new trick," said Jody laughing. "We're already registered for the game. I knew you wouldn't want to pass it up."

"Thanks," said Pleasure. "I'll see you later." Pleasure closed her cellular. She smiled enough to attract the attention of the cocktail waitress.

She produced a bottle of California North Coast Riesling wrapped in a towel. "May I?"

"Why yes. That would be very nice."

While the wine was being poured, Pleasure could not help thinking about how rewarding it would be to bring the Governor back to earth and get her money back. Nothing bothered her more than a poker player who could not pay his or her debts. In the Old West, they had a solution for that. It was called the hanging tree. Seemed fair to her. That's what table stakes were all about. You brought all the money you could afford to lose to the table, and you bet it. When you lost, you thanked the dealer for dealing a straight game, you thanked the other players, and you left the table. Hanging was probably the answer to poker honesty. It would give a gambler something to think about while bluffing.

Twenty-Eight

I spotted Olsen Saturday morning, and started to tail him.
It was easy. The man had more habits than a cat. I knew
he always stopped for coffee on his way to work. I didn't
want to stake out his house because he lived in a secure
subdivision southeast of town. I sat in a Boulder
Shopping Center parking lot waiting for him. Just like
clockwork he showed up at a local coffee house and
bagel shop. I laughed to myself. With the paunch around
his waist, Olsen sort of looked like a bagel. I expected
Olsen wouldn't enjoy the humor. You are what you eat,
they say.

Everybody hears stories about how boring it is to
do stakeouts and tails. Sitting in the car for hours on end.
You're either freezing cold or baking in the heat. Eating
cold pizza and drinking cold coffee. Nothing to do but try
and stay awake as you watch for your target to move so
you can proceed to the next location and do it all over
again. That's how it was when I was on the force, and
that's the way it is now.

At least most of the time. Other times you have to
blend in, and become part of the scene -- particularly in
Las Vegas. Now I'm prepared with the ultimate black bag.
I carry two cellular phones. I have a Bearcat police
scanner, and another one that picks up security at
McCarren airport. I also have a portable color television

and a built-in CD player with surround-sound speakers. I checked the sports pages and lined up my activities for the day. In the morning I'm following the ponies, and I've already placed my bets on twenty-to-one shots at four different racetracks. Tiger Woods is ready to win another golf tournament, and I'll be watching. The Sonics are in the playoffs and the NFL draft is getting close. I installed a personalized air conditioner in my BMW that runs off of a 12 volt battery. Just add ice. I can sit all day in the blazing heat with the engine off and be perfectly comfortable. Fargo Blue is on vacation.

Olsen walked out with a huge bagel loaded with cream cheese balanced on his coffee container. He also carried a small bag, probably for a mid-morning snack, I thought, as I bit into my own bagel. I was one step ahead of him. Always was, always will be. I prepared to follow by shutting off the television and the CD player. Olsen turned out of the parking lot and headed toward the Strip. My guess was he was heading for the MGM Grand, but I wanted to know the details of any extra errands he might be running. My cell phone rang. I figured it for Sheri.

"Hello, beautiful."

"Do you always answer your phone that way?" Abby asked.

Dead silence. I was lost for words. "I just knew it was going to be you."

"Sometimes I just don't believe you," Abby snarled.

"Now, how many people call me on my cell phone?"

"I don't know."

"Well, trust me, not many. What are you doing up so early?"

"Just checking on my favorite P.I. I figured if you answered your cell you're probably not in jail yet."

"You heard?"

"Yep. The talk at the Trop is you're the number one suspect and are going down for the big one."

"Nah. It's just a bunch of hype."

"I also hear you're a jewel thief."

"The only thing I ever stole was your heart."

"Such a guy. What are you doing?"

"I'm on an early morning tail."

"Still trying to solve the disappearance of Pleasure, are you?"

"Well, she's not exactly gone. But I still have not found Jody and recovered Pleasure's money."

"What about the MGM Grand? I thought you were working for them."

"Still am. Somebody's got to find the killer of the Jane Doe by the poolside," I said as I watched Olsen take a right toward Sam's Town. "Listen. I've got something happening here. I'll check with you later."

"There's been a car parked out in front of my condo the last couple of mornings. I think somebody is waiting for you to show up."

"Do they follow you to work in the afternoon?"

"Yep."

"What about when you get off work? Can you tell if anybody's following you home?"

"Can't really say. I've been watching carefully. Paranoia sets in and I think every car is following me. Being a dancer doesn't help. The girls always talk about the weirdo's."

"Let's do dinner tonight," I said.

"Sounds great," Abby said.

"It's a date. See you after the second set." I hung up as I too turned left onto Las Vegas Boulevard. So, somebody was following Abby. I had to guess they were some of Olsen's boys wanting to keep tabs on me. But I had to make sure. It's not the first time that chorus line girls are stalked.

The Sahara was at the end of the Strip, and I was entering no man's land. Once you passed the Stratosphere, you got to see a little bit seeder side of the Las Vegas Strip. The area was home to questionable wedding chapels, broken down Denny's, liquor stores, and really cheap hotels with clientele who were always suspected of either armed robbery or working the girls. Rumor has it that they're going to put in an entertainment park in back of the Stratosphere that Disney would be proud of. This would include a hotel without gambling. A frightening thought. I pondered this as I watched Olsen slow down behind a couple of busses.

Olsen must be headed for a meeting. I doubted he would go back to the police station after what Uncle Leo had done to him yesterday. I knew Olsen would be approaching Fremont Street and would probably go either left, which would take him into the older part of Vegas, or right, which housed more bars and motels.

I had to figure he was going downtown. Olsen continued past Fremont and then turned left down Ogden Avenue. I shot through the intersection and turned left on Stewart Avenue to set up a parallel tail. I knew I couldn't stay behind him with my Cad. Too obvious. I drove down two blocks and waited at an intersection. I looked to the right, and sure enough his Mercedes slid by headed toward a parking garage. I sped on down the street trying to put away all my electronic gear while attempting to get a block ahead of Olsen. I hung a right and a quick left and drove straight into a self-parking lot. I backed into a space and paid the attendant five dollars. I flashed my P.I. badge, slipped the attendant an extra twenty, and told him to watch my car carefully. It was worth protecting. There is honor among car thieves, sort of. It meant he wouldn't steal anything out of my car, but the rest of the cars were fair game.

As I left the parking lot I caught a glimpse of Olsen walking out of a parking garage that served a couple of different casinos. I couldn't imagine which casino Olsen was headed for so I had to get lucky here. Following him carefully I was able to spot him going into the Horseshoe Lounge, a leftover from the old days. What a lot of people didn't know is that many professional gamblers played craps at the downtown casinos and made a good living at it. Fremont Casinos had better odds. They weren't into the flash and glamour of the carpet joints on the Strip. These players hid behind tinted glasses and played grind out craps systems, which would not necessarily guarantee them a profit but would cut their losses considerably if they hit a bad run at the tables. Good advice for anyone.

I tailed Olsen into the Horseshoe casino and wondered what he was up to. Maybe he was going to visit a friend who was part of the security department. I stopped by a teller's cage and changed a fifty for some dollar coins in case I needed to kill time at the slots. I had been in this situation before and knew what might happen. I wandered through slot machine heaven still being able to keep Olsen in sight. The machines were making quite a racket. I watched Olsen scan a couple of crap tables. I never took him to be a gambler, but then everybody who lives in Vegas plays some form of the game. That's why they live in Vegas.

Olsen finally reached into his wallet and dropped a hundred on the table. This was scooped up and replaced with chips. Olsen started to scan the room, so I sat down in front of a slot machine that gave me a good view of the table while hiding me completely. My machine was a five-dollar feed with a lot of fruit. I watched Olsen. He scooped up the dice, threw a five-dollar chip on the pass line, blew on the dice, and tossed them to the end of the table. A roar went up and it was obvious Olsen had rolled a natural. I dropped five coins in my machine, pulled the handle, and watched the entire machine line up perfectly. Five watermelons all in a row. The siren that went off brought the whole casino to a standstill. I had hit the big one, with flashing lights, ringing bells, and people cheering. Here I was trying to hide, and I drew the attention of the entire place. Security showed up immediately followed by two of the casino's floor personnel, a cocktail girl, and a sad-looking clown. Someone slapped me on the back to congratulate me. They turned me around for a photo, and after the strobes had blinded me, I saw Olsen wave at me through a glare of white light. Over the confusion and noise I could hear Olsen, who had wandered over to see the big winner.

"Well, aren't we lucky this morning. I didn't know you hung out downtown, or maybe you're just doing your job."

"Just doing my job," I responded.

"I don't think so...."

"That's for the police to decide."

"We'll see about that," said Olsen. Another light from the photographer's strobe blinded me but I caught a glimpse of Olsen leaving.

"Congratulations," shouted a floor supervisor. "You've won the one-hundred thousand-dollar progressive. Where do you hail from?"

"I'm local. Look, how long is this going to take?"

"We should have you out of here in under an hour. After the slot supervisor verifies the win, there will be some tax forms to file."

The crowd surrounded the machine as the slot super opened up the machine. I was happy and disgusted at the same time. Olsen was gone and I had no idea what he was up to, but I knew it was not good. And of course, like a bad penny with poor timing, I came up a winner.

Twenty-Nine

I will be the first to admit I love Las Vegas and gambling. Sheri called me earlier in the afternoon and informed me that Pleasure had registered for a Texas Hold'Em poker game Friday evening at the MGM Grand. It was a no limit game with blinds starting at $500/$1000 especially arranged by the casino for a select group of players. Sheri comes through with the most interesting information at exactly the right time. She also told me somebody was going to be arrested later in the evening for the theft of the diamonds and the murder of McCaddy. This was not a good situation. Knowing the bail would be set at around five-hundred thousand was starting to look like a major obstacle. The office could handle it, but it would take some time.

Uncle Leo told me not to worry about the McCaddy charge since I had an alibi at the time McCaddy was hit. The timeline was going to be a problem for Metro. It was more important for the D.A.s office to arrest someone supposedly connected to the investigation. Makes the public feel good, and gives a secure feeling to other jewelry stores. Made me feel terrible. Bum raps come with the job, but this was going too far. Unless there was a turn of events, I would be charged.

A casino offers many chances to win and to lose, and have done a good job of opening up Hold'Em poker for gamblers. From low level limit games all the way to high progressive blinds in tournament play, it offered something for everyone. Walk through any casino and you will see a cross section of players dueling it out on the green felt. You will find grandmothers bluffing cowboys who are in town for a rodeo, or sharp players taking on the casino's local residence. The locals sometimes scalp the sharpies from the big city – thus the lure of Hold'Em.

Hold'Em poker at the MGM Grand is near the front entrance on the strip. Walk from the New York, New York into the MGM Grand and you come to a railing. Down below you will see the Hold'Em poker arena flanked by a state of the art sports bar. Monitors will let you know what tables are opening up and where you are on the list of players waiting to play. Strategically located at the entrance of the casino, Hold'Em is meant to draw attention to the casino and to the players. Marketing at its best. Motivation, greed, and sex all rolled into one - poker.

I felt comfortable in a basic black tux and tie as I stood by the railing overlooking the sports bar and Hold'Em area. From here I could gaze out on the casino floor and at the same time observe who was being seated at the poker table. Tonight would be my night. I observed the hustle of the casino as the casino employ- ees worked the guests, and the hustle of the guests as they worked the casino. People living ordinary lives - the ones who get up before dawn, take their kids to daycare, go on to work, back to daycare, and then home to confront the endless chores of domesticity. And here, for a brief moment, they can lose themselves in the opulence of all that is grand. That's what it's all about.

Pleasure was an exception to the rule. She walked across the casino, stopping briefly to observe the tigers in their cages. Pleasure was dressed in a black sequined gown with a plunging neckline. It didn't take any memory to know that Pleasure more than amply filled the dress. With her gown reaching the floor, her movement was more like a glide. Being tall, her body swayed in the natural rhythm of beautiful women everywhere. I thought about her unusual charm and confidence. She was a winner, and the management of the MGM Grand knew it. In the casino world, you don't screw with a winner. You go with the flow and let the winner bring you the notoriety required to be the best casino on the Strip. And when you are the best, the reward is a woman like Pleasure who would put the final touch on your casino for the evening. She was a magnificent marquee of beauty sought by all who watched her. These were the deep down, dark, private thoughts that casinos depend upon. Sex, and the greed to be a winner.

The crowds parted as Pleasure approached the Hold'Em area. She was greeted by the host for the evening and escorted to the table. One man already seated stood up and bowed slightly as she was introduced. She shook hands more with her eyes than anything else. She saw everything. Another host leaned over, there was a brief exchange, and he was gone with her order. The banker brought over a tray of chips, and she signed the marker. She was in for one-hundred thousand. That was enough to draw the crowds. The word had already gone out. It would be discreetly communicated throughout the casino.

The game was of course No Limit Texas Hold'Em, the richest card game in the world. Seven cards; two down, and five community cards up. Multiple levels of betting with multiple raises. There could be close to a half million dollars on the table before the night was over. The blinds were escalated as the evening wore on. The confident became more confident, and the losers began to chase their money with poor bluffing and bad hands.

I had made arrangements with the poker administrator for the evening game and knew who the players were and their descriptions. I spotted Anthony Kennedy Miller, known as the Governor, as he walked up and shook hands with Cliff Barley, who had just flown in from Texas. Both were big-time professional players. They knew each other and had played together many times in the past.

The dealer was named Drake Woods. He had dealt more Hold'Em poker games in Vegas than any other dealer. He was known for being cool under pressure. Tonight would probably mean several thousand dollars in tips, from both the rich and the professionals. Woods was playing in the hottest game in town surrounded by the rich and sometimes famous. The only problem was he was also surrounded by liquor, and that was his secret world; the inner torment he lived with every night. His first sip wouldn't come until two or three in the morning, and he wasn't scheduled tomorrow, so it was going to be a good night. His flask waited for him in his locker.

Two chairs remained empty. It was now my chance to turn the tables. I was dressed in a very expensive black tux I had just acquired. My trusty Glock rested in its waist holster in back, and my .38 snub nose nestled comfortably in my ankle holster. The Wild Wild West. I loved it.

The odds were simple. If Pleasure was a high stakes gambler, I too had to gamble. I had to know what made this lady tick. The risk was apparent. Sooner or later I was going to be nailed for the killing and the jewel robbery in which the gems had somehow ended up in her suite. I also needed some bail money quick. I strode confidently to the Hold"Em area and introduced myself to the host. After they checked my name I was taken to my seat and introduced to everyone. Pleasure's back was to me so she did not see me until I was introduced as George St. Clair.

"Call me St. Clair," I said as I nodded my introduction. I shook hands with everyone very politely, saving Pleasure for last, as any man would.

"George St. Clair, what an unusual name," Pleasure said. She was to the point. No sign of recognition. Bright lady.

The banker brought over my marker and I signed for $100,000, thankful for the winning slot machine. Nice round number. What I do for my clients. My accountant was probably breaking out in hives right now. I wasn't the gambling type. I was more like a shill playing with my own money. But a P.I. must take on many roles.

The chair next to me was still vacant, and it was politely announced that the last person would arrive within minutes. Drake started to shuffle the deck. In practiced moves he riffled the cards and split the deck into halves. He then quickly and effortlessly shuffled the cards again to break in the new deck. The table was ready. Stacks of chips in front of some players acted as a shield readying for battle.

It is not often in my life when I feel something is going to happen. The tiny hairs on the back of my neck went up in anticipation as I keyed my senses. You knew it was going to be important, but you didn't know why.

Without a prelude, like a sudden thunderstorm bursting its energy, a woman in a floor-length red gown with black gloves and matching handbag made her entry. Her dress appeared glued to her body. Probably a good defense in this place. Her shocking blonde hair added the final touch. She was even more beautiful than Pleasure. It was then that I knew who she was. I glanced at Pleasure and saw a sparkle in her eyes. It had to be Jody.

I knew then what was going to happen. Pleasure and Jody were going to take somebody big time in the evening's game. I noticed the Texan, Cliff Barley, smiling downright friendly to Jody and Pleasure. I glanced over at the Governor and knew at once he was their mark. He was smooth, but by watching his eyes I could tell he was nervous about the night's game. His eyes darted back and forth, and a small bead of sweat broke out on his forehead. The hotel was treating him with the utmost respect, and he had no problem obtaining his markers.

Jody offered her hand to us and we each politely rose from our seats and shook hands with her.

"Pleased to see you again," said the Governor.

"George St. Clair. You can call me St. Clair."

Jody turned to Pleasure.

"Welcome," said Pleasure, as she offered her hand. Gloves met gloves in a handshake that resembled an embrace. Softest handshake I ever heard.

The blind and double blind made a contribution to the pot. Gloves came off as aged cognac was poured into over-sized snifters. Already the onlookers were gathering for a peek. High-stakes Hold'Em poker with beautiful women and tuxedoed men epitomized the dreams of many. The house took a rake out of every hand as its fee for hosting the game.

"Wish me luck," I said to nobody in particular. I was not surprised that nobody answered.

Time passed. I lost some hands and won others. Everyone was trying to feel everyone out. It did not appear that Pleasure and Jody were in any way playing as a team, but then, who would know for sure? I knew they were working together, which in itself might make a few very angry gamblers. Twice already I suspected that Pleasure had won by pure bluffing. From a poker perspective she was a hard player to figure out. She cupped her hands carefully hiding the two down cards while she took a quick glance, never again looking at them. I spotted one of her possible bluffs right away. A King had dropped on the flop, and Pleasure quickly checked her hole cards. This was easily spotted by several of the players and they dropped out leaving her with the pot. The question remains, did she have pocket Kings, or was she decoying the table by looking at her hole cards right away. This was a common mistake by beginners wanting to make sure they had the pocket Kings in their hand, and it somehow had not turned into Jacks. There were few tells that gave any clues as to what she was holding. It was almost as if she didn't care.

Jody was similar, but better. She had the same built-in distractions that Pleasure did, but her innocence was immediately apparent. You got the feeling you wanted to protect her, but I bet she didn't need any protection. In fact, I'm sure you would be smarter if you protected yourself from Jody. There was hardness under her beauty. Where it came from was difficult to comprehend. She was the mystery woman of the evening.

Because Pleasure had hired me to find her, my job was over. The evening was bound to get more interesting, as I was anxious for a one-on-one conversation with Pleasure. Time to iron out a few details about her hotel room. I also wanted to find out from Jody when she had last entered Pleasure's hotel room so I could lay down a time line for my defense if I was arrested.

The focus of my attention became the Governor. He was sweating profusely. It was obvious he needed to win. It was his tell of desperation and it also meant he was going to lose. Everyone had his number early on in the game. But then, someone has to lose at poker. Cliff was also having his problems and kept making eye contact with Pleasure.

The crisis came in the middle of the third hour. We had just finished a hand in which I had won a considerable amount of money. I was lucky. I had held my own, even starting with the minimum buy-in. Pleasure was up $75,000. The Governor had lost and was betting wildly, backing bad hands hoping to bluff his way into a stack of chips. Jody and Cliff were holding their own. My beeper went off silently, and I stopped the slight vibration immediately. I didn't think it showed, but some pretty perceptive players were staring at me. A good poker player will notice even the slightest change in routine.

One major problem still remained. I was basically a billboard revealing my hand. I was so worried about my money I couldn't concentrate. As a consequence, if I got a good hand, everyone knew it. Even though I had stayed even, I knew I was no match for these pros. The blinds moved up and the cards were dealt. It was my turn. I bet $10,000 without looking at my pocket cards. Letting the cards lay made them all very anxious. There was a reason behind my madness. I was a neon sign of tells. One look at my cards and I felt everybody at the table would know what my hole cards were. If I didn't look, they had no way of telling what I was thinking. It was driving them crazy.

"Mr. St. Clair," said Drake, who had responsibility as the dealer to call attention to the small details of the game.

"Call me St. Clair."

"Those are your cards, sir." He pointed to the cards in front of me. Everyone looked at the face down cards and then turned their gaze to me.

"Yes, thank you."

"Don't you want to even take a peek?" said the Governor.

"Nope." I swung my head back and forth. I made no move. It was killing them. I started to like this game. I glanced at my beeper hidden beneath my coat jacket and saw what I expected: 711. Sheri was warning me as she'd promised. The warrant was out, and the Vegas cops were going to nail me. They probably would not figure I was playing under their noses in a black tie high-stakes poker game. This gave me a little time. But the police would for sure contact security here at the MGM Grand and Security would immediately spread the word. My only chance now was to leave the game without a commotion. With Pleasure and Jody in tow would be even better. A nightcap in my hotel suite might answer a lot of questions. The odds of leaving this table with these two beautiful women were as great as winning the lotto. Nearly three hours of playing had passed, and at one in the morning, it was time to call it a night.

"I'm sure, sir," said Cliff Barley, "that you would like to take a look at your hole cards before the round of betting. It does help, son, to know the full potential of the hand you are holding."

"I don't think so," I said.

"Pardon me," said Cliff, "if I may be so bold as to ask, but why would you not want to look at your cards?"

"Maybe I'll need it. Maybe I won't," I replied confidently while screaming inside you stupid idiot.

"You pulling a Maverick?" asked the Governor.

"I don't think so," I replied.

"I saw that movie," said Cliff. "I think he's pulling a Maverick."

"What's a Maverick?" asked Jody.

"Maverick was known to sometimes not look at his cards," Cliff said.

"Interesting," said Jody.

"Adds a bit of mystery into the mix," said Pleasure.

I just smiled. I was thinking about what my next move would be. I didn't have a clue. Jody was next to bet and she matched my bet, as did the others. The flop hit the table, two aces and a king. Everyone looked at the flop and then at me.

Two aces on the table, I thought. Someone could easily have another ace. Three aces a real possibility. I caught Jody's eye, and noticed that she had also caught Pleasure's eye.

All eyes were on me. "I'll raise another $20,000 as if I had all the money in the world. Actually, this was about all the money I had in the world, but nobody knew this pertinent fact. I placed the chips neatly in front of me, and met everyone's eyes evenly. I was full of confidence. I had no idea what I was doing, but it sure looked like I knew something they didn't.

"Sir," Cliff asked, "You sure you don't want to examine your cards?"

"Don't need to," I replied with a smile.

I caught Pleasure's eye and she forced back a smile. The pit boss and host were now hovering over the table. The Governor was agitated. Cliff was agitated. Was I bluffing? Probably, but you can't bluff if you don't know what you have. A technique probably not I covered in any book on Hold'Em poker. Not taking a peek at my pocket cards probably meant I was crazy. This had them confused. They were losing their train of thought. Everyone was in.

The Governor was sweating. He took one look at me and knew I was bluffing -- or was I? That's why he was sweating. I scanned the eyes of all the players, ending on the Governor. He was counting his chips and wondering what he should do. It was obvious he did not have a good hand. He should fold, but he didn't.

"I'm in," said the Governor. "And let's say, add another $25,000 to the pot, just to make it interesting." A stir of excitement went through the crowd when they heard the raise.

Pleasure tossed in $45,000. "I think you're bluffing, Mr. St. Clair. If nothing else, I need to know."

All bets in and the turn card hit the table. A seven. All eyes fell upon me again. I wondered how I had gotten myself into this mess. I paused and there was a great deal of silence. My two hole cards were sitting there, a mystery to all. I began to wonder myself what that last card held, not to mention the first two cards. I smiled a confident Fargo Blue smile, which was really my 'I'm in a whole bunch of trouble now' smile.

"I'm in." Without missing a beat I stacked $25,000 in front of me.

Jody observed Pleasure. If they were partners, it didn't matter whether she was in or not, unless she had the winning hand. "I'm in." She neatly pushed out two stacks of chips.

The table matched my bet and the river card hit the table. A king. Two kings and two aces on the table. Jody looked at her hand, Pleasure smiled and the governor frowned. Cliff Barley put his hands to his face. He needed a win. I was the only one safe, as I had no idea as to what I had.

It was up to me. "I'm all in." I counted $55,000 dollars and moved it out in front of me.

Jody folded.

Pleasure folded.

Cliff matched the bet and pushed the neat stack of chips into play in front of him. The Governor matched me and flipped over his cards and smiled as the third ace appeared. Everybody around the table figured the Governor for the high hand. I know I did.

Cliff Barley just dumped his cards in disgust. The focus of attention came back to me.

"Looks like it's time to play poker," I said. The tension mounted. I paused and then I flipped over my two pocket cards, exposing two kings, making four kings. I had won.

"Damn," said the Governor.

"Well I'll be," said Cliff.

Pleasure, who had moved forward on her seat in anticipation of the card, nodded her approval to me when I won. Jody put her hand on my shoulder. "Good for you. Congratulations. Interesting style. I'll remember that for a long time."

"I will too. But I'm afraid I'm going to call it a night. That's enough excitement to last me a long time."

The Governor, who was down by thousands of dollars, stood. "Ladies, I think I've had it also. It's been a good evening, and I'll look forward to another game with you all."

Everyone stood up. Handshakes all around. Cliff Barley looked straight at Jody and Pleasure, then nodded to them, as if giving a secret signal. Several casino hosts immediately started to secure the money. A marker was handed to me for well over $300,000. "Sir, this will be posted in your account. If there's anything the MGM Grand can do, please let me know." The host handed me a house card.

"Thank you."

Jody had already left and seemed to be following Cliff. I turned my attention to Pleasure. We were quite alone by then. "You play a mean game of Hold'Em St. Clair."

"I try."

"Well, you did all right. You won a nice tidy sum on the last hand. I'd like to try and win it back sometime."

"Perhaps. But right now, I've got another problem. Will you walk with me?" I asked looking around for any signs of Security.

She thrust her arm through mine and grabbed my wrist. We walked out of the poker arena, and into the crowd, which parted for us. "With you, I'll walk to the end of time."

"That's kind of where I'm headed," I said.

Thirty

PLEASURE AND I walked through the casino together, and I was relieved that the poker game was over. I would not want to do it again. Well, all right, I wouldn't mind winning the two-hundred thousand dollars, but I don't think I would ever be able to pull off a stunt like that again and win. A real poker player would be looking for a new game. Pleasure and I wandered.

"It appears that you have a knack for this game called poker," said Pleasure.

"I don't think so. Just wanted to get to know you better. I couldn't think of a better way than by playing some cards."

"Are you saying it was beginner's luck?" joked Pleasure.

"Not in the least. All skill. Planned the whole thing."

"That's what they all say when they win for the first time."

"I can understand that," I said. "Was it your plan to take the Governor tonight, or was it Jody's?" I caught a slight sideways glance from Pleasure, and then a smile.

"My, you are perceptive, aren't you?"

"That's my job."

"You're very good at it," said Pleasure.

"If you're thinking that I tracked Jody to the table, you're wrong."

"How did you know she would be there?" asked Pleasure.

"I didn't know. Just lucked out. What about the Governor?"

"What about him?" asked Pleasure.

"I think the Governor needed to win. I think the Governor is the one who owes you the money from your game in Los Angeles."

"He's the one."

"Has he paid you back?"

"Not yet. I believe him to be flat broke," said Pleasure.

"What are you going to do?"

"Jody should be with him right now. Care to join us?"

"Is this going to be a friendly visit, or are you going to beat the hell out of him?"

"Much worse than that," said Pleasure.

"I might as well tell you, I got a message during the poker game tonight...."

"I know," said Pleasure.

"How do you know?"

"Your whole body tensed up. I figured you had a beeper that buzzed. I saw you later look at something."

"Very observant."

"Thanks...."

"Anyway, the message was not exactly good news." I looked up and saw Peter Daily and another officer appear between two rows of slot machines. "Listen, would you care to make a run for it? I just spotted the cops and I think they're looking for me."

"Sure," said Pleasure. She grabbed my arm and we took a hard left directly into a hotel elevator. As the door closed I couldn't be sure we were not being followed. "We're we going?"

"Cliff has a room here for the evening."

"Okay. What floor is it on?

"The fifteenth."

"Sounds good to me," as I punched the button for the top floor and we were on our way.

"Why the top floor?" asked Pleasure.

"Once we get there, we'll take the next elevator down stopping at couple of floors on the way. Once we get to the fifteenth floor, we can hit about four or five floor buttons as we're getting out and they won't have any idea where we got off."

"Clever," said Pleasure.

"Keeps them guessing." I smiled at Pleasure and she returned a warm glowing smile that caught me completely off guard. I would have to remember she was a master poker player.

A short time later, Jody let us in to the hotel suite and smiled as we entered. "Congratulations, Mr. St. Clair. I enjoyed the game this evening. Maybe I will be more fortunate the next time we play. However, I don't think I have the nerve that you displayed this evening."

"To be honest with you, I don't either," and both Jody and Pleasure laughed, realizing that I was not the professional poker player I pretended to be. I smiled and glanced over at the Governor, who was sitting at a table holding a drink in one hand, his other arm strapped to the table. These poker players are serious about getting their money back, I thought to myself. I'd hate to owe them anything.

"Welcome," said Cliff, who walked up and greeted us. "Great game this evening. Pleasure, I'm glad to see you're here. We're about to start."

"I will have to ask, if I may, what is going on?"

"You know the Governor," said Pleasure. "He owes the three of us a considerable sum of money from previous games. Since Jody is leaving tomorrow, and the

Governor has not paid on his account, we're going to collect our share of the winnings."

I studied the Governor for a few seconds. He seemed more relaxed now than he had when we were playing poker. He took another sip of his drink, then nodded his head toward me, appearing agreeable about the whole situation.

"What's your feeling about this, if I may ask?"

"Well," said the Governor, "I have tried to convince our fine friends here that I could raise the money in the next couple of days, but I have failed."

"And how are they going to collect?" I asked.

"Here, feel this," said Jody, who walked over and rubbed the Governor's arm. I followed and could feel several lumps underneath his skin.

"What is that?"

"Diamonds," said Cliff. "Good ol' flawless diamonds."

"Diamonds!"

"We don't know how much it will get us in the market," said Pleasure, "but it's enough to start paying us back. Promises aren't worth anything if they aren't kept. He promised, then broke it. No more trust left."

Looking around. I was stunned by what I thought they were going to do. "So you're going to cut it out of his arm?"

"Yep," said Cliff.

"How did you get the diamonds in your arm?" I asked the Governor.

"Years ago. Instead of wearing a hustler's ring that anybody could steal, I had these diamonds sewn in my arm. One last chance. Once last poker game. After awhile they didn't bother me, and I never had them cut out."

"So now they're going to just slice open your arm and search for the stones?"

"That's what they tell me."

"Absolutely," said Jody.

"We've been waiting for this day for quite some time," said Pleasure. "This guy is a poker hustler who doesn't have a dime to his name. In the old days they would have taken him out to the desert and just shot him in a couple of unfriendly places, and that would have been the end of it."

"They'll do the same thing in Texas if they ever catch him down there," said Cliff. "Besides, he's into the hotel for over a quarter of a million. If we don't cut the diamonds out, someone else will."

Everybody turned and looked at the Governor, who nodded his head in agreement. Could you tell me, is this going to hurt?" asked the Governor.

"Yep," said Jody. "It probably will."

"Great, just great," said the Governor.

"I guess we might as well get this over with," said Jody, opening up a small handbag that had been sitting on the counter. She pulled out a bottle of alcohol and some large bandages.

"What kind of knife are you going to use?" asked the Governor. Jody immediately pulled out a dangerous-looking scalpel.

"That'll probably do it," said the Governor, starting to squirm a bit.

"You're really not going to do this," I asked. "You could easily take him to a doctor's office and have it done."

"We really don't have time for that," said Pleasure. Cliff and Jody agreed, and we all stood there and looked at the Governor.

"Listen," said the Governor. "Could I maybe have another drink? Might take away some of the shock when that knife cuts into my arm."

"I could certainly use a drink," said Pleasure.

"I could use one too," I said.

Jody walked over and pulled a bottle of Tequila from the portable bar. She grabbed five shot glasses and poured each glass to the rim.

"Here's to a successful operation," said Cliff, raising his glass in a toast. "May the diamonds be valuable, the pain short, with not too much blood." Everybody clinked glasses with the Governor, who was still tied up.

"Feel better already," said the Governor. "You know, you don't have to tie me up like this. It's not really necessary."

Pleasure stepped forward out of the little semicircle that surrounded him. "I think this will work out fine. This way you won't be jerking your arm when we cut into it."

"That's true," said the Governor.

"Now comes the question of the hour," said Cliff. "Who has the honors?"

"I think we should let the Governor decide," said Jody.

"Admirable idea," said Cliff.

"Only seems fair," said Pleasure.

We all studied the Governor and he studied us. "I think it would be appreciated that Mr. St. Clair, if I may call you that, be the one with the knife. He doesn't have a vested interest here."

"Me?" I squawked. "Now wait a minute. I'm just escorting Pleasure out of the casino. I had no idea I was getting involved in digging for diamonds."

"It's the only choice I have to make," said the Governor. "The others might just dig a little too deep, being that I owe them money and all."

"Nooo, I don't think so." I was starting to get nervous. A surgeon I'm not.

"Perfect choice," said Jody.

"I agree," said Cliff. "We need a neutral party to do the cutting."

"I don't think so," I repeated. These people had to be crazy. Cutting open a man's arm to remove some diamonds. I had never heard of such a thing. I was going to have to be more careful with the company I chose to keep.

Pleasure stepped forward. "Do it for me," she whispered. "I'd do it for you."

Yeah, I bet she would, I thought. "Well," I said, if anybody has to do the cutting, it might as well be me. It would give me something to think about, should I find myself in jail later in the evening. It would make a great jail story. Might keep my jail mates away from me, I thought.

"All right, I'll do it. But let's make it fast," I said as I took off my tux jacket and rolled up my sleeves. Jody poured alcohol over the blade while Pleasure gave another shot to the Governor, who was patiently waiting for this to be over. I had to admire the guy. He owed the money and he didn't have any qualms about how he was going to pay it back. I'm sure he wasn't crazy about the idea, but he was going along with it. Besides, he had to have known the surgery would eventually occur.

I grabbed the scalpel and studied the bumps that were right underneath the skin in the fleshy part of his arm. His arm was strapped to the table with his palm up, and it was easy to see what I was going to have to do.

"The only thing you want to do is not cut too deep," said the Governor. "There are some main arteries deeper down, but you should not be anywhere near them."

"How far down should I cut?"

"Less than an eighth of an inch."

"Do I have to make a cut for each stone?"

"No, I think you can squeeze them out once we get them started," said the Governor. "You should follow the outline of the diamond, but only cut about half of the outline. There shouldn't be too much blood."

"You've never seen me in surgery," I said.

"That's true."

I studied the faces of Jody, Pleasure, and Cliff. They were quite relaxed and enjoying themselves. I imagined they did this after every poker game. Being a poker player is a lot more dangerous than you can imagine.

"Here," said Jody, picking up a pair of rubber gloves and holding them out for me while I snapped them on. I held my hands up in the air like I was some kind of doctor about ready to save a patient in the ER.

"Hell of an evening," said Cliff.

"One to remember," commented Jody.

"I love diamonds," said Pleasure.

"Okay. Let's do this real fast," I said, looking around. Everybody seemed to be ready. Pleasure was heard sucking in air. The Governor closed his eyes. Cliff took another drink and Jody stood by ready to pour the alcohol over my pending incision. I studied them all again and figured what the hell. I shrugged my shoulders and got myself mentally prepared. Everything happens in Las Vegas. I was going to have to learn to take these things in stride. Tomorrow I might be called upon to perform knee surgery.

I made the first cut cleanly and was able to push a round two-carat stone out of the incision. It plopped on to the table all covered with blood.

"Pour some alcohol on it," Cliff said.

Jody poured alcohol on the diamond and every-body leaned forward to get a better look at it.

"My arm. The alcohol is for my arm, not the stone," winced the Governor.

"Sorry," said Jody. She poured some alcohol on his arm.

I tried to squeeze another one out, but it wouldn't budge. I made a second cut and the next diamond rolled onto the table. Two incisions and two diamonds. So far so good. I felt like I gave birth to twins. Surprisingly, there was not a great quantity of blood. I was getting into this. I had Jody pour more alcohol on the surgical blade and then I made the final cut. The third stone took a little more effort to remove, but it finally rolled out onto the table.

At that moment the door burst open and Olsen came rushing in, followed by a couple of his security guards.

"What the hell is going on in here?" screamed Olsen. We all turned to look at him, me holding the scalpel, Jody and Pleasure smiling their poker smiles, and Cliff grinning. The Governor just smiled. Of course, he was half-looped anyway.

"Nothing," said Pleasure. "Just an after-game celebration."

"Where's Fargo?"

I waved at him still wearing my surgical gloves. "Right over here," I said. Olsen took one look at the Governor and his expression was of pure horror.

"I thought his name was St. Clair," said Cliff.

"Somebody's got a lot of explaining to do," yelled Olsen. "And you, Fargo, you're just about buried."

"Nothing I haven't heard before," I commented. Behind Olsen swarmed a handful of police led by Peter Daily and Jack Johnston. It was easy for the hotel to find us in the Governor's suite of rooms, and had passed the information to Olsen and Daily. Jody and Pleasure stepped aside as the men stopped to look at the Governor.

"Greetings," said the Governor. "Care for a drink?"

"Not this evening," said Daily, who studied me, and then turned and faced Olsen.

Now Daily is going to let Olsen do the big bust and lead me out of the MGM Grand with my hands handcuffed behind me. I supposed Olsen had time to call the press and get them lined up. Out of the corner of my eye I observed Jody disappearing through the door.

"Vince Olsen," said Peter Daily. "You're under arrest for the theft of diamonds from McCaddy's and suspicion of murder."

"What?" screamed Olsen.

"We're placing you under arrest," said Daily, who signaled his men to grab Olsen's arms. Olsen was too surprised to put up any kind of fight. His hands were cuffed behind him.

"What grounds do you have for arresting me?" yelled Olsen. "What kind of crap are you pulling, Daily? I should have ended your career a long time ago."

"Your secretary found two bags of diamonds in your file cabinets. We also found your plane reservations to Rio. She turned you in."

"What?"

"You were headed to Rio, and I don't mean the casino."

"I have no intention of going to Rio," stammered Olsen.

"We have your checkbook and confirmed with Desert Travel that you purchased two tickets to Rio, and you paid by check."

"You're crazy," said Olsen, who looked at me. I knew what he was thinking before he even said it. "Its all Fargo's doing. He's the one setting me up. I'll get to the bottom of this and you'll be eating sand with the snakes."

"I'll have to say, Olsen, that you're looking dirtier than ever," I observed. "What security manager has the money to gamble at craps once a week?"

"I gamble once a week with my buddies. You don't have anything on me."

"I don't, but it looks like the police do." I put my arm around Pleasure. "And by the way, I would like you to meet Pleasure, my client."

Olsen was stunned. "Pleasure?"

Pleasure offered her hand to Olsen, which made him furious as he was cuffed.

"Yes. My client is very much alive. You should check into the Jane Doe that the coroner is holding." Pleasure snuggled next to me enjoying the attention.

"Why wasn't I informed of this?" snapped Olsen.

"Bad guys don't know everything," I said with just a hint of sarcasm.

Olsen started to put up a fight when I said that. No doubt he was going to lose his job as security manager for the MGM Grand. They led him, fighting, out into the hallway.

Peter Daily turned to us.

"Sorry this had to break up your evening." He walked over to where the Governor was sitting, still holding a drink, his arm strapped to the table. "What on earth is going on here?"

Pleasure moved forward. "We've just performed a little surgery on the Governor to remove a few diamonds from his arm. He owes us."

Daily turned to the Governor. "What do you have to say about this?"

The Governor raised a drink. "I have no problem with the arrangement. I've wanted to get these diamonds out of my arm for the last couple of years. Saved me the cost of going to a doctor's office. Insurance probably wouldn't pay anyway." Pleasure moved in and removed the straps around the Governor's arm and started to dab the small cuts with cotton and alcohol.

"So, you are not requesting any help from the police," Daily said. "Is that correct?"

"I have no need for the police. I'm okay. Drunk, but okay."

"And apparently poorer," replied Daily.

"What's going to happen to Olsen?" I asked as I looked around the room. I noted that Jody had not returned. Smart girl. Who needs all this attention from the police.

Daily turned back to me while Cliff helped the Governor up. "He'll be taken downtown and booked. He's got a lot of explaining to do. I would think a former cop would be smarter than to hide diamonds in his file cabinet."

"Diamonds," I said.

"Yeah, quite a few of them."

"Some thieves aren't very smart, just clever," I said.

"Sometimes clever is enough," said Daily, walking to the door. He turned toward me at the last moment. "And it looks like you're off the hook," he said indicating Pleasure.

Pleasure nodded to him, and he left.

I was grateful.

Thirty-One

I caught up with Daily and I was thrilled. It was like the parade of parades. Daily led the party down the hallway and into the elevator, followed by a uniformed police officer. The best part is that Vince was handcuffed. Detective Jack Johnston followed Olsen, and I, along with two hotel security guards, wrapped up the celebration. My job was complete. Olsen had placed the diamonds into Pleasure's safe. Olsen had the opportunity, being the head of security. We just had to find the motive, but I guessed that would be the easy part. Tony Botello would be pleased that his information was right on. The street always knows what's going down. Especially when it is a crooked cop.

We approached the elevator. I was having visions of being comped at the MGM Grand for at least two weeks. Time would only tell what I had uncovered. By the time the MGM Grand and the police finished their investigation into Olsen, they might come up with all kinds of stuff.

"Fargo, you're digging in the sand. Real deep."

I turned and faced Olsen. "You don't look so honest in handcuffs. Actually, you look like I always imagined you to look. Guilty, and on your way to jail."

"You're going to be surprised, Fargo. Real surprised," Olsen said.

"I love surprises." We exchanged stares as the elevator door opened.

The ride was uneventful. I smiled, Olsen scowled, Johnston did his detective thing, and the police officer watched both Olsen and the flashing numbers.

We reached the management floor, went past reception, down a hallway, and into Olsen's office. It was crawling with police and suits from the hotel. Lieutenant Daniel was impressive at six feet, two inches tall and weighing two hundred-ten pounds. His short-cropped springing-into-the-air hair and up-and-down-slanting eye brows was a surprise to most. "What have you turned up, Lieutenant?" asked Johnston.

"Plenty," answered Lieutenant Daniel. He picked up a small parcel and poured about thirty sparkling diamonds onto the table. "He's probably got more of it stashed around here."

"I've never seen those diamonds before," said Olsen in one of his tough-guy voices.

"Here we go," said another plainclothes policeman. He pulled a file drawer out a little farther and picked up another packet, then two more.

"My, my, my," said Detective Johnston. "Haven't we been busy."

"Look, I don't know what you're trying to pull here. But I assure you, I have never seen those diamonds before in my life. Somebody placed them there." Olsen spat the last few words.

"Keep it down," said Daily who had tight hold on Olsen's left arm.

"Everybody's innocent," I commented.

"You're getting in over your head," said Olsen. "The boys here are going to figure out that I had nothing to do with this, and then we're going to be looking at you real close. Jail-time close. Know what I mean?"

"I don't think you should be talking to us," I said. "I think you should be talking to your lawyer. And I would recommend a pretty good one."

"Cut the crap, Fargo. You know I wouldn't pull a stunt like this."

I turned toward Detective Johnston. "You got enough evidence for a Grand Jury hearing?"

"We'll see," said Johnston. "It's up to the D.A." He nodded to Daily and several of the policemen. With Daily leading the way, they escorted him out of the office.

"I hope the press is outside," I said as Olsen passed. "I had Sheri call them. I figure you'll be the lead story all day tomorrow. I know you like the attention."

"Screw you," said Olsen. "We're going to have a little talk as soon as I get out of jail."

"I'm going to retire in about twenty years, so I won't be around when you get out in thirty. If you get out."

"We'll see about that."

Thirty-Two

I couldn't believe it. I was standing facing Harry Lanning in his MGM Grand office bright and early Sunday morning. The night before we had taken the diamonds out of the Governor's arm. Beside me was Vince Olsen, who had just been released on bail by Lanning personally. How Olsen accomplished this, I had no idea.

As soon as Peter Daily had hauled Olsen out of the hotel for booking downtown, the party broke up quickly in Cliff's hotel suite. Pleasure had informed me my employment with her had ended. Jody had turned up, and with the diamonds I had cut out of the Governor's arm, Pleasure was more than paid back for the money she had won in the L.A. poker game.

Vince Olsen kept on screaming that I had planted the diamonds in Pleasure's hotel room, and in his office. I now knew how the diamonds got in Pleasure's hotel safe. Olsen had planted them there. But what I could not figure out was why the young lady was killed at poolside. The dart was probably meant for Pleasure. The only person who had any motive was the Governor, who was in deep with both Pleasure and Jody for some serious cash. Gamblers, for the most part, always owe money. The Governor was a stand-up guy, only he was broke. It was rumored he was having some serious meetings with the hotel over the unfortunate results of the poker game the night before.

Sheri had called my room at the MGM Grand bright and early Sunday morning informing me that Lanning wanted to see me in his office at eight sharp. This was unusual for Lanning to be in his office so early. I was expecting some praise and possibly a bonus. What I found was Olsen also waiting to see Lanning.

Lanning slammed down the phone.

"Which one of you idiots do I bring to the carpet first?" Lanning said. He was seething merely at the sight of us.

"What's the problem?" I asked. Every time I open my mouth my rule of silence falls by the wayside.

"What's wrong?" screamed Lanning. "Here I am running one of the most popular hotels in Las Vegas, and I've got two clowns giving me stories on how they didn't do this and didn't do that. I'm surrounded by idiots, that's what's wrong!"

"I don't understand," I said. "Olsen was arrested for the robbery of the Desert Sage and McCaddy's murder."

"What?" stammered Olsen. "Is that what you think?"

"Sure. It fits perfectly."

"Fargo," said Lanning.

"Yes, sir."

"The night that McCaddy was hit, Olsen and I were dining at my country club. He could have not been out robbing and killing, like you assume he was."

I was completely taken by surprise. "He was with you?"

"Sure, that's why I had to bail him out."

Olsen was smiling now. "And that still puts Fargo as prime suspect on the robbery and killing at Desert Sage. Not to mention the killing at poolside - whoever

256

that was. You're going down, Fargo. You're connected in some way."

Lanning ignored Olsen. "So how did the diamonds get into Pleasure's hotel room?"

Olsen and I both pointed at the other. "He did it!"

"I did not," said Olsen. "You're the one who had opportunity."

"You had the jewels in your office," I countered.

"I...."

"Cut the flak, both of you," said Lanning. "Your both in deep crap over this. Let's start from an interesting point of view," said Lanning. We stood and waited. "I don't think either of you committed any of these crimes."

Olsen and I eyed each other. I still thought he was guilty as hell. And I could tell from Olsen's expression that he didn't believe a thing I said either.

Lanning continued. "Now, as partners on this case...."

"Partners?" screamed Olsen. "He's not my partner!"

"Hey," I said. "Fargo Blue works alone. I've got a reputation to live up to. What's it going to be like for me to be seen with Olsen? We know what kind of a guy he is."

"You two guys are officially partners," said Lanning. "I've had enough of this fooling around. I've had enough of finding diamonds in hotel safes, in file cabinets, and everything else that's been going on. I want three things accomplished immediately. I want a reasonable explanation as to why we had a murder in the pool area. I want to find out who committed the robbery and murder at the Desert Sage, and I want to find out how those diamonds ended up in one of our guest's safe as well as your office, Olsen. That's it. You've got twenty-four hours."

"First of all," I said, "there's no way I will work with this loser. I work alone."

"Likewise," said Olsen. "I've got one of the best security teams in any hotel at my disposal. I don't need a former flatfoot to hamper my investigations."

"Well, I got news for the both of you. Olsen, you're dismissed as head of security until you answer those three questions."

"What?" Olsen screamed.

"Fargo, I'm holding your winnings from last evening and you will lose your comp privileges from this hotel if I don't have the answers in twenty-four hours."

"You can't put a hold on my winnings."

Lanning picked up the phone, dialed a number, and waited. "Jeff, this is Lanning. I want you to put a hold on an account...Mister St. Clair...The poker player from last night...Right...Yes, thank you." He slammed the phone down and looked at me.

I looked at Olsen and he looked at me. Damn, the luck of the draw. Only one thing for sure was that I hated Olsen a lot more than he hated me. I knew he had strong feelings about me, but he had no idea how much I didn't want to work with him. In the back of my mind I kept remembering my incredible suite of rooms, which I would like to take advantage of and just hang out in for awhile.

"Okay, you two are outta here. I've got work to do, and you've got to catch a killer."

Olsen and I found ourselves standing in the middle of a boxing ring in the MGM Grand's Garden Arena. It was set up for a heavyweight match that was being bantered around in the press as being the biggest fight of this century. Nothing like a good copy editor to put a little zing in your advertising. Advertise the event enough and it becomes the biggest fight of the century. The Grand Garden Arena has seen every type of performance Vegas could think of. What it guaranteed was couples dressed to the nines parading around the casino like they owned it. Of course it made the everyday tourist dressed in shorts a little envious of all the glamour, but that was all part of visiting Las Vegas. Neon lights and diamonds. What the nap sack-carrying tourists didn't realize is that the glamour guys and gals also were tourists and were spending a lot more money on their five days of fun-in-the-sun.

Olsen had taunted me to climb inside the ring, which was surrounded by armed guards who patrolled the area, making sure everything was shipshape for the fight in a couple of days. Olsen mumbled something about having never had the chance to stand in the middle of the ring, and this was as good opportunity as any. I glanced around at the work lights and imagined what it would be like to step into a ring like this in front of screaming fans. Whether you win or lose, it was worth anywhere from five, to thirty million, even if you got knocked out.

I turned to face Olsen and saw his fist about two inches from my jaw. It was the Mike Tyson of punches. A roundhouse slam that could have brought down a battleship. I staggered, and then slumped to the floor faster than Gabby Hayes does in a barroom fight. Great partner. As my head hit the canvas I kept thinking that if I had time, I would pull my .38 and blow him into a ring-side seat.

"That's for setting me up by planting the diamonds in my office," screamed Olsen as he stood over me. I kept waiting for my manager to run out and rescue me, but I figured it wasn't going to happen. I also knew I wasn't going to win any twenty million for hitting the mats like a two-hundred-pound sack of potatoes. Some security guards leapt into the ring and started to pull Olsen away, and he vented his anger and frustration out on them as well as on me. Once they realized he was head of security, they all backed off. They didn't know he was sort of fired. I crawled to my knees and tried to focus on the three Olsen's who were dancing in front of me.

"You got me on that one, boss," I said, trying to stand up, stumbling as I did so. "I figured those diamonds would hang you and I could go on with my life."

"That's what I figured," bellowed Olsen. "I want the whole story now, or I'm going to beat it out of you."

"Hey you guys! Out of the ring," yelled a cigar-smoking event manager. "Nobody plays around in my ring. I don't care who the hell you are."

Olsen grumbled and knew he was outranked. He looked at me in disgust, then started to climb through the ropes. That's when I hit him with my upper cut, which could be ranked as one of the greatest uppercuts ever thrown. It was the Tiger Woods of golf shots. It was the snap-crackle-pop of rice krispies. The snap was Olsen's jaw giving way, the crack was the sound of broken teeth, and the pop was Olsen's nose breaking in a smashing blow. I always wanted to know if Olsen was a bleeder, and I soon found out. It was good that he was wearing a cheap suit. Olsen was hanging on the ropes with one leg twisted and locked down. I shouted at him. "Just for the record, I didn't plant any diamonds in your office." It did no good. Olsen just groaned.

"Hey, you guys," yelled the event manager. "I don't care if you want to fight. Find a bar down on Fremont Street if you want to throw some punches."

I waved my understanding of the situation and un-twisted Olsen's leg from the ropes. He crashed to the stadium floor like the best of knocked out heavy weights.

A couple minutes later Olsen started to come around. He was holding his nose, which was bleeding profusely.

"You're screwing up my career, Fargo. I had you nailed a long time ago for all this stuff. Why don't you just take the fall and I can get back to work."

"Listen. You're the one who is stashing bags of diamonds in your filing cabinets."

"Not me," said Olsen.

"Then who...?"

"Listen. I just want you to know that I have no intention of working with you, Fargo. I don't like you. I'd rather go ten rounds with you than work with you. And I'd rather lose my job here at the casino than work with a has-been detective who now has his own agency and thinks he's in the big time."

"Just because you couldn't cut it on the force, Olsen, is no reason to get upset now," I replied through my hands, which were holding ice to my eye -- conveniently brought by one of the guards.

"I was a great cop," whimpered Olsen.

"Great at stealing stuff."

"I never stole anything."

"You were a one-man crime spree. All those times we were in single patrol cars. You were always answering the burglary calls on your own. Everybody knows the scam. You pick up some goodies on your first walk through and someone else gets blamed."

"Just doing my job, Fargo. I at least captured the crooks instead of filing away twenty years of reports of how they got away."

"I caught my share," I said.

"Remember who got promoted to detective first," said Olsen.

"Politics...all politics," I said as I slumped down next to Olsen on the hard concrete floor. I just hated the idea of working with anybody. That's why my card reads, Fargo Blue -- Detective. It doesn't say anything about a partner. Just detective. But I figured I would be a much better detective with my money in my account than in the teller's cage at the MGM Grand. "We've got to work together. Pool our information and figure this thing out."

"Not going to work, Fargo. I'm doing this alone."

"You can't afford to, Olsen. You're in bigger trouble than you care to admit. You might lose your job at the MGM Grand, and Lanning is not going to let you get hired by any of the casinos in this town. You might have to move to Atlantic City. Me? I just go on to the next case."

"I hate Atlantic City," Olsen said.

"Just think about all that snow in the wintertime." Olsen squirmed a few more minutes while trying to repair his nose, and then he started to come around.

"I suppose you're right...."

"Always am...."

"Cut the crap, Fargo!"

"It's a good thing I didn't give you my one-two punch," I informed him. Olsen just glared at me, hatred filling his eyes.

Thirty-Three

OLSEN AND I were comfortably seated at the Fiamma Trattoria & Bar. Comfortably might be a bit of an exaggeration. I had a black eye and the knuckles on my right hand were bruised. Olsen had a bandage below his chin where I had scored an upper cut. My body ached, and I suspected Olsen's did too, although he would never admit it.

Fiamma is one of the newest restaurants to open at the MGM Grand. Sleek, sexy and sophisticated, Fiamma Trattoria features signature dishes and hearty pastas. I figured in an Italian Restaurant we could yell a lot and no one would pay any attention to us. We could just wave our hands and everyone would think we were having a normal conversation. It was mutually decided this is where we would work out any disagreements between us so we could get on to the problem at hand: finding the "poolside killer" and the killer of McCaddy during the Desert Sage jewel heist. In some way all these events were connected to each other, but neither of us had put it together yet.

We both had to clear our names, although secretly I was happy they arrested Olsen. It evened the score. Olsen was out on bail, and his job at the MGM Grand depended upon his swift and speedy action.

I arrived early and located a seat where Olsen and I would be able to see the entrance of the restaurant -- a custom you learn in the private-eye game.

"You look well rested," I said. He didn't really look that good, but I wanted to be friendly.

"That supposed to mean something?"

"Listen, get off it. We're here to work."

"It doesn't mean we have to like each other."

"Well, I suppose it doesn't," I said.

I flagged down a passing waiter and we were served two steaming hot cups of coffee. We both needed it.

"Well, I know I didn't do it," said Olsen as he reached for the cream.

"And I know I didn't do it," I said. "You shouldn't use so much cream. It's going to kill you."

"I should worry about cream when I'm having lunch with you?"

"Go ahead, use the cream. Maybe that's the best way to solve this case. Here, have some butter." I picked up a small dish stacked high with butter squares and handed it to Olsen, who put it aside and smiled. It wasn't a happy smile, more like one you reserved for a light moment at a funeral.

In Vegas, a destination town for the rich and the poor, diets are non-existent. A tourist might diet all year, but when they hit this town they eat everything and anything. It's the nature of people.

The perky waiter arrived dressed in the traditional long white apron. Always sparking clean. If I worked here I'd go through three or four of those each night. The waiter seemed as if he was trying to look Italian. It didn't work. He looked like someone who had made it across the border in the middle of the night. Just then Olsen's cell phone rang. He answered and turned away to hear better, one finger in one ear, and the cell phone jammed in the other ear. I'm glad he wasn't driving. I thought I'd order.

"My friend here will have your fettuccini alfredo, double order, extra cream sauce. Throw in a half dozen garlic bread slices. He's a big eater."

"And for you, sir?"

"I'll have the chicken salad."

"Dressing for you, sir?"

"Low-fat Italian. On the side."

"Very well, sir."

"Oh, why don't you add some Italian sausage on the side with some freshly sautéed peppers. Don't want him to go hungry."

"He is a big eater, isn't he?" said the waiter as Olsen hung up the phone.

"I took care of your order for you. My treat." The waiter departed shaking his head.

"Thanks."

I took several papers out of my attaché case. "I've done some work. I went over a few reports and came up with a list of people who were at the various crime scenes."

"So, you're a list maker."

"It's a gene trait. You wouldn't know about it. It's generally connected with competence."

"Cute. I work with a comic."

I ignored Olsen. "I have three lists of people. One is a list of who appears to have had access to Pleasure's hotel room. The second is a list of people at the pool shooting."

"Pool shooting. Why that? Doesn't make any sense."

"Let me finish."

Olsen waved his hand in the air for me to continue.

"And third," I said, with a more of an aggressive voice, "are all the people who had access to the McCaddy crime scene. Take a look for yourself." I handed the paper over to Olsen.

As Olsen examined my notes I took a look at the wine menu. The waiter saw me and was hovering at my shoulder. "I would like a the 2001 North Coast Pinot Noir."

"Very good choice, Sir."

Olsen was absorbed in the list. "What do you think?"

"I have a hard time with lists."

Just then the wine arrived with a loaf of warm Italian bread. I went right for as Olsen grabbed another roll and slapped some butter on it as he started to read the document.

The waiter made a big scene of opening the wine which I tasted and approved. Then we got back to business.

"So, nothing here that I can see."

"That's the point. There is nothing but cops there, including you and me."

Olsen glanced at the sheet again, and then looked at me over his half glasses. "So you think some cop did it?"

"I think we're missing something, someplace, somewhere."

"I could have told you that a long time ago."

I ignored his comment. "The point is, the number of people who had access to the poolside murder scene were several hundred, according to the MGM Grand's records. The only people who had access to the Desert Sage, and Pleasure's room, were the police. Something's not right. I think the McCaddy killing is somehow tied to the poolside murder."

"You're crazy." He wadded up the paper and threw it at me. I made a great one handed catch. I was always good at sports.

"Consider this," I said in my most convincing voice. "If we find a connection, then it makes sense, doesn't it?"

"No. Doesn't make any sense."

"Well, consider this. I know I didn't do it. And you say you didn't do it."

"You better believe it."

"Okay, so I'm going to trust your word on this for the minute."

"I didn't do it!" yelled Olsen. His loud voice caused a couple of people to turn their heads.

I continued. "So we know for a fact, based upon our word as P.I.s and former Vegas cops, we didn't do it. Right?"

"Right."

"You're willing to shake on it?"

Olsen stuck his paw across the table. We shook hands. Maybe he didn't do it, I thought.

"So what do we do?" Olsen said.

"We start with the police. Perhaps there is something they haven't told us."

"They've told me everything," Olsen said in an accusing voice.

"You're sure? You're absolutely positive they've told you everything? If that's the case, you would have known you were a suspect."

"That's true. Think they're holding back something?"

"We always did when we were on the force. Only way to control the information."

"So we have to find out what they're not telling the public?"

"Right," I said.

"Okay, I can buy that," said Olson. "Makes sense that they wouldn't tell us everything."

"So how do we start?" I asked.

"Carefully. Very carefully."

The waiter appeared with an abundance of food. He served Olsen's fettuccine alfredo with a flourish. The plate was steaming hot and the aroma of the garlic bread floated through the air. The smell of the rich alfredo cream sauce and garlic was killing me. This was followed by the Italian sausage and sautéed green sweet peppers. Lastly, my chicken salad was put in front of me with an attitude that suggested I personally had insulted the chef.

"Fresh pepper?" The waiter waved the peppermill as if ready to Knight us. He should get a job across the street at the Excalibur, I thought to myself.

"Look at this," exclaimed Olsen. "I've never seen so much cream sauce." He turned to the waiter. "No, I don't want any pepper." His voice was a little too loud. He turned to me. "What are you trying to do, kill me?"

"Never occurred to me."

"What are you having?"

"Fresh chicken salad with low-fat dressing on the side."

"You're trying to kill me...."

"You don't exactly act as my best friend." I pressed a little further, picking up the butter dish. "Have some butter."

Olsen's look could kill. He suddenly got up, acquired another plate from a passing waiter, and dumped half the fettuccine on to it. Then he grabbed my salad and dumped half of it on his plate. Following this he grabbed several garlic rolls and tossed them to me. Not satisfied, Olsen got up again and split up the sausage and green peppers.

"Eat. If you don't, I will kill you," he said seriously. He waved at the waiter. "Bring a side of blue cheese dressing, enough for two. And bring a slab of blue cheese for the both of us. There, that should do it. You can die right alongside of me."

We both dug into our food. I had to admit it; the fettuccine was the best.

"So, what's the next move?" I asked.

"I think we should visit Las Vegas Metro."

"How are we going to make a visit when we're both suspects?"

"Go in and hope for the best," said Olsen.

The blue cheese dressing arrived along with two slabs of rich blue cheese. Olsen stabbed one with his fork and kept right on talking. He never missed a beat. I had a feeling I had missed a lot of good meals with Olsen. Perhaps he and I were going to be good friends after all. I stabbed the other hunk of blue cheese, doing my best to imitate Olsen.

"Next, how is everything connected?"

"The pool killing, Pleasure, the jewel theft and murder?"

"Right," I said, my mouth full of fettuccine.

"Maybe the target wasn't Pleasure."

"If that's the case, this is a bigger problem than we both suspected. Have you seen the autopsy report of the woman killed by the pool?"

"No, but it should be in my office by now."

"Okay. We'll start there."

"What's next?" said Olsen, tearing off another piece of garlic bread.

I grabbed one too. I didn't want to be left out. "I think we have to consider how the jewels got into the safe."

"That's nothing. How did they get into my file cabinet?"

"If you didn't put them there...."

Olsen started to turn about thirty shades of red.

"...And I know you didn't put them there," I continued,

"Then someone did. And that someone was either very good, or had inside connections."

"Or both."

"True. Or both. Perhaps we need to talk with the

office manager up there to see if there was any unusual activity."

"Let me ask you a question, Fargo. In your best estimation, how many people did it take to shake down the Desert Sage?"

"I would say a minimum of two. Awfully big job for one. Lots of details."

"That's what I think. Had to be one person pulling the strings, setting everything up, and another that goes in." Olsen poured on the blue cheese dressing.

"And we don't really have any crime scene forensics to back us up. Not a lick. Scene was as clean as they come."

"There's always something."

"True."

"Right, so that means we're after two people. At least two people."

"And they're pros," I said.

"Yep, we're dealing with professionals," Olsen said.

"And that means it's going to be a tough case to crack. And I mean tough. These guys are good, and they're not helping us any. Any chance we could run the MO through the various bureaus?"

"Possible. Let's put it down. What's next?"

"Perhaps we should run a decoy and flush them out."

"How so?"

"Let's drop by Metro to, say, inspect the diamonds."

"Do we act like we're the best of friends, Fargo?"

"In front of those guys? Nope, it would be out of character."

"So you're going to be your usual asshole self," said Olsen.

I ignored the remark. "We drop a hint that the accomplice to the Desert Sage robbery has indicated that they're going to turn over their partner, and the accomplice wants you, as head of security, to bring them in to headquarters and to arrange protective custody."

Olsen took one last sip of wine. "Okay, what does that buy us?" as the waiter to clear the table. We're probably the only people in the restaurant who actually ate all their food. And I mean everything.

"We'll just see what happens."

"Okay."

"So let's tag onto the story that this accomplice doesn't want the police there."

"Good," Olsen said. "I like it. We'll be firm. No police."

"Anything else?"

"Like what?" challenged Olsen.

"We plant a second story."

"A second story. I like that."

"I have a street contact. We'll plant gossip that the diamonds from the Desert Sage robbery are going to be delivered to the MGM Grand tomorrow morning at ten o'clock."

"Then we'll wait and see what happens."

"Right. But we're taking it one more step."

"I'm afraid to ask."

"It's like this. We're going to plant a story that we have photographs," I said.

"Good idea. Photographs make people nervous. You're all right for an ex-cop, but I don't trust you for a second."

"Thanks. I'll be watching you're every move, but I think we can still work together."

"We have to. I don't want to, you understand."

"I understand. Now we've got stories to plant, and police stations to visit."

"Right. Work," said Olsen.

"Think of it as keeping us out of the slammer."

We left the restaurant and ambled through the casino. The food was doing its work, and moving around was particularly difficult. Real food really slows you down. We took the elevator to casino business floor where Olsen's private office was located. It had a one-way mirrored window that overlooked the casino gambling floor. Without sound it presented an odd picture.

"Nice view."

"Yeah, not bad. Helps to keep track of things when we got something going down. I can get from here to the secure section above the casino floor. But it takes awhile even for the head of security."

"Must be a complex system?"

"Mostly videos now. But you still have to have the pros watching for the card sharks. They're always trying."

A beautiful smiling face appeared from around the corner. I was introduced to Olsen's beautiful administrative assistant named Sheila. Her smile was framed by hair the color of autumn that accented her freckles. "Coffee, gentlemen?"

"No thanks," Olsen said. "We just ate the entire dinner menu at Fiamma Trattoria. If I had anything else, I'd explode. How about you, Fargo?"

I held my hands in the air. "I'm with you. Couldn't eat or drink anything else."

"Okay, just yell if you need something. I'm right here."

Olsen was right. My metabolism was slowing down to a point where I think I could hardly move. It felt like the alfredo cream sauce had just entered my blood stream. Probably why they call fettuccine heart-attack-on-a-plate. Olsen looked worse than I did.

Olsen tossed me the autopsy report. "Here, check this out. I'm going to check personnel before their shift ends." He walked out of the room with a little bit too much energy. I bet he was faking.

I settled into the couch that gave me a good view

of the casino floor. People were moving about. New people were arriving, while others were preparing to leave. I started to read the autopsy report that had just been released by the medical examiner. As I labored over the details, the couch became uncomfortable. So I lay down, propped my head up for reading, and continued. No question about it, I fell sound asleep. Dead to the world.

I was dreaming I was on a sand-covered beach. White sand and aqua water. Pleasure and Jody were running up out of the surf topless. Beaded water dripped off onto my chest in slow motion. Pleasure began poking me in the ribs. The more she poked, the more I dreamed.

"Fargo!" yelled Olsen. "I can't go away for ten minutes without you falling asleep."

"Damn." Good dream, bad ending. It had been Olsen hitting me in the ribs. So much for Pleasure and Jody. I made a mental note to eat more fettuccine.

Thirty-Four

OLSEN AND I headed downtown and reviewed the autopsy report as we drove. I was fully awake and had started to come out of my stupor. My short Sunday afternoon nap had not helped to digest the food. More simply put, I felt like I was going to explode. The oversized meal didn't seem to phase Olsen a bit. Either he was putting on the biggest act in the world to make me look bad, or the guy was superhuman, able to eat large Italian meals in a single sitting. I feared the latter.

Olsen, at the wheel, said, "Well, we didn't learn anything in the autopsy report. Nothing unusual except it was a poison dart gun of some sort."

"Peculiar MO I wonder if the police put it through the computer. Seems like we'd hear about that kind of killing if it had happened before."

"I checked. Nobody in Las Vegas has gotten murdered with a poison dart. Of course, there are a lot of bodies buried in the desert and we don't know how they died, but I'd put poison darts low on the list."

Olsen pulled into the side lot for visitors. Each of us had lost parking privileges when we left the precinct. We were waved though after getting visitor's badges. Upon entering the detective's bullpen we received the usual waves and disgruntled remarks. Several hookers were being booked from an undercover operation, which tends to keep everybody awake. It always made for an interesting scene.

"You two the best of buddies, I see," said Charles "Cookie" Bentley. Cookie was one of the senior detectives, now that I had left. He favored western boots and lots of cookies. Few people had ever seen him eat a regular meal. Lean in figure, with a face as rough as they come. On several occasions he has easily been mistaken for the robber who had just pulled a heist. His claim to fame was making a big bust several years ago when he was able to pull together a motive from an almost impossible abduction case. He liked to think through a case before taking action.

"I'll never be the best of buddies with this scumbag," said Olsen as he shot Cookie the finger.

"How about you Fargo? All love and kisses with your partner?" teased Cookie in the midst of some general heckling and laughter.

Taking my cue from Olsen, I said, "I only work with the real losers. You guys don't even come close." Olsen gave me a dirty look.

"Why are you guys here? I understand you're both about to be busted for various crimes, misdemeanors, felonies, etc." Laughter from the gang.

"We're here to look at the evidence from the Desert Sage robbery," I said.

"Going to see if the diamonds match the ones you got?" More laughter.

I made a move toward the bastard but Olsen stopped me just before I nailed him a good one. "I should bust the guy just out of general principles."

"Save your energy," said Olsen. He pulled on my jacket and dragged me toward the stairway leading to the evidence room on the lower floor.

"You guys can't look at that stuff without our authorization," yelled Cookie. Olsen was heard to be yelling something about kissing something he owned. The boys loved it. Made their day.

We proceeded down the stairs and into the bowels of the building. The green and white linoleum floor had taken on a beige and brown color over the years, and the room smelled of floor wax that had been repeatedly applied, layer after layer. Each door in the hallway bore old-fashioned safety glass with chicken wire embedded in it. This was either to keep people out of the offices, or to keep the detectives trapped inside.

We entered the evidence room. "Need to see the Desert Sage evidence collection," I announced.

"You boys were the last ones I expected to see here," said Brent Jacobs, an old timer assigned to the evidence room. He took his job seriously, which wasn't going to help us any. "You're going to need to get some signatures with those I.D.s."

Daily walked into the room. "How did you get in here?" He waved Brent out of the room.

"We have come to observe good police work, to take a look at the evidence, and to generally gear up for tomorrow's action," said Olsen.

"Oh, so what's going to happen? You're going to catch the bad guys?"

"Yep," said Olsen.

"How? Give me an education."

"Well, it's not going to be that easy," I said. "But that's the general idea."

Olsen stepped forward, as I knew he would. "What my gay friend here is trying to tell you is we have made contact with an accomplice who is going to turn themselves in, to guess who. You're looking at heroes in the making. And when we do, and after we talk to them on official MGM Grand business, we will eventually, and I do mean eventually, bring them in under protective custody."

Daily was agitated. "You can't do that."

"And why is that?" I asked. "Which part don't you like?"

"It's police business. We'll throw additional charges and pull you in."

"We'll tell you what we think you ought to know," said Olsen.

Daily ignored Olsen. "I want to know where."

"Where?"

"Where you're going to meet the alleged accomplice."

"Why?"

"I have to be there! It's my job. It's what I get paid to do."

"But you don't know where," I interjected.

Daily was now beet red and pissed. "Listen, you can't just go around playing cops and robbers like this. You have to bring us in. Otherwise we'll get you for obstruction of justice and get you off the street."

"No," I said right in Daily's face. "That's our job. We're both P.I.s. We investigate matters of interest to our clients. And right now, we're the clients. It's obvious that you can't do your job. You couldn't find a con in a prison."

Olsen stepped in and broke us up. "Listen, don't take what my friend says seriously. He's good but he's not that good. We came here to look at the Desert Sage evidence. Sign us in, and it's not a question. I'm telling you to."

Daily wheeled around and stalked out. You could hear Daily yell at Brent out in the hall. "Give them what they want."

Olsen turned toward me and whispered, "Think we came on too strong?"

"Nope," I whispered back. "He just wants to make the bust. We'll bring him in when we need to. It's our show right now. Daily's a good guy. He's under a lot of pressure."

"Aren't we all? How come you didn't tell him where the meet was going to be?"

"We'll drop that as another clue in the net. Somebody will pick up on it."

Brent walked back in and shoved a clipboard at Olsen.

"Sounds good," said Olsen, signing for the evidence. Since it was valuable, it was in the safe, and we had to go to a special room where the contents were placed on a table. Brent, the evidence man, stayed with us. Each diamond had been accounted for, as each alone would be a magnificent contribution to anyone's retirement fund -- particularly a cop's.

We went through the diamonds. Some of the stones were loose, while others were in special waxed slips of paper common to the diamond industry. Notations on the outside of the packets indicated grading, color, and a buy date. The rest of the evidence consisted of crime scene photos, fibers from an unknown garment, dry glue from the safe's door, and other evidence all numbered and catalogued. Nothing special.

The photos revealed a sprawled-out McCaddy, who had come to rest with his head against a drawer that had been ripped out of the wall. He was dressed in a very nice suit, and had a flower -- a red rose in the lapel. His shoes were highly polished and had small specks of blood on each shoe. Cuff links, expensive-looking ones with diamonds clearly showing, were neatly in place. I wondered if this was his regular wardrobe, or was he dressed up for something special. I would have to find out. Details led to clues.

Then we looked at the inventoried list of Jody's luggage, and then examined the contents. Nothing out of the ordinary.

"Had enough," I said to Olsen in a low voice as I examined the last of the photos.

"Yeah," said Olsen. "It will take us a month of Sunday's to find the one clue that gets us off the hook. We don't have the time."

Thirty-Five

I slid into the passenger seat and Olsen took the wheel. He pulled up sharply at the police-parking exit, long enough to make sure everything was clear, and then he hit the gas. He made a sharp left and accelerated into traffic.

"Makes you stop and think when you start to add everything up, doesn't it?" I observed.

"In this game, I don't like to think."

I gave him a look. "Can I quote you?"

"No, you can't quote me. What I meant to say is you never know until you know." Olsen turned onto the Strip.

"Let's put phase two into motion," I said as I dialed Tony Botello's number. He came on the line instantly. The world of cell phones has made it so easy to keep in touch with the pimps, con men, and general sleaze bags you need in this business.

"Who's this?" said Tony.

"Your best friend when you're in trouble."

"Is that you, Fargo?"

"Yeah. Listen, I got some news for you. I want to spread it around."

"Costs money to do that."

"How much?"

"Depends upon the news."

"How much?" I asked being a bit more firm.

"A hundred."

"Good. Here it is. The diamonds from the Desert Sage jewelry heist are going to surface at the MGM Grand tomorrow at ten A.M. Got that?"

"Yep. I'll repeat it. Fargo Blue says the hot ice is going to melt at the Green Corner at ten tomorrow."

"Good, but drop my name."

"That's going to cost you extra, Fargo."

"You are the biggest slime ball I've ever dealt with."

"It's a way of life. You'll learn to love me over time."

"Okay. I'll throw in another hundred."

"That's what I like to hear. A businessman, making deals, making money, making my day. When do I get paid?"

"I'll take care of you when I see you."

"That's going to cost. Throw in another fifty and I'll carry you, no interest"

"You're a real businessman."

"That's me. Think of me as a consultant. Say, didn't I tell you? I was right on the money. Olsen. He's the one. Just like I said. Bad cop. They'll love him in the joint. People waiting for him up there. They're getting in line and selling positions."

"Later, Tony."

Olsen glanced at me as he caught the tail end of a yellow light. "What did he say?" He hit the accelerator and the car almost went airborne.

"He sends his love."

We headed back to the MGM Grand and decided to split up. Olsen was going to snoop around his office, and I was going to plant another seed. I walked over to the Sports Bar. And as I suspected, Uncle Leo was playing the ponies. I like a lawyer who is dependable.

"Afternoon."

Uncle Leo looked up and raised his eyebrows, forming deep furrows on his forehead. He was reviewing the morning line and checking it against his own system. One of many. "And the same to you. I hear you and Olsen are now the best of friends."

"Not quite the best, but we're working together."

"Good. Why don't you sit down? Play a few races. Enjoy."

"I've got a lot of work to do."

"Listen. Take it from me. You can't play the horses in the joint. Relax a little bit."

"That's not what I hear."

"Yeah, but not with this ambience." He motioned to the surrounding scene.

"Television monitors everywhere featuring race tracks all over the United States, a deli just off to the right, beer delivered right to your table...what more do you want?"

I sat down.

"Rumor is they're going to renovate this whole place."

"Again? I don't think so."

"I heard about the pool, but not the Sports Bar."

"Who knows? Every year they do something different."

I looked at his scratch pad filled with mystical numbers. "Which system today?"

"The usual. I handicap based upon their last four outings. Are they moving up in class, or coming down after a win?"

The monitor showed two minutes to post time at Belmont.

"Time to bet. Are you in?"

I followed Uncle Leo to the betting area, all the time keeping an eye on the tote board. I got in line and was able to place a bet with about ten seconds to spare. I went over to the Sports Bar and picked up two drafts.

Might as well enjoy the event. After a short wait, I turned around and saw the horses rounding for home. Looking good.

I shoved the draft beer in an iced mug toward Uncle Leo. "My treat."

He tore up his tickets in disgust. "Why your treat?"

"I wanted to say thanks for meeting with Darlene McCaddy. And besides, winners always pay."

"You won? How did you pick that twenty-to-one shot?"

"Simple. I picked the twenty-to-one shot."

"Purposely?" He sounded stunned.

"Yep. I bet all twenty-to-one shots to win. If there are three, I bet them to win. If there are only two, I bet them to win and to place. And if there is only one, I bet them to win, place, and show."

"I've heard of a strange part of society betting that way. But never really met one."

"That's me. On this one I played her across the board. Might have picked up some change on that one."

Uncle Leo was shaking his head.

"So, since I'm buying, I need a favor."

"I already did you a favor."

"You're right. How did that go?"

"Fine. Mrs. McCaddy will be okay. I've got the Desert Sage attorneys running around in circles to please her."

"Thanks."

"What's the next favor? I know. Don't tell me. You want me to keep you out of jail."

"Nope. A lot simpler than that. I want you to drop a piece of information on the street."

"What do you want dropped?"

"That the dart gun used in the poolside killing is going to surface in the casino tomorrow at around ten A.M."

"No kidding."

"Yep. No kidding."

"How do you know that?" asked Uncle Leo.

"I don't. It's a trap. Olsen and I are going to try and smoke out a suspect."

"I see. And who's the suspect?"

"Do you really want to know?"

"Yep. It might help me catch the killer if you happen to get whacked."

"A lot of faith in me, I see."

"No, just an old wise lawyer doing his job. So who's the suspect?"

"We really don't know yet. Just testing the waters."

"Why is it I don't believe you?"

"You've just known me too long."

"Mistakes happen," Uncle Leo said.

Over the next three races and two beers, I proceeded to update Uncle Leo on our plan of filling the streets with some phony facts just to see what happens.

"These are desperate times," Uncle Leo said.

"That they are."

"Anything else I can do?" he asked.

"Nope. Just be careful if you're over here tomorrow in the morning. It might get interesting."

"It's already interesting. I just want it to get uninteresting."

I looked up and spotted Pleasure walking toward the poker area. I waved and she headed in my direction. She was some package. She was dressed in black again, and her hair actually glowed.

"It's good to see you," I said. "We have some things to discuss."

"Yes, I know." She leaned over and gave me a peck on the cheek. I felt like a hero. "Why don't you buy me a drink and we'll talk."

"Sounds good to me. But first..."

"I know, the famous Uncle Leo," Pleasure said.

Uncle Leo stood up and bowed. "It has been a long time."

"And I feel like I owe you a lot," Pleasure said. She leaned over and gave Uncle Leo a kiss on the cheek.

"That's enough. I don't feel like sharing right now," I said. They both laughed.

The announcer broke the silence with the quarter turn, and the sound in the casino sports arena picked up.

Leo gave a short wave and was back to his racing form. "Go on. I've got work to do," he said.

I escorted Pleasure out of the Sports Bar area and we headed toward Starbucks Coffee next to the Studio Lounge. I ordered two coffee lattés, and we found a couple of seats.

"I do appreciate your help," said Pleasure.

"I've still got a way to go before this is all over."

"Did they find out how the diamonds got into my safe?"

"No. But they arrested Olsen."

"Why?"

"Diamonds turned up in Olsen's files and in his desk."

"That can only mean an inside job."

"True. But it can also mean that someone is clever at making things appear different from what they really are." Pleasure sipped her coffee. "Have they questioned you?"

"Yes," Pleasure said. "They questioned me right after the incident in Cliff Barley's room, and told me not to leave Las Vegas."

"Are you going to leave...?"

"No. I checked out of the MGM Grand and into the Rio. Officially. That's where I'm at now."

"Are you playing tonight?"

"Yep. That's all I care about. Another hand. One more chance."

"That's the only thing you care about?"

Pleasure's smile was brilliant. "No. I do care about other things."

"Like...."

"Timing. Timing can be everything."

"True."

"So, you have completed your contract. Jody showed up. We got our money back. I appreciate your help."

"Thanks. How long are you going to be around here?"

"I'll be here for a while yet. This place grows on you."

"Particularly if you're winning."

Pleasure smiled.

"You are winning, aren't you?"

"Yes, I am."

"What happened to Jody?"

"She's long gone. As soon as we got our money and the diamonds from the Governor, she left. Said she had enough of this place."

"It happens."

Pleasure stood up to leave, and I did the same. She put her arms around my neck and looked up at me. She was completely oblivious to the people, the casino, everyone around us. She possesses one key essential to being a poker player. She can concentrate.

"I'll probably see you again," I said. "I know I will. But I want to say thanks. If you need help, call me. I'm at your complete disposal. Anytime. Anywhere."

She kissed me. Call it a retainer.

Thirty-Six

I had been up too many hours, and stress was beginning to take its toll. A black and white art deco pattern stared at me as I tried to focus on it through fuzzy eyes. It was early Monday morning. In front of Olsen and I were mounted about thirty monitors that covered all the entrances and exits of the MGM Grand covering the entire gambling floor. Larger color monitors were used when they want to zoom in on suspicious activity.

Troll had a crew handling technical support. With the push of a button, cameras could be moved to focus on one particular table or player.

We were in the video monitoring control center, the backbone of the security operation for the MGM Grand. The video cameras worked hand in hand with the floor personnel who roamed the casino keeping watchful eyes on all the tourists that chose this carpet joint to drop their money in.

Technology changed Las Vegas more than people realize. The only hitch to this electronic wonderland is the cameras are only as good as the operators who sit hour after hour watching for any signs of trouble. If a crap table is winning big, the cameras focus on the hands of anyone who touches the dice. Anybody trying to bring new dice into the game with a palm switch would be spotted immediately. Sophisticated video recorders taped everything for future use.

It is a common fact that even with the most elaborate measures taken to make sure the dice are honest, there is always somebody who thinks they can put a phony set of dice into a game. The players watch to see what numbers come up, and the pit bosses watch how the dice spin and tumble. Any sign of something unusual, the dice are inspected right away. Throw a set of dice off the table and an army of eyes arrives to check for any kind of switch.

We had been at it since four A.M. Waiting. Killing time. Making small talk. "Hey Olsen, did you find anything out about who planted those diamonds?"

"Enough to know I've been screwed. Seems there was a strange visitor a couple of days ago that took an unauthorized tour of the facilities. I think that's when the diamonds were stashed."

"So, who did it?"

"I haven't the foggiest. I think a female did the plant, but I don't know who hired her."

"A female? Any description?"

"One that really doesn't help. Brenda now feels the lady was a complete phony. She suspected a wig all along. But you don't just walk up to someone and say, hey, nice-looking wig."

I glanced at Olsen's hair, then back to the monitors.

Olsen gave me another dirty look. "Screw you, asshole."

I laughed. "Well, it could be worse."

"How could it be worse?"

"What if they suspected only you and not me?"

"Yeah, you're right. That would be worse," said Olsen.

I laughed again, then saw Olsen tense up.

"Oh oh."

I turned my eyes to his monitor. "What have you spotted?"

"I've got him," commented Olsen.

"Who?"

"Daily!"

"Daily? You're kidding. Where?"

Olsen pointed to the third monitor from the left. "He's in the shopping arcade."

"What's he doing in that part of the casino? How did he get there? I didn't think there were any entrances on that side."

"Just employee entrances. I should have guessed somebody would try something like that," said Olsen.

"Notice he's dressed as a tourist...."

"Yeah, I caught that." Olsen picked up a walkie-talkie. "Crew twelve. We've got our party spotted in the arcade and moving toward the casino. Move to positions four, five, and seven." A crackling of radios were heard.

"Not very clear."

"They're just clicking to let me know they heard the news. Look at that."

"What?"

"Troll, could you get us a closer view?"

"Sure, boss."

"What's going on?" I asked.

"Check this out." Olsen snapped on a large monitor. Daily's back was to the cameras.

"There's Daily, but I don't see anything unusual."

"Wait till he turns around...there...see it, the cord?"

"He's wearing an ear piece," I exclaimed.

"I'll bet you dimes for quarters he's listening to us."

"He's trying to come in undercover."

"Yeah...that's what he's doing all right. Watch this." Olsen turned to the Troll who was busy tracking Daily with the video cameras. "Give me a wait-and-see scenario for the Wolfgang Puck's."

"Right," said the Troll.

"What the hell is a wait-and-see...?"

"Just hang on," Olsen said.

"This is control. All units approach and watch Wolfgang Puck's for a possible nine-seven," said the Troll.

There were five cameras trained on Daily. As soon as the Troll made his announcement, Daily turned to his left toward the Wolfgang Puck Bar and Grill.

"He's listening," said Olsen. "Otherwise he never would have turned in that direction."

"What are we going to do?"

"We'll put a wrinkle into his listening." Olsen picked up the hand mike. "All units. This is a nine-seven. Move to channel twenty-three. Possible conflict."

"What does that mean?" I asked, more and more impressed with Olsen's ability to handle the situation. It was impossible to know all of the internal codes of every casino.

"The nine-seven means not to pay any attention to what follows. Look at Daily. He's trying to switch to channel twenty-three. He's starting to listen now." Olsen turned to the Troll and nodded his head.

"All clear on the floor," said the Troll. "All units resume normal patrol. Will stay on this channel until further notice. All clear now."

"That will hold him for awhile," said Olsen. "Keep up the chatter." The Troll nodded and continued with security info, which Daily monitored.

"So Daily thinks he's now on the right security channel?"

"Yep. He has no idea we're onto him. We can now bring in more undercover people if we have to. But right now we can watch him anywhere in the casino."

"Have to say I'm impressed, Olsen. It's no wonder you were able to track me when I was walking through the casino. I just can't figure out how you picked me up."

"That was easy," said Olsen. "It was your hands."

I looked at my hands. "I don't get it."

"The ring you wear on your left hand."

"So...."

"You are the only person I know who wears a Hong Kong Jockey Club ring in Vegas. Plus the fact you always hang out in the Sports Bars. Never in any other part of the casino. We watched only those people who sat down in the Sports Bar. After that, I just got a close-up of your hands and spotted your ring."

"You're kidding...."

"Yep. Pretty good outfit, if I do say so myself."

"Felt like a tourist...."

"Looked like one too," said Olsen, studying the monitors. "We won't even talk about your use of a cellular phone in the Sports Bar. Any other day we would have busted you for that one."

I smiled knowing he had me dead to rights.

Olsen moved toward the monitor. "Daily's on the move again. He's now walking past Wolfgang Puck's and is headed into the main casino."

"He's headed for the jewelry shop," I said.

"I think you're right."

"Should we join him?"

"Not yet," said Olsen. "Let's see what he actually does."

We watched Daily as he made his way through the gaming area. He walked casually, but you could tell there was something on his mind. He wasn't watching the action of the tables. He seemed to focus more on the people around him. Two uniformed security officers walked by, and Daily turned to his left and pretended to be interested in some slot machines. Once they passed he turned and continued to walk until he eventually took a seat at an open Bar.

"What do you think?" I asked Olsen.

"He's waiting for somebody. Now the question is, who and why? How did he know the bust was going down at the MGM Grand?"

"He picked it up on the street," I said.

Olsen looked at me. "He's in my court, and if he wants to play, we'll just have to give him a game."

We both got up at once. "Suits me fine. Been wanting to have a little talk him."

"Watch him, Troll. You'll see us make our approach." We headed for the door.

"Just a minute," said Olsen. He crossed the room, picked up the phone, dialed a number, and proceeded to have a quick conversation with somebody. I watched the monitors. Daily had ordered a drink, but was not sipping it. Olsen hung up the phone.

"Just called the watch commander. Daily is supposed to be investigating a robbery of a furniture company."

"Looks like our boy is not paying attention to his job."

"Let's have a talk," said Olsen as we exited the security offices. It took us only a couple of minutes to make our way across the casino, where we picked up Daily still sitting at the open Bar.

"How do you want to attack this?" I asked. "Friend or foe?"

"I think he's on enemy ground. I think we should lay into him and see what kind of reaction we get."

"What the hell. We'd better lay into somebody or neither of us is going to have a job in a couple of hours."

"Good point," said Olsen. He pulled out his two-way radio and clicked it over to channel twenty-three. He looked at me, I nodded, and we moved closer. Daily was sitting with his back to us. Olsen spoke into the portable radio. "Control, we've got the diamonds and the suspect is in custody."

With that remark Daily almost shot out of his chair. He kept staring toward the entrance. Olsen and I moved closer, and then I tapped him on the shoulder. This made him jump about a foot off the ground.

"What the hell are you doing here, Daily?" I asked, pushing him back to his chair. Olsen moved to the other side of him. A couple of tourists gave us strange glances. We both pulled out our I.D.s and displayed them, then inserted them into our front coat pockets. Procedure. We wanted everybody to know we were the good guys.

"Just a few questions, if you don't mind." Olsen stated as a matter of fact.

"I'm just here to make the diamond bust," said Daily. Olsen and I looked at each other.

"How come you didn't check in with my office?" Olsen asked.

"Didn't think it was necessary...."

"That's procedure. You know the routine. You're in my hotel. What the hell are you doing here?"

"You're supposed to be interviewing witnesses in that furniture store robbery," I pushed.

"I finished up early."

I turned to Olsen. "I don't like this. He's operating outside of the department. Must have a reason."

"I don't like it when somebody goes undercover in my casino and doesn't inform the security office."

"I just thought...."

"Looks like you're trying to pull a fast one," I said, jamming my finger into his chest. "What else aren't you telling us?"

"Why the hell are you so interested in the diamonds?" demanded Olsen.

"Listen, you guys. We're on the same team. Right?"

"We don't know what team you're on," said Olsen. "With a little investigation by my partner here, it turns out you had access to all the diamonds and crime scenes."

"Partner. You guys are partners? You guys hate each other."

Olsen looked at me. "Yeah, that we do."

"Couldn't agree with you more," I said.

"Hell, it looks like you've been fighting...." Daily said glancing back and forth between us.

"We have. Olsen's got a glass jaw," I said.

Olsen gave me a quick sideways look. "Watch it Fargo!"

"So, what are you doing here, Daily?"

"I wanted to be the first detective on the scene."

"Want to get a big promotion, is that it?" I asked.

"Yeah. I want the big promotion. Get off my back you guys. You're talking the wrong guy.

"Let's throw him out," I said. "He's got no official business in the casino. He can be thrown out."

"I'm just visiting," said Daily.

Olsen snapped his fingers and two large security guards appeared on each side of Daily.

"Please escort him to the front door," said Olsen. "We only want police in here who are on official business."

The security guards grabbed each of Daily's arms and hoisted him out of his chair. Olsen reached over and grabbed the radio out of his belt and yanked the cord out of his ear. Daily flinched at the cord being ripped from his ear.

"Next time, call before you visit my casino. And no secret radio stuff or I'll arrest you for interfering with the security of this casino."

Daily was furious. "I'm going to report this. You'll be hearing from the department," he screamed as he was dragged away by security.

We watched him for a few seconds.

"Time to hit the road," I said.

Olsen radioed security. "Secure one, this is Olsen. Pull out Fargo's car at the north entrance."

"It's nice that your team is behind you," I observed.

"What do you think?" questioned Olsen.

"We'll hang here for a bit and then leave. What do we have now?"

"I think we got crap. He has a network on the street just like we do."

"We got something," said Olsen. "We got one shook-up detective who was caught being someplace he wasn't supposed to be."

"Playing by his own rules."

"Most cops would have checked in with security. That's the procedure for any casino in Vegas. Check in first and let them know what you're up to. Add the radio and the monitoring of our security chatter, and you've got one suspicious character."

"At least we shook him up," I said.

"Kind of fun."

We had a good laugh over that.

Thirty-Seven

RUBY ANN BARRE rose from her seat, leaving a ten-dollar bill to cover her drink and tip. She wore an all-white evening dress complete with a plunging neckline. She turned and headed toward the casino entrance.

*   *   *

Olsen spotted her and examined the package. He gave me the nod to take a look, so I twisted in my seat to take a peek. Las Vegas attracted the most interesting people. In Vegas, no one would give a second thought to anyone's dressing in an evening gown in the early morning. The tourists loved the drama of somebody dressed for an evening on the town -- no matter what time of day. For most tourists, it was completely different from their hometown where women got dressed up only for church and funerals. Las Vegas was different. It had class and attitude. Anything goes. Just look at Olsen and me. Heated enemies working together. I would never have guessed it. I turned back to Olsen and gave him the thumbs up approval. What's not to like.

*   *   *

Ruby Ann Barre, alias Montoya Martinez Colorado, alias Marilee Phillips, never turned back when she left the Bar.

Street info had brought her here. She had seen and heard everything when Fargo, Olsen and Daily were talking. Ruby Ann was shocked when she heard the voice of Daily. It was her partner. She knew that now, and time was running out.

Thirty-Eight

OLSEN AND I climbed in my BMW with the engine running. I was at the wheel and was intent on beating a rusted Toyota out of the lot. I won. I figured I would. There is justice in the world, sometimes.

Olsen radioed security and they informed him Daily was pulling out of the back lot headed down Tropicana. We turned in pursuit.

"This Daily is a strange guy. He is either as straight as can be, or he's crooked as a banker on his way to Brazil."

"Nobody is that crooked," I said, checking the cars behind me with a glance at the rearview mirror.

"A politician. You'll go far on someone's ghost payroll."

I checked the back seat to make sure my black bag was there. You never know when you're going to need it. We spotted the black Ford, and took up an inside left tail position. We were in Daily's blind spot when a car pulled into our lane just as Daily turned left onto Marilyn Street.

"Oh shit!" said Olsen.

I revved up the engine, and hit it. "Close your eyes." I waited until I had just enough space and punched it. The car rocketed out into traffic, and I cranked the wheel to the left and punched it again. The result was an accelerating turn from the wrong lane that made the wheels smoke and horns honk.

"Great, he'll never know anyone is behind him now."

"It doesn't look to me like he is really concerned with who's behind him."

Daily was weaving in and out of traffic and accelerating. We moved down Marilyn Street, staying in the right lane to keep in his blind spot as much as possible. Daily turned on to Sahara and headed north toward the Las Vegas Strip.

I followed. "This is going to be a good show for the tourists."

"I don't want to be in any show for the tourists," said Olsen. "I've got enough trouble with my own show."

It was apparent Daily was agitated. He went past the Strip and headed farther up Sahara heading north. We barely made the light. Then he pulled into a Strip shopping center and brought his car to an abrupt halt. Olsen was hanging on for the ride.

"Man's in a hurry," said Olsen.

"Yep, he's in a hurry all right."

Daily jumped out of the car and rushed into a travel agency. Olsen and I looked at each other.

"My, my, my...a traveler," said Olsen."

"I wonder what brought this on." I focused in with a high-powered set of binoculars. I could see Daily on the inside sitting at a desk. Some pretty little thing was working feverishly. I handed the binoculars to Olsen.

"Here, take a look." I grabbed the car phone and dialed the precinct. "Yeah, Fargo here. Connect me with homicide. Yeah, thanks. I'll see what the station has to say." Back to phone. "Yeah, it's me, Fargo. Who's this?"

"It's Duffy."

"Duffy, give me Daily. I've got a hot lead for him."

"He's not here. He's out."

"What do you mean he's not there?"

"He left. Was agitated about something. Said he'd be in tomorrow."

"But I've got a lead for him. Who else is working the case?"

"No one. It's his. No one else wants it."

"Can you call him?"

"Yeah, I'll call his pager."

"Great. Thanks. Tell him Olsen and I've got a hot lead."

"I'm doing it as we speak."

"Thanks, bye. Duffy is paging him," I said glancing at Olsen, who was still right on top of him.

"Yep. I can see him reaching for his pager."

"What's he doing now?"

"He's using his cell phone."

"Great. Come on. This is going to be fun."

We jumped out of the car, and moved around to the front hood. We were parked a little past him one row out. With the angled parking, he would have to pass us when he left.

"This will be interesting. I wonder what kind of reaction we're going to get."

"I don't know. Guilty or not guilty? We'll soon find out," said Olsen."

"Are you carrying?" I asked, both of us keeping our eyes on Daily through the front window.

"Always."

"The Wild Wild West," I said thinking of Pleasure. I pulled a Glock from under the seat and secured the waist holster to my belt. Olsen checked his SIG in his shoulder holster, and then added one nice touch. He clipped his badge wallet to the front of his jacket. The MGM Grand security badge glittered in the sun. I followed suit with my gold P.I. badge. There we stood, casually leaning up against the car, guns and badges showing.

"Well, at least we look official," I said. "Man, does he look upset."

"We'll know pretty soon. Here he comes."

Daily hurried out of the travel agency clutching airline tickets. He jerked his car door open and dove into the front seat, starting the engine in the same motion. He peeled out going backwards into the lane of traffic, cutting off a good-looking blonde who immediately flipped him off. Nice lady, I thought. Good for her. Daily punched it at the same time he saw us standing there, and he hit the brakes coming up right next to us. Engine revving. Daily's chest heaving.

"Afternoon," I said.

If Daily didn't have high blood pressure, he did now. Easy diagnosis. His face was one tense, red, swelling piece of flesh. He looked mean, pissed and ready to do damage. I could see him take in our guns and badges.

"What are you guys doing here?" screamed Daily.

"We have an investigation in progress. Can't talk about it much," I commented.

"Client confidentiality," chimed in Olsen.

"You assholes. You're dead, you're both dead. I'm going to have you both arrested. We're going to throw the book at you."

Olsen walked up to Daily's car window and came face to face with him. We were watching for gunplay. I moved to the Ford's right side. We each had our hands on our weapons, which really pissed Daily off.

"Taking a trip?" asked Olsen in the calmest voice I've ever heard him use.

"What's it to you?" Daily clutched the wheel.

The back seat of his car was a complete mess. Almost as if he had been living out of the car. One disheveled bag looked like it had been packed in a hurry.

"Yep, he's taking a trip," I said.

301

"Where to?" asked Olsen, never taking his eyes off Daily.

"Up the river," I replied. "And it ain't no lazy river where he's going."

With that, Daily punched the accelerator, causing us to jump back. He burned rubber all the way to the end of the aisle, slid into the turn, and shot out into traffic, causing several horns to go off. He then punched it again and screamed through the traffic.

"Guilty," I said.

"No question. Guilty. But guilty of what?"

A black and white was passing by at the same time and hit the lights and siren. There is justice in the world.

"Get the car," said Olsen. "I'm going to find out where he's going."

Olsen ran over to the travel agency, and I could see him showing his badge. The gun was obvious. Most people don't take a second look at a badge. I got the BMW, and backed it up right in front of the agency's door.

The police radio came alive. "Fifty-two is stopping a black Ford, license plate 234UYT. Ten-four."

Olsen jumped in, clutching the pocket notebook all detectives seem to carry.

I hit it and we left, a bit slower than Daily had.

"He's off to St. Thomas."

"Ahaa, the islands. Nice place to go to. I've got to get back there."

"Land of water, women, and off-shore banking."

"Exactly what I was thinking. When?"

"Tonight. I'll have a man at the airport just in case."

I spotted Daily, who had been stopped by the black-and-white. I pulled over, as I wanted to hang back. We could see the officer move back to his patrol car, as Daily moved into traffic.

The police radio came alive. "This is fifty-two. Cancel the records search. He's with the department. Ten-four."

The police officer pulled away, and we pulled into traffic far behind Daily.

"Now let's see where he goes," I said.

"Yeah, he would never suspect we're behind him now."

Daily turned left into another Strip mall. He stopped in front of another travel agency named The Get-Away.

"He's a mover."

This time we stayed back and watched. The scene repeated itself. Daily went in, and about fifteen minutes later came out clutching more tickets. He left without looking around, and turned right heading back down Sahara.

I pulled the car in front of the agency as Olsen jumped out. No communication needed. I backed into a space and waited for him.

Olsen got back into the car. "He's going to St. Thomas."

"He already has a ticket for St. Thomas."

"Now he's got two. Only this one is for tomorrow at six P.M."

"He didn't cancel the first set?" I asked.

"Apparently not. Looks like a decoy."

"Yep. He's a man with a mission."

Thirty-Nine

PETER DAILY must have been thinking of running. That's the only thing a man can think of when the law starts to close in. It's human nature. But Daily, like so many other criminals, feels he has a certain amount of invincibility. He will never be caught. He's smarter than his adversaries. Daily felt secure because no action was being taken against him from the department. He would have picked up on the rumor mill simply by the way people treated him on an everyday basis. Even saying hello, when you're under suspicion by the department, is as different as night and day. The stunt at the MGM Grand shook Daily up, but he felt he had fared well. They were just testing him.

When Daily opened the door to his condo he was momentarily startled. He heard something. He recognized "Morning Mood" from the Peer Gynt Suite I, Opus 46, by Edvard Grieg. The C.D. was one of his favorites, and it was playing on his stereo. It held special meaning for him, and now he knew it was also important to somebody else.

Something caught his eye and he looked down at the floor. Diamonds were everywhere! He began to hyperventilate, his heart pounding fiercely in his chest. Somebody had invaded the very privacy of his being. They had thrown the diamonds in his face and left them lying around like sand on a beach.

Daily studied his empty apartment. He proceeded to check out his entire home while Greig continued playing. Moving from room to room, from shadow to shadow, Daily examined every square inch of his domain. He found his suitcase in his bedroom that surprised him. His fear rose. The suitcase was always kept in a storage compartment in the hallway. Impossible! He opened the suitcase carefully and found his personal belongings packed for a trip. He turned and opened a closet door and found another valise. It was empty. This was the one he had packed only hours before. Who could have entered his residence and switched his clothing from one suitcase to another? Madness. And why? Who could have found his diamonds that were so carefully hidden in his Edvard Grieg C.D. cases?

Knowing that he did not have much time, Daily moved to the living room and pulled a plastic case from his C.D. cabinet. One single diamond rolled out of the case onto the floor. He had carefully planted his loot from the Desert Sage robbery there thinking that nobody would look in his personal collection of C.D.s.

"Damn..." said Daily, and he began to sweat even more. He looked at the diamonds on the floor. His life of future pleasures and revenge were disappearing in front of him. Daily jerked his head toward the front door at the sound of somebody moving quietly in the hallway. He reached for his four-fifty-four Casull. It could take out a four-wheeled drive sports vehicle at one hundred fifty yards. Daily took careful aim at the doorway. Nothing happened. He lowered his Casull and began the task of gathering the diamonds and placing them in his pockets. His life's work thrown on his living room rug like Easter eggs on Sunday morning.

At that precise second, the front door crashed open and Daily turned and opened fire.

Forty

I lowered my weapon. Olsen was boiling in anger. "Damn it, Fargo. You were closer to him. You shouldn't have missed." Olsen shoved another magazine into his Glock and checked to see if the safety was on.

"You don't appear to be a crack shot."

"I was trained not to shoot cops," said Olsen.

"That's not what I heard...."

"Watch it," said Olsen.

"I should have waited by the front door to make sure Daily didn't do an end run on us," I said as I backed away from the window.

Olsen smirked at me with his usual look. "We came in like the cavalry and he left like an Indian. We look like idiots. Nice work, Fargo," Olsen said.

"Sorry. I thought I could fire a warning shot."

"Never fire a warning shot when you're about to die."

"I'll remember that."

"He's going to bolt. We'll never catch him now."

"You never know. Daily doesn't have his diamonds, or at least all of them."

"He'll split. He knows we're on to him."

We moved across the bedroom into the living room and studied the floor. Diamonds all right, and we had a hunch they were from McCaddy's. We knew we had Daily dead to rights. But why were they scattered all over the floor? Could Daily have dropped these as he was trying to make his escape? Olsen went in one direction while I examined the kitchen and the hallway before entering another bedroom, which I took to be Daily's. Olsen was already there.

"Airline tickets and luggage," Olsen said. He opened the suitcase and we examined a very careful packing job. "No doubt about it, he was planning on going somewhere."

"Everybody needs a vacation," I said.

"Especially crooks. Daily could maybe use a few years of R&R at one of the federally owned prisons. Chow's not too good, but then you can't have everything."

"I don't know. Seems our guy here was thinking of a lifetime of beaches based upon his trips to the travel bureaus."

My cell phone rang. "Hello?"

"Fargo, its Sheri."

I indicated to Olsen that the call was safe.

"You looking for Daily?" asked Sheri.

"Yep. He just ran out of here a few seconds ago."

"I'm on to him. He's two cars ahead of me."

"You found him?" I turned to Olsen. "Sheri is following Daily."

"Who's Sheri?"

"Works in my office," I said.

"Yeah."

"Okay, where are you now?"

"I'm on Eastern Avenue."

"He's headed straight for the Strip."

"So far so good," answered Sheri. "He's turning left on to Desert Inn."

"Okay, we're leaving here and I'll call you as soon as we get rolling." I shoved the cell phone into my pocket and waved at Olsen to get his attention.

"What's going on?" he asked.

"I'll tell you as we go."

Olsen and I raced across the living room, out the door, and jumped into my BMW.

"Sheri is following him now. We can try and catch him."

It didn't take us long to get rolling. "Olsen, call in the shooting at Daily's to Metro to keep us legal."

Olsen pulled out his cell phone. "I'll be as vague as I can."

I nodded as I dialed in Sheri on my cell phone.

"Sheri. You still have him?"

"I've got him three cars away," Sheri said. "We're approaching Las Vegas Boulevard, and he's turning left."

"Daily just turned on to the Strip." I took a hard left and pulled onto Maryland Parkway. Olsen snapped his cell phone shut and pulled his Glock to check it, preparing for anything.

"Glove compartment," I said.

Olsen took a look at me and then opened the glove compartment. "It's empty," said Olsen.

"Hit that black button right by the latch."

Olsen punched the button and a fall-away-panel revealed a secret storage compartment filled with guns and ammo. Good guys need lots of guns.

"My my...what do we have here?" Olsen was very impressed with my set up.

"Time to load up," I said as I reached across and pulled a handful of magazines for my Glock, and also pulled out my Russian Makarov and some ammo. The Glock stayed in my leather shoulder holster and the Makarov went in a concealed carry behind-the-back waist holster. I also pulled out a .38 with an ankle holster and slipped it around my ankle for additional security. A bit tricky while driving, but I've done this before. "There are extra magazines for your Glock."

"Great," said Olsen. "Next time I get caught in a fire fight I'll remember that you come fully equipped."

"I've got another .38 and some speed loaders in the trunk if you need a back up," I said.

"No. I'm in good shape. I'm packing two Glocks."

"Sheri?" I asked picking up my cell phone again.

"What happened?" said Sheri.

"We flushed him out. Thought we had him there but he made a quick exit we weren't counting on."

"He's your man?" Sheri asked.

"He's the one. Diamonds all over the living room floor. Must have dropped them when we crashed in through the front doors."

"He's turning," said Sheri. "He took a left onto Tropicana."

"He's at the MGM Grand," I said to Olsen.

"Why would he go back there?"

"Don't know."

"He's turning right into the Remo," said Sheri.

"He's turned into the Remo," I said to Olsen.

"Daily's just dropping the car. From there he can make it across the street and into the MGM Grand," said Olsen.

I remembered a second entrance into the Remo. "Sheri, take the second entrance into the parking lot."

"Right," said Sheri.

"We're turning off Maryland onto Tropicana," I said. As soon as I turned the corner and straightened out the BMW I held the wheel with my knee and removed the magazine from my Makarov and checked the magazine for a full load. I had one round already chambered so I was seven plus one, and ready to go.

"Don't plan on using that, Fargo. You're the worst shot I've ever seen."

"If I get enough rounds off I can usually hit something."

"Try packing an Uzi. Might save your life some-day."

"Thanks. I've actually thought about it."

"Be careful though. Think of all the tourists you could blow away."

"He's crossing the street," said Sheri on the phone. I told Olsen, and he realized Daily was going for the main entrance. "Let's cut him off."

I swung the car toward the main entrance and could pick up the figure of Daily as he moved into the Porte Cochere that was lit with thousands of lights.

"I don't think we're going to be able to cut him off," I said.

"Jump the curb," yelled Olsen.

I went for it. I had no idea what it would do to the BMW, but I had to do something so we could stop Daily from getting into the MGM Grand. What a great entrance. We crashed into a gold Lexus and slid to a stop between Daily and the MGM Grand. Onlookers just stopped and stared in horror. It's not often you get to see a gold Lexus smashed beyond repair.

"Nice driving," said Olsen. "I'm sure you will get to meet the owner of the Lexus."

It sort of went downhill from there. That's when Daily pulled his gun and shot me. I saw the whole episode in slow motion. I was getting out of the driver's side as Olsen tucked and rolled out the passenger door. I was impressed. Never saw him move so fast. Here he was rolling to the ground and I was falling into the sights of Daily's gun. His .38 police special looked like a monster when you were looking down the gun barrel. One pop and I was rolling to the ground gushing blood. I had been hit in the upper arm, and flying glass also had cut me up pretty bad. I'm glad he wasn't using his Casull.

Daily fired one more shot and then ran through the screaming crowds into the MGM Grand. Olsen would have nailed him but there were too many tourists he could have hit. Olsen took one look at me as I tried to stand, clutching my arm.

"Get 'em!" I shouted clutching my arm. Olsen turned and ran for the entrance. I made my way to a standing position by the side of my now wrecked BMW, and then collapsed to the ground.

Forty-One

OLSEN dashed through the doors of the MGM Grand and studied the lobby. A few of his security people were also running for the entrance, but Olsen ignored them. He continued to walk into the Casino, watching for any signs of Daily. Why would he enter the casino? What could bring him back here? Olsen entered the main casino gaming area. Many times he had watched people do exactly what he was doing. He wondered if his security forces were also watching him. Another security man approached.

"Mr. Olsen...."

"Mack...give me your radio."

The guard handed it over.

"Check the entrance and see if they need any help out there."

The guard turned and raced toward the Porte Cochere.

"Troll? You there, Troll?" asked Olsen into the radio.

"I'm here, Vince."

"What you got from your end?"

"Disturbance at the entrance. You tracking somebody?"

"Yeah. A cop named Daily. You'll remember him. It's the same cop we tracked through the casino earlier this morning."

"Right."

"Check for him. He had to pass this spot no more than thirty seconds ago."

"Hold on." Olsen knew Troll was putting his team to work. It was only a matter of time before he would spot Daily. Olsen was walking continuously past rows and rows of slot machines. Bells and sirens kept going off accompanied by flashing red and blue lights. The clanging of coins made a constant racket -- music to the tourists' ears.

"Two rows down from where you are. Man at a machine. We think he's holding a gun behind a coin cup," said the Troll. "I'll send extra units."

"Put them outside the exits," said Olsen. "We've got to move him out of the casino. We can't have gunfire inside."

"I'll move them into position," said the Troll.

Olsen continued to move forward until he was just one row away from Daily. He pulled his Glock from under his shirt and carried it straight down near his side. Taking a deep breath, he turned the corner and faced his prey. Suddenly from his left a cold metal object was put next to his head. It was Daily.

"Drop the gun, Olsen."

"Not on your life."

"We're talking about your life, scumbag. Drop the gun or I'll start popping tourists." The Glock fell to the floor and Olsen figured his days as the head of security had ended. He had found Daily, but now he was really screwed.

"We're just going to back our way toward an exit," said Daily. "I'm not taking the fall for this thing."

"Whatever you want," said Olsen. "Whatever made you put together a scheme like this?"

"For love and money...but you wouldn't understand that. You were too busy ruining my career. Stepping over me for other more qualified individuals."

"I was just doing my job," said Olsen as they moved backwards through the casino. Security guards were clearing a path and trying to keep the tourists out of the way. Some were watching and others were running.

"Tell your men to let me through. I want no trouble," stammered Daily.

"They wouldn't try anything unless I say so," answered Olsen.

Forty-Two

I struggled from slot machine to slot machine and finally found Olsen and Daily. I leaned against a video slot as blood dripped to the floor. With the way casino floors are designed, you couldn't even tell I was bleeding.

"Fargo. Get the hell out of here," yelled Olsen.

"Officer down. Officer down," said Daily into a portable radio.

If the cops arrived, I knew we would be perceived as the bad guys. I looked at Olsen and guessed he was thinking the same thing.

"Fargo...." Olsen began.

"Tell Fargo to take a hike," said Daily, beginning to panic. "Officer down. Officer down. Two white-males with weapons inside the MGM Grand. All units respond." Daily continued to shout into the radio. "Code thirty, at the MGM Grand."

"Get the hell of here, Fargo. I've got everything under control," stammered Olsen.

I laughed. "Yeah, right," I said. "Given the fact that Daily's got a gun to your head. And I might add, a rather large one."

"All part of my plan."

I slumped down a little more against the slot machine. "I thought we should just end this right here."

"Now don't try anything, Fargo!" screamed Olsen. "You know you're a terrible shot. Daily does have a gun to my head."

"I see that," I said. "I think I can put a bullet in his gun hand."

"Don't do it, Fargo," screamed Olsen. "You hit his wrist and he'll squeeze the trigger."

"We don't know that for sure," I said, getting weaker and weaker.

"Don't let him try it, Olsen," screamed Daily. "I'll blow your head clean off."

It was a stand off. Everybody just stared at each other. I raised my Glock. One quick POP and Daily's hand snapped back causing him to drop the .38 revolver. Several of the bystanders screamed and ducked out of the way. More people moved in to see what was happening. It was a mess. The slug slammed into a slot machine and the bells proclaimed it a winner.

"Fargo! You could have killed me," Olsen screamed as he grabbed Daily.

"A one shot take-down," I said.

"Drop the gun, Fargo," said a woman's voice behind me. I knew that voice. Everybody turned to see Julie Fuller, the assistant to Lanning, holding a 9mm Beretta to the head of Pleasure. By Pleasure's facial expression, she was in some pain. She sort of hobbled forward, being pushed from behind. Her arms were cuffed in back, and her legs were bound with a short piece of rope to keep her from running. Julie, minus her dark rimmed glasses, looked like she knew what she was doing. That's how she had gotten Pleasure all the way into the casino. Pleasure's eyes were wide, and I knew she was scared.

"Julie! What the hell are you doing here?" I said. "I thought you were on a trip."

"Drop the gun, Fargo."

"Why Pleasure?" I asked, not making any moves.

"Our insurance. Remember when we had the discussion about your client? You would always save your client. That became our ace in the hole. You won't try anything now that would endanger her. Not good for business if word gets around Vegas that your clients get killed."

"You've got a point there."

"Drop the gun, Fargo," said Julie.

I let the Makarov fall to the casino floor.

"Olsen, let go of Daily." Olsen was strong and Daily squirmed. "I mean it, let him go."

Olsen let Daily go, and he quickly picked up his weapon and moved to the side.

"Now, what are you going to do Julie?" I asked.

"It's not working out like Daily and I had planned, but we'll make the best of it," said Julie.

"You and Daily!"

"That's right. That creep, Olsen, put my brother in prison on a phony robbery charge. Olsen should have been locked up in jail for the Desert Sage robbery. That was the plan. Would have served Olsen justice for all of the injustice he's done to us. An eye for an eye."

"The two of you," I said, not believing.

"The two of us," said Julie. "We worked it out together. A brilliant plan."

"You're framing Olsen?"

"He deserved it. He's a bad cop."

"What about me?" I asked.

"You just got in the way. You're too damn good at what you do."

"And the Desert Sage robbery?" I asked, stalling for time.

"Daily organized it. He hired the thief, whoever she was."

"She?"

"Yeah, some babe."

"Why?"

"It was our drop dead money for a life filled with clean sandy beaches, good weather, and no worries. All bought and paid for. You had to ruin it. You had to keep after Daily, who was just giving Olsen what was coming to him. A cop's justice. When they're bad, put' em away."

"Julie, you'll never get out of here. Let Pleasure go. We can work something out."

"I've been in tougher situations," said Julie. "Right, honey?"

"Yeah," said Daily as he held his crippled arm.

"We'll get out of here," said Julie. "We're going to back toward an exit, and we'll take out Pleasure and anybody else who gets in our way. A plane's waiting."

Suddenly, the sound of a gun startled everyone as Julie's head snapped back. Tourists screamed and ran for cover. Security guards hid behind multicolored slots. I turned and saw Sheri holding a Glock. Smoke drifted up from the end of the gun. Pleasure fell to the floor as I dove across the room to pin Julie to the carpet. But, it didn't matter, she was dead.

In the confusion, Daily disappeared in the crowd of tourists behind them. Olsen lunged after him. Two tourists saw Olsen jumping at them, stepped aside, and watched Olsen slam into a slot machine. I rolled over and saw Sheri standing in a locked arm position holding her weapon. She moved her arm up so that the Glock was pointed toward the ceiling.

"Sheri?"

"Hi, boss. Hadn't heard from you so I thought I would do a little back-up. Just like you taught me. Hope you don't mind."

"Not at all." I smiled knowing I can always count on Sheri. I got up and gathered Pleasure into my arms, pulling her to a standing position. She was helpless. I tried to get the cuffs off, but they were secured with a lock. I gave Pleasure a hug and all she could do was to press her body into mine as a way of saying thanks. As uncomfortable as Pleasure was, she always found a way.

"Glad I hired you," smiled Pleasure.

"Well, you're welcome," I said.

"Sorry for this mess."

"These things happen."

Olsen was lying by a slot machine. He shook his head to clear it.

"One out of two isn't too bad," said Olsen.

"Don't worry about it. The guards will get him at the door."

Olsen rubbed his head.

"You all right?" I asked.

"Yeah. Just took a header into slot machine."

"Bad habit to get into," I said. Sheri moved over and I wrapped one arm around her.

"Thanks, lady."

"No problem, boss," said Sheri.

"Where did you learn to shoot like that?" I asked.

"Sort of runs in the family."

"Military?"

"Nah, gunslingers...."

"Glad to hear it." I laughed.

Olsen walked over sore as hell, blood dripping down the side of his face. "You son-of-a-bitch, Fargo. You could have killed me with that stunt you pulled."

"I just looked at the downside of the situation and thought, what the hell. Besides, partner, you would have done the same thing if you were in my position."

"I'm not that good a shot, Fargo."

"I'm not either." I smiled. "But hell, this is Vegas. Anything is possible.

Forty-Three

I lounged by the pool. The sun was hot. Las Vegas hot. Enough to make you sweat without moving. It was Sunday afternoon, and Uncle Leo, Sheri, Pleasure and I were by the pool at the MGM Grand under a huge umbrella, where I had first met Pleasure. Lanning had comped me a room for a week, everything except food. But I took care of that. We were celebrating. A never-ending line of chefs decked out in white billowing hats paraded by our table, providing a catered lunch direct from Wolfgang Puck's. One of the best meals I had ever eaten. Several nearby groups were wondering where all the fine cuisine was coming from. They kept giving us dirty looks as they downed their deli sandwiches.

"So, Sheri, what do you think about all this detecting?"

"I think it's great as long as they're not after you."

"Well put."

Uncle Leo looked peaceful as he did his usual routine with his Racing Form. "They're always after Fargo," Uncle Leo said. "You'll just have to live with it."

"True," I said. "Comes with the territory." I turned and studied Pleasure, who was working on her tan and reading the paper.

"Fargo, is Abby coming?" Sheri asked as she lounged in the sun next to Pleasure.

"Nope, she's mad at me. I dumped her for dinner this week and it will take a month of Sundays before things are right."

"Doesn't she understand the trouble you were in?" Sheri asked.

"Yep."

"The never-ending battle between the showgirl and the detective," Sheri commented.

"That's about it. But I've got a plan. I'm going to take her on a trip...I'm thinking the islands. Maybe St. Thomas."

"Fargo, I've got another question for you. Who killed the Jane Doe?"

"Daily," I responded.

"How do you know it was Daily?"

"The Jane Doe turned out to be an unfortunate accident. Daily had targeted Pleasure with a dart that would make her really sick and put her in the hospital. Her safe would have been opened, and the diamonds would have been found from the Desert Sage, which eventually would have tied Pleasure to Olsen with the diamonds in his filing cabinet. What happened was the Jane Doe had an allergic reaction and it turned into murder."

Pleasure sat up holding her Las Vegas Times. "Oh my God, Fargo! Look at this story!"

I leaned forward and glanced at the paper, and read the headline out loud. "Las Vegas Cop Found Executed in the Desert." When I read that, I grabbed the paper.

"What's happened?" asked Sheri.

"Daily's dead! Murdered. Single bullet to the back of the head," I said. "A real pro. They found his body in the desert thirty miles outside of town. No marks. No witnesses. No immediate clues."

"Forensics will turn up something," said the doubting Uncle Leo.

"Are you sure it's Daily?" asked Sheri.

"Yep. It's him. No question about it." I raised the paper and the face of Daily was unmistakable. I paraphrased the rest of the article. The story went into the details of the shoot-out at the MGM Grand and how Daily had gotten away after sacrificing Julie Fuller. Daily had been shot in the hand, then established an 'Officer Down' scenario and created a mob scene of police and tourists. Airports had been checked as Daily had a reservation for St. Thomas, but he never showed. "There are no known leads in the desert murder, and the investigation remains open."

"Fargo, you're in a lot of trouble," yelled Olsen arriving at the lunch in his usual sport coat attire. He carried his walkie-talkie in one hand and a cell phone in the other.

I raised up the newspaper so Olsen could see the headline. Olsen grabbed the newspaper and scanned it. "I got a call on this about an hour ago. Metro is really buzzing."

"Are we in trouble?" I asked.

"Not even a suspect."

Everybody turned as Pleasure stood. "This is too much for me." She started to leave, then turned back. "Fargo, meet me in my room in about an hour. I've got something for you." She waved good-bye to everybody.

"Okay, what room?" I yelled after her.

"Room 2345."

I glanced at Pleasure as she disappeared around a palm and wondered.

Olsen's walkie-talkie buzzed with a call. "So, you didn't invite me to your little party here."

"You're invited. Sit down. Enjoy," I said.

"Can't. We've got a situation going on."

"Anything I can help you with?"

"Yeah. Just leave it alone. That will help me the most." He hit me on the shoulder in a good-humored jostle and turned back toward the casino. As he left he picked up the check. "Promise you'll stay out of it and this one's on me," he said smiling.

Olsen left holding his walkie-talkie to his ear. About the same time he glanced at Wolfgang Puck's tab for the lunch. You could hear him all across the pool. "Jeez Louise! What the hell did you all eat?"

* * *

JODY lowered the newspaper featuring the article on Daily. Ruby Ann Barre, formerly Montoya Martinez Colorado, also known as Jody, smiled. Actually, they were her aliases -- former aliases. He new name was Ms. O. Ramos. She looked down through the small circular airline window at the expanse of ocean beneath her, and closed her eyes in complete contentment. Her father sat sleeping next to her. They were now on their way to Rio. Daily's connection had released her father before Daily had been murdered. They were lucky. Timing was everything. She knew someday she might team up with her friend, Pleasure, but for now, South America was her new home.

* * *

I knocked, and Pleasure opened the door immediately. She gave me a kiss on the cheek, and moved over to the bed and sat down and picked up a deck of cards. She looked quite ravishing. She had changed for another play at the tables. Her plunging neckline was suggestive and enticing.

She patted the bed besides her. "Care for a game?"

"And what are the stakes?"

"What they always are. What I always play for. Everything. Your soul, if you'll bet it. The money in your wallet. The clothes on your back."

"I'm in swim trunks."

"In strip poker, the first rule is to pick your opponent."

Pleasure didn't give me a choice. She dealt the cards, and they floated aimlessly out and down into a nice neat stack. She leaned over as she dealt.

It was then I knew I was in trouble.

"The winner wins, and there is no backing down. And I play to win," said Pleasure.

I sat on the edge of the bed and hesitated, then tentatively picked up the hand. I was looking at two queens. Three, if you included Pleasure.

I tossed three cards out hoping for another queen. Pleasure drew three cards. She was also building on a pair. Although she didn't need to.

"Let's see 'em," she announced.

I thought it should have been my line. Two queens it was.

She had two Jacks. I won. Pleasure lost.

Pleasure looked at me, stood up, and slid out of her evening dress. She wasn't wearing anything underneath.

Pleasure isn't that good of a poker player, I thought. She could have taken off her shoe.

About the Authors

Don McKenzie

Don continues to write and develop plays, screenplays and novels in Oregon where he and his wife Sandra live. Don graduated from Foothill College, Los Altos, California with an Associated Arts degree, and Humboldt State University, Arcata, California with a Bachelor in Theatre Arts.

Ron McKenzie

Ron lives in Illinois his wife Pamela and continues to develop novels and screenplays. Ron graduated from Foothill College, Los Altos, California with an Associated Arts degree, and California Polytechnic State University, San Luis Obispo, California with a Bachelor of Architecture degree.